# Chinook, Wine and Sink Her

## Morgan Q. O'Reilly

**LYRICAL PRESS**
Kensington Publishing Corp.
www.kensingtonbooks.com

First Electronic Edition: September 2008
eISBN-13: 978-0-98411-322-4
eISBN-10: 0-9841132-2-3

First Print Edition: September 2008
ISBN-13: 978-1-61650-897-5
ISBN-10: 1-61650-897-3

Printed in the United States of America

*How does a gold mining fisherman catch the girl of his dreams? Ask the moose and the dog.*

Linnet Greenbriar has a job to do on the isolated Alaskan Yukon River. Hoping the remote area will keep her away from men for as long as possible, she is shocked to see the handsome stranger walking up the river and singing a little song. All her hopes change when a mishap sends her falling into the river and also into the arms of said handsome stranger.

Creed finds himself in the wrong place at the right time and becomes a self appointed hero when he rescues the beautiful Fish and Game Officer from the icy river. All he wanted was a little peace and solitude, but one look at this city girl has him changing his tune.

# Books by Morgan Q. O'Reilly

Frozen
Chinook, Wine and Sink Her

*Open Window Series*
Til Death Undo Us
Courage to Live
Weathering the Storm


**Published by Kensington Publishing Corporation**

# Acknowledgements

Many thanks to author Carolyn David for the title, and to all my critique partners for all their words of wisdom and help. Special thanks to Liz Selvig, who can be my co-pilot anytime on wild and crazy research trips. We certainly made it to Circle without busting anything!

Last, but certainly not least, I dedicate this book to my husband. In our early dating years he sang the song Squaws Along the Yukon on occasion, and at one point had the words programmed into his digital watch. Mention of it usually earned him a smack on the shoulder. The slight word change of "salmon-colored" to "salmon-scented" is his contribution to the song. Apologies to songwriter Cam Smith and recording artist Hank Thompson for the minor twist.

## Song Credits

Squaws Along the Yukon
Recorded by Hank Thompson
Words and music by Cam Smith
Originally recorded in the 1950s

# Foreword

Certain artistic license was taken regarding the location of Creed's cabin and the village of Circle, Alaska.

While there are working gold mining operations all along the Steese Highway, which leads from Fairbanks to Circle, Creed's is entirely fictional. The Steese Highway ends at Circle on the banks of the Yukon, and there are no roads leading to hidden cabins so far upstream. River travelers, who put in at Dawson or Eagle and float down to Circle, find many camping places along the route. There are also public-use cabins maintained by the Bureau of Land Management. Slaven's Roadhouse is a real place, reachable only by river. Whether they have sat-phone or not, I don't know.

The people of Circle are mostly Athabascan and live in a very small village. They live a mainly subsistence lifestyle with few modern conveniences. The roads are unpaved and the villagers haul water much as our characters do. The Washeteria does exist, pretty much the way Linnet sees it.

The few people we met on the late July day a friend and I made the drive from Fairbanks were very kind. We didn't see many residents, but those we did looked curiously at our 'Circle or Bust' sign on the back of my dusty minivan.

The proprietor of the one and only store told us most tourists make it to Circle by accident, thinking they're going to the Arctic Circle. No, we told her, we were writers who'd made the drive to Circle on purpose. Yes, she thinks we're nuts, as well as a few dozen other people we talked to about our trip.

Many thanks to Ron and Sylvia of the Chatanika Roadhouse for good coffee, good food, good conversation and information. Ron gave us a personalized tour which included the official outhouse of their annual Outhouse Races held each March. If you're ever there, be sure to mention the crazy romance writers who stopped by. We left our dollar bill under the nightlight display near the entry.

Of note, there is a wonderful essay and a collection of photos detailing the history of the Steese Highway to be found at: http://www.steesehighway.org/steesehistory.html

# Chapter 1

*"There's a salmon-scented girl, who sets my heart awhirl..."*

Linnet Greenbriar closed her eyes and grimaced. Despite the pleasant male baritone singing the annoying song on key for a change, she'd heard the lyrics one too many times in her life. Her fingers clenched around the long aluminum pole in her hands. Each time she'd stopped in Circle some joker had made a point of singing it within her hearing. Out here, miles from the small village, the song was no more welcome than it had been there.

"Manley," she snapped at her borrowed dog without looking around. "Attention."

His whines subsided and she knew he stood alert, watching for the stranger approaching along the trail from the cabin. Hopefully the man would see the dog and just keep moving downstream.

Leaves crunched and twigs snapped under his footfalls. He could be the friend George had said might come by for a week of fishing. Or perhaps he was someone else who'd beached his boat at the small gravel shingle in front of the cabin. Screened by the trees, she couldn't see that far. He certainly hadn't floated past her. Probably George's buddy.

Even that possibility didn't quell the sudden fear turning her blood to ice. With great control, she forced the automatic reaction away. Using rehearsed words, she reminded herself he was just a citizen, entitled to fish wherever he wanted along the river. Men who made the effort to reach this remote location were looking for solitude and a meaningful relationship with the river, not women to party with.

*"And she lives along the Yukon, far away..."*

Just what she needed, some macho man escaping town for a week of fishing. The least he could do was camp someplace else. Determined not to give in to the urge to dash onto the bank and greet him with a .357 aimed his way, she focused on the job in front of her.

*Morgan Q. O'Reilly*

Steadying herself, she made sure her legs were solidly braced, then swiped her dipnet through the strong current of the mighty river trying its best to suck her under. Insulated hip waders protected her from the icy flow, thick and gun metal gray with glacier silt. The Yukon was not a river to be taken lightly. It was a good thing she was tall and her active lifestyle kept her muscles strong, or with one misstep, she could have been swept away by the deadly water pushing at her legs.

The little backwash she'd found was popular with the fish as a resting place where the current wasn't quite as strong. Not to mention easier for her when standing in the river for most of the day. Did her visitor know this spot for that very reason?

The net jerked and she pulled it back, fighting not only the flowing water, but the fish inside. The lifejacket she wore made movement difficult and the mosquito netting draped over her hat and around her head impaired her vision. At this moment, she wasn't so sure she loved Alaska. She loved the land, just not the biting black flies, mosquitoes or gnats, and many of the men were debatable.

"Hey there, Manley." The male voice had stopped singing, and she guessed he stood on the edge of the small clearing on the bank behind her.

She could hear Manley's tail whacking at the stand of alder defining the space.

"How are ya, boy? Where's George?" The voice held the same rich baritone quality as his singing.

Great, Manley knew the stranger behind her. Then this could only be George's friend. She didn't have time to worry about the dog greeting his buddy. To drop her attention now would mean an unwanted swim in the river.

"You do know dipnetting is illegal, right?" the man asked, closer than she expected.

"Fish and Game," she growled and carefully stepped backward, lifting the net so the fish couldn't escape. By the weight and fight, it was a big one. Since it was still hidden under the gray silt of the river she could only guess by the drag on the net. A sixty pounder? Holy crap! No wonder her boss had eyed her up and down before shrugging and sending her out to this post for the rest of the summer. Most of the fish didn't get this big, and damn few like it made it this far up the river, but snatch just the right king salmon and a girl became a fisherman's dream woman. Hell, even a forty pounder would impress most men.

"Fins and Feathers, eh? Want some help with that?"

"Got it." Fighting the monster fish, resisting the current, keeping track of the dog, and speaking politely to a taxpayer was a little more than she could handle all at the same time. The last thing she wanted to do was trip and fall into the river. The water was cold and moved faster than it appeared on the wide flat surface. Even if the stranger nearby could pull her out—doubtful—getting wet was not on her agenda. Weighing and measuring this bad boy was. But first she had to get him onto the bank and that job required her full concentration.

She also didn't need Manley running around on shore once she landed the fish. "Manley, sit."

"Better do as she says, Man."

Ignoring both of them for a moment, Linnet focused on the job at hand, praying the net wouldn't slip from her hands. She worried not so much for the loss of the fish's statistics, but if he remained caught in the net it would be a senseless death. One more step... she grit her teeth and set her heel on the muddy ledge just above the water. Without taking her eye off the wildly thrashing net at the end of the long pole, she shifted her weight, pushing up from the small sandy spot in the water.

Powerless to stop the motion, her heel slipped as the wet bank under it began to crumble. The extra weight of the fish? Her heart jolted in fear. *No!* Her fingers automatically tightened their grip around the handle of the net and she shifted her weight back, praying her torso would land on the solid ground. The bank was high enough that she might very well miss and slide down into the water.

"Whoa there!"

Still clinging to the net, she felt the hard ground spank her bottom and not her back.

"Ooof!" The involuntary sound left her on a whoosh of air.

Strong hands held her under the armpits and dragged her backwards until only her feet and the long pole hung over the edge of the bank. Stunned, she didn't have the presence of mind to protest, much less the time to tell him to keep his hands to himself, before the pole was jerked from her hands and the fish hauled out to lie on the bank beside her. In the next second she had eighty pounds of chocolate lab wiggling onto her lap.

"Manley, down!" She tried to push the eager lab off her.

All his attention was on her now and made the situation all the more awkward. She breathed a sigh of relief when he obeyed, lying at her side with his head across her thigh. "Good boy."

"Nice catch," the male voice said with a tone of amused appreciation.

*Morgan Q. O'Reilly*

"Yeah. Thanks." Shifting uncomfortably, Linnet took stock of her situation. The stranger had made a good catch himself by not letting her fall into the river. Other than a bruised butt, she seemed relatively sound. Shaking her head to toss off her confusion, she looked at the man now crouching beside her as he gently worked to untangle the fish fighting for freedom.

"Thanks for ca-cat…ching me." Her breath caught, making her stutter over the word as she stared into warm brown eyes only inches away. Hot coffee-colored eyes surrounded by thick dark lashes. The kind of lashes she wanted when dressing for a date.

Right, who was she kidding? It had been two years since a date had required clothing fancier than her current apparel. Two years since she'd had any kind of personal relations with a man. Two years since she'd even thought about wearing mascara, much less makeup of any kind. Wincing, she pushed that memory back into its deep, dark hiding place and used her hand to swish away a buzzing insect

"Um, yeah, thanks," she muttered again and pulled her eyes away. Petting Manley to assure him she was fine gave her a moment to let her heart calm down.

"You okay?" Amusement still laced the warm voice and any cold she'd felt from the water or wet ground disappeared. Had she looked in a mirror and seen her face glow bright red she wouldn't have been surprised. Funny, the blush seemed to cover her entire body if the all-over body heat was an indication. The only other explanation would be a hot-flash, but she was too young. "Would have been a nasty dunk if you'd fallen in. That silt is a pain to wash away. Not to mention to clean out of a weapon such as the one you have on your hip. Use it much?"

"Yeah, um, yes, I'm fine." He was right. A swim in the Yukon could have resulted in her being dragged under and found somewhere out in the Bering Sea, if she'd ever been found at all, even with the life jacket she wore. Fallen trees and strong eddies were just some of the dangers lurking in the water. "I carry the weapon to scare off desperados and ravenous beasts."

Nudging Manley aside, she placed her hands on the ground and pushed herself up. Let him wonder which category she placed him in. A strong hand gripped her arm and helped, doing most of the work of hauling her to her feet. "I just need to get this one's statistics and put it back in." The moment she was stable she stepped away, effectively shaking off the stranger's hand as quickly as possible.

With supreme concentration, she crouched over the huge fish, using her feet to keep him from wiggling back into the water. Even though he appeared to be tiring, there was still plenty of power in his tail. Looked like his gills had been caught in the net. Probably the only reason she'd been able to pull him out at all. Nearly the size of a newborn beluga whale, she bet the damn thing would probably reach her shoulder if she stood it on its tail.

"I don't want to leave him out of the water too long." She hoped her explanation sufficed. Looking in the newcomer's face again was just out of the question. There was work to be done and melting into a puddle at his feet wasn't on her checklist.

"Let me help. He's at least sixty-five, maybe even seventy-five pounds. Too bad you have to toss the mighty Chinook back. Good eatin' there." Large tanned hands expertly finished extracting the fish from the net.

Linnet passed him a handheld scale and he attached it to the monstrous mouth.

Protesting probably wouldn't work, so she dug her tape measure from a pocket and stood when he did.

"Oh yeah, what a beauty," the man crooned. "Seventy-six pounds. About twenty pounds under trophy weight, but still a mighty monster. The big kings like this don't usually make it this far up river," he added with a tone of respect.

Linnet stretched out her tape measure. Four feet, three inches. "The size of a small, skinny pre-teen." It wasn't easy to ignore how easily he handled the huge fish. Probably worked out often to have that kind of strength.

The man laughed and she snuck a peek at him. Eyes danced over sculpted cheeks dark with two day's growth of beard. It would come in darker than his sun-streaked honey blond hair, which was long enough it touched the collar of his shirt in loose waves. "Where I come from, this is the size of a child about seven years old."

Linnet felt her heart sink even as her eyes cut to his hands looking for a wedding band. No ring and no sign he'd ever worn one, but that didn't mean anything. Besides, what did she care? She wasn't out here to find a man, but rather to avoid men on the make in general. She stared at him again and noticed she had to look up. Not just aim her eyes up a little, but tilt her head as well. That was unusual. Must make him well over six feet. Six-four?

Concentrating on her job again, she quickly made her other measurements and jotted them down on her clipboard. Figures George hadn't told her more about this mysterious friend of his. Probably never occurred to him to mention the man was a walking wet dream.

Good lord, where had that thought come from? Shaking her head to rid herself of a brief fantasy where she looked down at him framed by the curtains of her hair, she tried to remember what George had told her about the man. Not much. Apparently she was lucky George, man-of-few-words, had mentioned him at all.

Finished, she set down the clipboard and reached for the fish as the man lifted the behemoth in his hands. "Done?" He waited for her nod. "I'll put him back."

"Really, you don't have..." her protest faded away as he flashed a wide grin of white teeth and strode past her to the river. Normally teeth didn't impress her, but the last month had shown her a horrifying array of what poor dental habits could do to people. Damn, if his straight, white teeth weren't one of the sexier things she'd ever seen. Not to mention those tight buns as he bent over, the giant fish cradled in his hands. *If he could hold the fish that easily, he could probably lift me...* Just the thought made her head spin with conflicting emotions as she watched him expertly hold the fish facing upstream until it began to move again, then flipped out of his hands.

"Okay, buddy, there you go. Hang around here and I'll catch you fair and square."

*He talks to fish.* She'd seen stranger things and people were different up here. The thought reminded her of an old quote about Alaskan men. *The odds are good, but the good are odd.* Just how odd, was the question that plagued her most.

The man straightened and watched the beast flick his tail and move sideways then float downstream where Linnet knew the fish would rest as if assuring himself he was still alive. In a few minutes he'd surge upstream again.

Linnet watched the man's body shift under the almost-regulation outdoor clothes. Mosquito-proof shirt, camo fishing vest, faded jeans, brown hip-waders encasing long, long legs. Unlike her, he didn't wear a hat and netting. Must be one of the lucky ones the blood-sucking, vampiric insects didn't like. If there was even one mosquito in the neighborhood, it would beeline straight to her. Guaranteed. It was a sure bet her back was covered with the blood suckers.

As the man turned back toward shore, she bent to pick up her tools. She'd already decided that fish was the last one for the day. The tape measure was quickly tucked into its pocket and the scale attached to one of the many loops of the fishing vest covering her life jacket. Two quick snaps and her chest gratefully expanded, relishing release from the confining flotation device. A deep breath filled her lungs with cool, fresh air as she straightened and stretched.

Each fish she'd pulled from the river had been larger than the last. After a month of the grueling exercise, her arms had toned up and weren't so tired as they'd been the first week. Still, the last beast, combined with her slip, put the exclamation point on her aches for a day that wasn't quite over yet. She finished her notations and slammed her notebook shut with the pen tucked inside.

"Sooooo," the drawn-out drawl drew her attention to her helper again. "You're hanging with Manley. Where's George?" The hand he extended towards her was large. "I'm Creed Willis."

Remembering how he'd pulled her onto the bank and the feel of his grip around her arm, she wiped hers on her hip then clasped his cool, damp palm. Of course, he'd just rinsed it in the river.

"Linnet." Better to avoid her last name in case he recognized her first name was a type of bird. Kind of like being named Robin. Thankfully she didn't have to endure jokes about red breasts in addition to shrubbery. Once men figured out a linnet was a species of bird, the jokes that followed about a bird in the bush were too hard to resist. And since they were in 'the Bush' of Alaska, the layers just increased.

"Just Linnet?" He held her hand warm and secure as she stared. Not hard, just… secure. Like she tried to pull it away. Not. His twinkling eyes messed with her composure again.

"It works for now," she muttered and, unbelievably, felt her face flush.

He released her hand and pushed aside her vest to show her badge. "Greenbriar. Linnet Greenbriar. Pretty name. Pleased to meet you." Before she could finish jerking away from the unwanted touch, the spreading grin on his face told her the jokes were already processing in his head.

Telling herself he was only being friendly, she kept her curled fist at her side. "Save 'em," she said shortly, and stepped back. "I've heard them all, and I do mean all." Now if only the blood roaring through her ears would dissipate.

"What?" His hand dropped to his side and a confused look creased his face.

"The jokes about my name." Using the opportunity to avert her face, she bent once more and picked up her dipnet. For the first time she noticed his fishing gear lying on the ground. Probably meant her head was clearing. Still, a good time to put some distance between them.

Thoughts of barring the cabin door until he left seemed at once prudent and childish. "Anyhow, I'll leave you to your fishing. Or should I ask to see your license?"

"George Nyuchuk checked it six weeks ago, but I'd be happy to show it to you," he said as he reached for his wallet. "What happened to George anyway? This is his beat and you're with his dog."

She held up her hand to stop him from pulling out his fishing license. Looking at his license would only prolong this contact. "I believe you. George slipped in the mud and broke his leg. He's in the office for the rest of the summer, so they called me up from Anchorage. He thought Manley would keep me company and provide a measure of protection at the same time."

Creed shoved his wallet back into his pocket. "Sorry to hear about that. George is a good man to fish with. Manley makes a good guard dog, though. Knows the regulars on this stretch of the river and he's an excellent judge of character. Do you fish?"

The animal under discussion wiggled and rubbed up against Creed in a shameless bid for attention. Attention Creed readily provided. Linnet almost envied the dog writhing under the big hands stroking his body. Was it possible to feel that much pleasure from the touch of another? With great effort she pulled her mind back to the question.

"No. I just net, measure and toss them back. That's enough for me."

"Nothing like fresh salmon cooked over a birch fire on the riverbank." The look in his eyes made her want to wiggle under more than just his hands.

Immediately after that thought she wanted to slap herself. Men who looked like him felt like they were God's gift to women. She didn't need to be a groupie on his ego trip. *Been dragged down that road already.*

"If you say so." She adjusted her grip on the dipnet and notebook, looked around the cleared bank to make sure she had everything, then shook her head to clear the unwelcome thoughts suddenly inhabiting it. "We'll leave you to it. Have a good evening. Manley, come."

The dog reluctantly came to her side. After a month of being her obedient and enthusiastic companion, his action was telling. Definitely George's friend. Great. What had George said about the man? A loner who liked to spend hours in the river fishing. She patted Manley's head and took her first step.

"Wait." Creed's tone more than his word stopped her. As if he wanted to keep her there. At her heels, Manley stopped as well and sat down.

"Are you staying out here? I pulled up at the cabin back that way and noticed the truck outside." He pointed upstream toward the cabin.

Good manners said all travelers were welcome at the old log cabin, which was open for public use. George had told her it was on private homestead land, but the owner purposely allowed river travelers to use it as needed. Silly to bar a perfectly warm and dry cabin to those who floated the river. It was just the Alaskan way, and all who used it knew the rules and savored the experience of living in a genuine, pioneer log cabin built in the early nineteen thirties.

Most only stayed one night before they moved down the river. If more than one party arrived on the same night, they shared the space. They stayed longer if the weather was bad or they were tired. So far she'd only had to share it one night with a family canoeing the river from Eagle to Circle and another with an older gentleman who stopped because of rain. All the others had opted for the gravel bar downstream, away from the mosquitoes and biting flies. Smart people.

Only a handful of people knew how to access the cabin over land, via a track not worthy to be called a road. Since neither vehicles nor road could be seen from the river, the secret stayed secure. Even with a detailed map, she'd needed GPS coordinates to find the final turn-off from the Steese Highway to travel the last twenty miles over the four-wheel-drive-only track between the trees. A drive that discouraged her from daily trips to the nearest town for groceries. In four weeks, she'd only been out once by the road.

"Yes, that's my truck. If you want the cabin, I can set up my tent. I'm prepared to give way to citizens." Damn. Because Manley and any bears in the area weren't a good mix in a tent, she'd chosen the cabin. The truck was big enough they could sleep there again. George had assured her Manley knew all about camping. He'd never mentioned whether or not this friend stayed in the cabin or pitched a tent.

"No, don't move out. There's a tent in the shed I can use. Since it's a good place to park, I hope you don't mind if I set up near there?"

"No. No problem." Yes, there was a problem, but she could bar the door at night and had a couple of weapons handy, not to mention Manley was well trained with voice commands and would attack on order. Creed didn't look like a murderer or rapist, but you never knew out here in the wilderness.

Looks, as she well knew, could be deceiving, and she was miles away from anywhere… A moment of panic iced her blood before she shook it off. Manley knew him. Would Manley protect her from a man he knew? Who was more dangerous? The two- or four-legged predator? Nevertheless, Creed was right; it was one of the better camping spots with the flat ground around the cabin, a fire pit and an outhouse.

"Nice truck."

"What about it?" She stared at him through narrowed eyes. This is where he'd say something cute and patronizing about girls out in the wilderness.

"Hey, I'm not trying to harass you. I just like the decal on the back. It's wrong, but I like it." He gave her a boyish smile and she felt one side of her mouth curving up to return it before she could stop herself.

"Yeah, well, you're allowed to have your own opinion." Teasing? Where did teasing come from? Seeking to regain control, she forced her expression to fade into the neutral cop face she was learning to cultivate to hold strangers at bay. "Enjoy the fishing. There are some big ones out there right now."

"No kidding. A hog like that one would feed me all winter. I'm not usually so lucky."

"Well, remember your limit. Good night." Feeling as if she fled, she turned and strode into the trees with Manley at her side.

* * * *

*Good night?* Creed glanced at his watch again. Early August meant the days were still long. No, his time sense wasn't that far off. It was only seven in the evening. Maybe she just knew fishermen. He was likely to stay out here until it grew too dark to see or he couldn't keep his eyes open any longer. A couple of times this summer he'd fished all night and not realized it. It was easy to lose track of time out here when the sun didn't set long enough for even dusk to settle. This close to the Arctic Circle the sun didn't set at all for a week on either side of the Summer Solstice.

But not tonight. It had been a long day and all he wanted tonight was fresh salmon cooked over an open flame for dinner. He'd get to the more serious fishing tomorrow. The sooner he caught the fish, the sooner he could get back to camp, set up, and find out more about his neighbor for the next week and a half.

Intimately familiar with his gear, five minutes later he stood knee deep in the water. As the river pushed at his legs, the soothing flow washed away all the cares of the outside world. Standing on the edge with the mile wide, flat river before him put life in perspective. The sheer vastness of the river and the land around him reduced his problems and worries to specks no larger than the swarm of gnats hovering nearby.

The last four weeks had seemed endless, but now he was here. Just twelve hours ago he'd eaten breakfast a few hundred miles to the north. Less than an hour off the plane and he'd been in his truck for the four hour drive to the river, the last forty miles pure dust and grit after several weeks of sun and little rain. He'd dreamt about this every night for the last week. This was the life. Just him and the river. One trying to hold onto the fish, one trying to steal them out. An ancient battle. One he was very good at.

The image of Linnet standing in the current came back to him as he made a deep cast out into the water. He'd noticed right away that she was taller than most women when she stood next to him. Despite the layers of clothing and the life jacket, he'd known she was a woman at first glance. No red-blooded male could have missed the shape of those hips. Not even the wide brimmed hat with concealing netting had hidden her appeal. Wide, light-colored eyes had made his heart thump double time when she'd finally looked at him.

Gripping the pole, his hands remembered the feel of her arms. Firm and strong. He bet the rest of her was firm as well. Her breasts had made her lifejacket burst open when she'd released the latches. Good thing she hadn't been looking at him then, or she would have seen his tongue hanging out.

*Get a grip, man.* He should just pack up now and hike up stream. Fish far away from this stretch. It had been ages since he'd camped out along the bank, away from the cabin. Maybe he was going soft. Until he had to go back to the North Slope, he wanted to be as far away from people as possible. For a private guy, living two weeks on and two weeks off was tough on his need to be alone. Working a double shift of four weeks was murder.

Living in Prudhoe Bay housing for the *on* portion of his work schedule meant little or no privacy. He shared a room with his alternate, so he had no space to call his own while on the job. Sure, it was his during his weeks on, but it didn't have private facilities. Bathrooms, showers, laundry and dining were all communal experiences. He'd give it all up but for just one thing.

The money.

It always came back to the money. The money and the two weeks of seclusion to balance out the two weeks of remote camp life with its twelve-hour workdays. It sure as hell beat the normal day-in-and-day-out, Monday-through-Friday, eight-to-five work schedule. Two weeks off, every month, to do as he pleased.

In the summer, that meant fishing on a lonely stretch of river. In the winter it meant holing up in Fairbanks. It was a good life and he enjoyed the solitude. Books, DVDs, and woodcarving filled those hours of peace and quiet. At least once a year he'd fly out to someplace warm. Scuba diving in Hawaii was mighty fine in January. Cancun added variety. This winter he wanted to dive Belize. It would be his turn for four weeks off. Could probably do both Cancun and Belize.

He should move on and leave Linnet in peace to do her job. A little short on sweet manners, still, at first glance, she'd seemed capable enough. Until her foot had slipped. He grinned, thinking of how he'd pulled her from near disaster. That should earn him some hero points.

Not a delicate little flower, she had some meat on her bones. Not fat, not even stocky, just solid, like she spent a lot of time outdoors or in the gym. *What did she look like without the loose fitting shirt? Would the rest of her match her curvy ass?* Strong enough to pull in a seventy-six-pound king salmon. *Damn, what a fish that had been.*

Who was he kidding? He wouldn't move on. A woman out here alone was trouble and who the hell had let her come out here? Sure, she had a well-trained dog with her, but Manley wouldn't stop a determined bear or man. Creed frowned at the river, not really seeing it.

Like him, George had been raised out here. He knew the dangers, knew how to take care of himself. But this chica looked as if she'd been city raised, and not even Anchorage. Probably from California, if he had to guess. Her truck had screamed city slicker, especially with the decal in the back window.

"*Silly boys, trucks are for girls.*" Just saying it out loud made him laugh.

Without the decal, he wouldn't have guessed it was a woman's truck. The decal had sent him wandering down the trail instead of fishing right in front of the cabin. Brand new, the bright blue paint had shone through the heavy layer of tan-colored dust that came from driving the remote highway. Fully outfitted with a shell on the back, Linnet could probably live in that thing if she needed to.

A tug on the line told him he had a live one. Was it the big king? Or was it a Dolly Varden? It was a fighter for sure. With the tune he'd been singing now playing in his head, he turned his attention to pulling dinner from the river.

Could he talk Linnet into eating with him? More importantly, as prickly as she'd been, how long would it take him to seduce her into being his dessert?

# Chapter 2

On her way back to the cabin, after washing her dishes in the tiny clear-water creek that ran into the river, Linnet heard his singing before she saw him.

*"Where the Northern Lights, they shine, she rubs her nose to mine, she cuddles close and I can hear her say... Ooga-ooga mooska, which means that I love you. If you'll be my baby, I'll ooga-ooga mooska you. Then I take her hand in mine and set her on my knee, the squaws along the Yukon are good enough for me..."*

He finished up the chorus as he strolled into the clearing. "Hey there," he said in greeting.

Linnet stopped by the picnic table under the deep gable overhang of the sod roof. "Hi," she grunted. Then rolled her eyes as he hummed the tune. "Please. Don't you know any other song? That is if you absolutely must sing."

She felt the need to harden her defenses. This one was a charmer. The worst kind of man. The kind who could slip into a girl's bed before she could pull back the covers and invite him. Exactly the kind she didn't want to be near.

"What? Don't you like my voice? I was almost the lead singer in a rock band in college. I returned to Alaska instead." The wide easy grin only convinced Linnet she had him sorted out properly.

"You have a fine voice. It's the song I object to." A mosquito buzzed her ear and she waved her hand to whoosh it away.

"Ah, now see, you just don't have an appreciation for fine music." He dropped his tackle box on the bench and flopped a large plastic food bag down on the table. It was stuffed with deep pink salmon fillets. "That song is a Hank Thompson classic. Was real popular forty—fifty years ago."

*Ah, Neanderthal days. Better to let that subject drop.* "Didn't catch the big guy?" A nod at his catch neatly changed the subject.

"Nah. Too early in the trip. I want to catch one like him just as I'm heading back into town. This is just right for dinner tonight and lunch tomorrow. Hope you'll join me."

"Thanks, but I just finished washing up my dishes. Manley had his yummy kibble and I had a nice bowl of pasta." She clanked her metal plate down into the pot she'd just washed.

"Don't tell me you're a vegetarian." He gasped, and she had a hard time not laughing at the horror on his face.

"Those radical liberals," she scoffed. "I'm a vegan."

"A what?"

This time she did laugh at the blank look on his face. "Just kidding. Actually, I'm worse than vegan. I hate salmon." And the bugs loved her. Fanning them away with her hand didn't work for long.

"No! How can you live in Alaska and hate salmon?" Hand over his heart, he staggered back a step.

She shrugged. "Easy. I don't keep what I catch, so I don't have to clean it or eat it. Just measure it. Now if you want to talk halibut or shellfish..."

"You must be from California."

The teasing look on his face shored up her resolve to hold him at arm's length. "And that has to do with what?" Too many digs about Californians over the past year had her hackles rising. Why did everyone on the West Coast pick on Californians as a whole?

"Hey, no offense meant." In a silent gesture pleading for peace, he held up his hands and gave her a smile most women probably found irresistible. "I've just noticed people from California, the Bay Area in particular, love their shellfish. East Coasters too, but the accent is West Coast."

"Right. Well, I have some things to do, so I'll leave you to your dinner." She turned toward the cabin door only to stop cold at his touch.

The warmth from his big hand gently holding her upper arm burned through her shirt as if it didn't exist. The first instinctive fight-or-flight adrenalin rush hit her then faded into something else.

This man didn't want to hurt her, she knew it on a deep, inexplicable level, but she'd been fooled before. Because of that one exception, where a nice guy had turned out to be a beast, her body stiffened, preparing... waiting... Panic held at bay for the moment, she stared down at his hand, willing him to release her. Instead he tugged her back around to face him.

"I didn't mean to hurt your feelings. It was a joke. I'm sorry."

With no netting to shadow her face now, she reluctantly looked up at him. Serious with his apology, his brown eyes shimmered as he stared at her. Their gazes locked. She watched his soften and a smile lit up his whole face.

"Don't worry about it." Could she sound any more insipid or dead? "I'm used to the slams."

Creed shook his head slowly. "Not a slam. Just an observation, meant to be friendly teasing."

"Fine. Now, if you'll release me, I do have some work I want to finish up tonight. I hope you won't object to the sound of my generator for an hour." Speaking civilly was damn near impossible and the tiny quaver in her voice didn't help. Torn between wanting to hit him with her best karate chop and wanting to wrap her arms around him, Linnet was desperate to put sanity-restoring distance between them.

Something of her inner battle must have showed in her eyes because his regard turned curious as his hand slowly uncurled from her bicep. "No, that's fine. As long as it doesn't run all night." The white teeth flashed at her and the return of his easy smile nearly melted her.

As much to clear her mind as to agree with him, she shook her head. "I enjoy the peace and quiet too much, but I do need the power tonight. I don't run it every day." Besides, the generator blocked out sounds she wanted to hear at night. Sounds of bears or other beasts trying to break into the cabin.

"By the way, you're very pretty without the hat and netting."

Rolling her eyes helped cover the jump of her already thundering pulse. "Most people look better without it. Speaking of," she batted at the gathering of buzzing insects, "time for me to get this chore done and then get myself inside before they eat me alive. Good night."

\* \* \* \*

Dismissed. Again. Twice in one evening. If a guy were emotionally invested it could be a blow to his ego. Had her eyes showed the slightest hint of disgust he probably would have felt offended. Instead he felt challenged. Interest was there, without the netting over her face it had been as clear as the pulse beating at the base of her throat and her faint blush.

What confused him was the other emotion he'd seen deep in her eyes. Fear? If he wanted to get anywhere with her, it would be best to move slowly. Like he had time to move slowly with not quite two weeks until he was gone again.

Hands working automatically to start a cooking fire in the concrete fire pit a half dozen yards away and downhill from the slight rise the cabin sat on, he let his mind sort through the fresh memory of her. Like an Alaskan strip tease, she'd removed the hip waders and vest along with the netting to reveal more of the luscious curves he'd guessed were there. The oversized long-sleeved shirt had to go. He wanted to see under it.

In a face worthy of a super model, she had big, clear, pale green eyes framed by thick lashes and delicately arched brows. Sun had glinted off red highlights in the rich brown hair pulled back into a thick ponytail. Let loose, her hair probably fell to the middle of her back. He'd wanted to pull off the tie holding it back and see.

The flush of heat across her cheeks had enhanced the high cheekbones, rounded like small apples. And her lips. A man could wax poetic about those lips. Perfectly proportioned and naturally red.

He'd love to see her smile without restraint, though the little crooked quirk was down-right adorable. Each feature in itself perfect as if sculpted by a master artist.

But no artist could have captured the beauty of her skin. Marred only by a few mosquito bites, her flesh was lightly tanned. Was the tan limited to her face and hands? Her top hadn't been unbuttoned enough for him to see. His fingers still itched to pop the buttons on her deep green shirt just as she'd popped open her life vest earlier.

Satisfied the fire burned properly, Creed laid the cooking grate over the flames, placed the frying pan on it and turned to his food box. Practiced hands quickly seasoned the fillets with a dry rub made up of his own blend of herbs and spices. That task completed, he moved to the next while the pan heated. Finding a flat spot to the side of the cabin, he erected and secured his tent in a matter of a few minutes, sleeping bag and gear just as quickly organized inside. The simple life. After dinner he'd secure the food box in the cabin and then set about getting to know Linnet better.

From the corner of his eye, he watched her exit the cabin and walk around behind it. The unfamiliar slap of a screen door snapping shut made him do a double take. When had the screen door been installed? The wooden frame looked as if it had been there as long as the log cabin. A bit of curved antler formed a handle and a simple spring pulled it closed. A few minutes later the purr of a generator rumbled in the quiet, not as loud as he'd expected. Not bad. Almost soothing. He hadn't noticed it earlier, so maybe she had it stashed in the trees or in the back of her truck. She'd need a couple extra-long extension cords if that was the case.

Setting his dinner into the hot pan, he kept half an eye on the cabin. What did she need the power for? A laptop? City girl for sure. He added a freshly sliced onion to the fillets in the large, well-seasoned cast-iron frying pan. Bet she didn't have a cast-iron fry pan, not one with the years of history behind his.

Rumor, and family legend, said his great-great grandfather had carried this very frying pan up and over the Chilkoot Trail alongside Jack London. Creed's father had once bragged his sourdough starter dated back equally as far. His mother had later told Creed she'd had to restart a fresh batch in the seventies. Still respectably old, but certainly not any more special than most Alaskan starters.

The whine of a power tool broke into his thoughts and he looked up. She was still out of his view so he couldn't identify the tool immediately. Not a circular saw, yet it didn't sound like a drill either. Unable to resist, he turned the salmon in the pan and pulled it off to the very edge of the grate. He stepped to the side far enough to see her concentrating on the side of the cabin with a tool held about eye level. *A reciprocating saw?*

Wagging under the force of his tail, Manley left Linnet and came over to Creed.

"Hey, boy, what's she doing, eh?" Creed scratched Manley's neck and accepted the animal's need for human comfort. "Making a lot of noise, isn't she?" The dog pressed against his legs and Creed patted him. "Did George give her permission to make improvements?" Why the hell hadn't George called him?

Manley, having no answers, merely wagged his tail and tried to knock Creed over.

Torn between his sizzling dinner and curiosity over her actions, he hovered until she put down the saw and reached up. "Stay," he told Manley. One could only hope the dog wouldn't try to steal the salmon.

"Need a hand?" he offered. Had he surprised her? The flinch took him by surprise as much as the fact his question seemed to have startled her.

"Nope. Got it," she grunted out the words and carefully lifted down the ancient rectangle of glass with gloved hands. He was impressed she wore safety glasses. A good-sized tool box lay open at her feet. That sucker had to be heavy and her truck was easily a couple dozen yards away, down the backside of the rise.

"What are you doing?"

She shot him a mildly irritated glance before answering. "Modifying the windows so they open. It gets stuffy inside the cabin, but since the mosquitoes love me, I want to cover them with screening."

"Wow, we're going high class now." The lines of her body stretched to reach over her head distracted him for a moment. He could see her in a clinging evening gown, or better yet, a clinging negligee.

When she struggled with a bit of wood stubbornly stuck to the upper frame, he reached over her head and pulled it down.

"Thanks," she mumbled and stepped to the side, barely missing the pane of glass. "I seem to use that word with you a lot."

Yeah, and he liked it. "Come sit with me while I eat and then I'll help you. Two will make it go faster." Waving his hand toward the fire, he felt like a teenager asking a girl out for the first time. Odd.

"I like doing this. Besides, now the window is open I don't want to leave it that way any longer than necessary," she gave him the brush off. "Too hard to flush the blood suckers out, even using the smoke coils."

Fair enough, he could see that. It took away some of the sting from her rejection.

"Honest, I can do this myself. I already did the window on the other side. Go take a look and see, if you don't think I'm competent." She used a wide-bladed chisel to clean the surfaces of the window frame set into the log structure.

"I have no doubt you're competent, I'm just looking for an excuse to talk to you." Maybe a sheepish admission would win her over. He gave her his best attempt at a boyish smile.

"You'd better stick close to your dinner or Manley might forget he's a well-trained dog." She smirked over her shoulder. "Go on. Eat your hard-won fish. Maybe you can hold the frame when I'm ready to put the hinges on and reinstall it."

He stared at her for a moment, waiting for her to turn and look up at him. Standing this close, he got a better sense of her height. He wouldn't have to bend far to kiss her. No neck strain. Moving without a conscious thought from him, his hand reached out and tucked a stray lock of hair behind her ear. "Promise?"

Why did she flinch and why did she refuse to turn toward him? He wanted her to turn and smile at him in the worst way. Instead her shoulders stiffened.

"Yes."

He barely heard her husky response and trailed the back of his fingers down the side of her neck. The sensation made her swallow deeply. There was that pretty flush again.

"Linnet…"

Abruptly she cleared her throat and dropped to a crouch. "Smells like your dinner might be burning."

*Shit.* He didn't care about his dinner. What he wanted was a kiss... and a whole lot more. Didn't look like he'd get it right now.

Linnet breathed a sigh of relief when he finally turned away. Another minute and she would have leaped into his arms or slammed an elbow into his midsection. Conflicted, trying to determine if he were friend or foe, chances were she'd probably try to do both at the same time. Complications out here weren't needed.

There was work to be done and she was the new kid. A Cheechako. An Alaskan greenhorn. Proving herself was number one on her list. Using her forearm, she wiped away the sweat gathering on her brow. The day's heat didn't seem to be dissipating and the long sleeves she wore to protect against bugs didn't help.

Fitting the glass into the frame she'd built last night, she carefully tacked it into place with strips of wood molding. Not properly glazed, it would allow for the expansion and contraction of the wood as the seasons cycled. The cabin only had three windows; one on the east and one on the west, both set high in the walls, the last next to the north-facing door.

The ones in the walls were two feet wide by one foot high. Just barely large enough to let in light. The window by the door was larger, four panes of glass, each two feet square, providing a good view to the river. Simple shutters were made from plywood covers that dropped down over the outside of the windows when the cabin was unoccupied.

Using the same principal as the shutters, she'd designed a frame that could be pushed open from the inside to let air in. A stick pushed the window out and held it open. Fiberglass screening tacked in place with a staple gun would keep the winged ravening hoards out. One window on each side in addition to the screen door would provide ample cross breeze to keep the cabin cool when the summer temps outside reached an unbelievable one-hundred degrees. A hundred degrees in Alaska. Who'd a thunk?

The thermometer had been stuck in the high eighties since mid-morning and the bugs' usually frantic drone seemed slow and lazy because of the warmth. The ventilation would also be great with the RV style three burner propane stove and oven someone had been clever enough to salvage and install.

The work required enough of her attention to keep her from thinking about Creed sitting on a log by the fire. Carefully keeping half an eye on him didn't help much. If her mind wandered even a tiny bit she felt his gaze on her. Manley—the traitor—lay by his feet, gazing up at him with utter doggy adoration. Probably hoping for handouts.

Using her cordless power screwdriver, she'd just set the last screw in the hinges on the frame when she felt man and dog approach. Easing the cramps out of her legs, she stood.

"Good timing," she said without looking around.

"Are you sure about that?"

How did he get so close, so fast? She felt the warmth of his breath against her neck stirring a few loose hairs at the nape. A shiver of undetermined meaning coursed through her and he chuckled.

"Do you want the inside or outside?" she asked. One step to the side put a little distance between them.

"How did you do it before?"

"Very carefully. Here, you hold the frame while I put in the screws. After that it's a simple matter to put up the screening."

"You can do it from here." Even though he made sense, the suggestion almost didn't stop her from running away into the cabin.

Not really wanting to run, she gave in and felt his chest brush against her back while she reached over her head to position the window and secure the hinges. Fortunately it only took six screws. The way her hands shook made the job take twice as long as it should have. Dropping one of the screws didn't help either.

"Wait," he said as she prepared to squat and look for the screw. "You hold the window, I think I see where it landed."

The way he had her trapped against the wall, she could just see her butt pushing into his groin if she bent over to find the screw. It was that, or find her face at his groin level if she crouched. "Sure."

Okay, so his face was level with her butt, his hand resting on her waist to steady himself as he crouched. She looked down to watch his long fingers reach into the decaying leaves piled up against the base of the wall. His fingers plucked the screw from the ground and there was a heartbeat of hesitation before he stood again.

Had he been staring at her butt? Had he been thinking about biting it or something? Oh God, she was so not prepared to deal with this. A moment before she considered hip checking him to his ass, he stood and held the screw under her nose. His arm under hers, his arm against the side of her breast.

"You're pushing your luck, buddy," she growled. Too bad the waver in her voice ruined the effect.

"Sorry, didn't mean to intrude so deeply into your personal space." Damn if she couldn't hear the amusement in his voice. At least, thank goodness, he returned to holding the window and stepped back a few inches.

"Did you make the screen door as well?" he asked when the final screw was secure.

A finger of smoke curled out of the window. The back of a hand pressed to her nose suppressed the need to sneeze. She nodded.

"Great idea."

"I still need to attach the push stick." That would mean turning around, facing him. Trapped between him and the wall of the cabin. With her hands up over her head. Oh, God. Let him continue to be a gentleman.

He moved back half a step and she escaped long enough to get the pieces. Sure enough, he left only two inches of air space between them again while she attached the part with two screws.

"Okay, let's double check the fit," she was able to say at last.

Without stepping away, he gently lowered the window and slid it into place. "Very clever idea, Linnet. Perfect fit." Somehow he'd managed to step close enough to erase the slight distance without her personal space alarms going off.

The way he said her name and stared down into her eyes lit a smoldering fire deep inside. His chest rumbled against hers so she could feel his voice as much as she heard it. The slight friction made her nipples tighten and ignited a tenuous heat deep in her core. Was he talking about the window or how their bodies fit together? Squeezing her legs together didn't help much and a suspicious dampness grew while the tiny voice in her head screamed out, *no no no*!

"Glad you approve," she managed to say, though how she couldn't imagine. "I need to get the screen in place."

He sure seemed to be in place, his hands resting on the wall beside her head, his body touching hers from chest to thigh. Dizziness assaulted her and once more fight or flight fought with the need to wrap her arms around his neck. Incredibly, the latter seemed to be winning.

"Is it ready to go up?"

He was certainly already up if the presence against her stomach meant anything. Or was he asking if her fireworks were ready to go up? The answer was yes… but to what question? *Oh, the screen. Right.*

He smelled good. Wood smoke from the campfire, and mint. No salmon? Come to think of it, he'd eaten dinner rather fast. Gum? Or did he travel with breath freshener in the woods? What would he taste like to kiss? Certainly there was a scent of pure male about him. Soap and fresh air. *No!* She didn't need to be thinking these thoughts. Remember...

*Answer. He's waiting for one.* Where in the hell had her brain gone?

"Yes. I have it cut already."

"I suppose getting it means one of us moving."

Sounded like a horrible idea to her. "Right. I need to get the screen. It's inside. I'll get it." *Babbling! Stop babbling!*

"Would you like me to staple it on out here?"

"Sure. While you do that I can check on the coils already lit inside." That was her opening to escape, but did she take it? Oh no.

His gaze left her face and traveled down her neck. "You also need a touch of calamine on those bites. You have some new ones."

The minute he said it she had the overwhelming urge to scratch. Releasing the wall, he grabbed the hand flying toward her face.

"Don't scratch. If you want, I can help apply the lotion. You do have calamine, right?"

Yeah, she had antihistamine cream, but it wouldn't do anything about the heat of his hand on her wrist. Gently gripping her arm, he applied just enough strength to hold her nails away from her face. Ragged nails on rough hands. She curled her fingers into her palm. Filing her nails was already on her list for the night.

"Benadryl, but it works the same. Okay, let me go, I'll go take care of the bites and hand the screening out the window. I'll also prop it open from inside. The staple gun is already loaded and in the tool box."

Creed let out a sigh of regret when she moved away. She'd fit him. Perfectly. Her lips had only been a few inches away and as tempting as ripe strawberries, her breath as sweet. Why hadn't he kissed her? The fact she alternated between tensing and softening might have something to do with it. That, and the salmon he'd just eaten.

He'd tossed the onions and most of the meal into the river, eating just enough with a piece of bread to kill the growling of his stomach. Good thing fresh fish didn't have the over-powering aroma of most seafood. Still, even chewing on wild mint while he cleaned up in record time hadn't completely cut the taste in his mouth.

Hyper aware of her, he listened to her movements inside the cabin. He was able to look through the window, and saw her press a hand to her flushed cheek before she reached for the section of screening.

"Duct tape?" He laughed when she opened the window and slid the material through. She'd edged it with the all-purpose, fix-everything solution most favored by Alaskans living in the Bush. Pilots had been known to repair wings well enough to make it home using this stuff. Hundred-mile-an-hour tape they called it. The only thing missing was the blue tarp. Give an Alaskan a blue tarp and a roll of duct tape and they could fashion everything from a tent to an apron out of the materials.

"It'll keep the edges from fraying and make it last a little longer. Hopefully longer than one winter."

"Brilliant. One more use for the books." He smiled wide to let her know he approved. Holding the screen in place he attached the first staple with a truly satisfying snap. "Is it straight?"

She nodded and he set another staple.

"I might get my name in the *Book of Sourdoughs* yet, eh?"

Her sarcastic bite made him laugh. "How long have you lived up here?"

"You tell me first." The challenge came back at him without hesitation. "I want to know who I'm talking to."

"Oh, well, I guess you could just say I'm Alaskan through and through."

"Native?" An arched brow rose nearly to her hairline. "Forgive me for saying so, but you don't look…"

"Eskimo? Indian? Ah well, must be the Russian, Swede and Irish getting in the way. And yet, there is that tiny bit of blood, one-sixteenth to be exact, which holds me to the land."

"There's a family story there I'm dying to hear."

"Oh, now that would take hours, days, weeks, nay years to tell." He tacked the last staple in place. "What do you think? Tight enough to protect your fair hide?"

He watched her face as she tested the screen from inside. "Should catch all but the most determined ones. You know, the ones that can squeeze through a hole half that size."

Most people didn't believe it, but Creed had sat once and watched a hungry mosquito do exactly that. Voracious buggers when sweet blood was around. Even now they began to swarm on the screen. By morning it would be black with the greedy little things. Just like her back had been at the river this afternoon.

"So, which flavor of native are you?" Her question drew his attention back.

"Aleut." Ah, that surprised her. Cute the way she raised her brow. "All right, I'll give you my lineage, but you have to tell me your story too."

"Fair enough I suppose."

Decidedly reluctant to part with her past. What little secret did she hide? Everyone had secrets. Some were just more interesting than others.

"I want to clean up first." She moved away from the window.

"I'll get the gear outside. Is the back of your truck open?"

"Yes. You'll need the keys to lock it up again." She paused and turned to look at him through the window, her lips curled up on one side in her quirky half smile. "Thanks."

Would she thank him after a long night of loving? Just turning that smoldering gaze on him was almost thanks enough. Ms. Linnet Greenbriar was going to make a most interesting companion for the next several days. A small part of Creed was very glad good old George had broken his leg. He'd have to thank his cousin later.

# Chapter 3

"What about the generator? Are you done with it?"

Damn that voice of his. She didn't want the thrills coursing through her body at the sound of it. Didn't need him interrupting her peaceful existence just when she was relaxing and no longer dreading each boat floating down the river.

Creed stood on the other side of the screened window, his head barely clearing the rafters of the eaves, peering into the cabin.

"Let me check." She turned toward the box in the corner and checked the dials then looked at her laptop on the table. "I need it to run maybe another thirty minutes. My batteries aren't quite fully charged."

Creed's snort made her look up at him with a frown.

"Can't leave civilization behind for a few weeks?"

Before she could stop herself, she straightened and with fists on hips snapped out her response. "Unlike you, I'm out here to do a job. I need the laptop for my work. It's more efficient to just type everything in from the get-go."

He threw up his hands in surrender. "Okay, okay, I'm sorry. Didn't mean to get your dander up again."

Linnet forced herself to release her tension with a huge exhale. *Blow it out.* She was out here to get some perspective on life while doing routine data gathering. *Mustn't take offense at every hint of criticism. You're too touchy. Just relax and go with the flow. You know your job, now learn the people skills to go along with it.* Re-learn.

Reminding herself of the words her supervisor had spouted didn't help a whole lot, but it did help her back down. "Would you like a cup of cocoa or tea while waiting for the generator to finish?"

That put the wide friendly grin back on his face. "I'd love some. Cocoa that is."

"Bring your mug. I'll heat the water."

Creed ducked to move from under the low eves and she sighed. The man was simply overwhelming.

As a wildlife biologist, she worked primarily with men, when she worked with people at all. During the summer, she spent most of her time outdoors and had worked toward positions just like this one. Frank Newbauer, her boss, had made it crystal clear, this was a test. If she did well here, she'd be given more remote assignments.

As far as she was concerned, her entire career depended on doing this right. Failure meant office work and small jobs in town. Either desk work or public relations. Neither appealed to her.

Through the screen door she heard Creed and Manley approaching. She lit the burner on the stove and felt a glow of satisfaction as she set the kettle over the flame. Lighting the stove in the closed-up cabin had made her nervous. Now she had plenty of air flow to do it safely.

"Wow." The quiet word from Creed made her glance his way.

She saw a look of awe on his face as he looked around.

"George gave you permission to make all these changes?"

She shrugged. "After my first week up here I drove back to Fairbanks, told him what I wanted to do and he said he was cool with it." In fact he'd had sort of a confused expression on his face as if he'd only just realized the cabin needed some work. "Didn't think the owner would mind. Do you know who owns this piece of land anyway?"

Creed gave her an odd look, as if considering his words. The moment passed and then he shrugged. "I do. I mean, I own it."

Mouth open, anything she might have to say froze in her throat. Linnet stared at him and felt all heat leave her body.

In the space of one heartbeat Creed held her in his arms. "You okay? You went pale rather fast there."

"Oh." Didn't she know any other words? *Shit.* First she barred him from his own cabin and then she got caught making changes. No matter how needed repairs were, to touch a cabin was a huge no-no on the Federal- and State-owned public-use cabins, even more so in privately-owned cabins. As thanks for staying there, she'd hoped to do it quietly and anonymously, but no, she'd had to get caught red handed.

"I like it. Honestly. The improvements are long overdue. Thank you for taking the initiative."

She stared up at him. Had she done something right for a change? Henry, her ex-fiancé, had nearly had puppies when she'd rearranged his houseplants so they'd get more light. It had taken him a week to admit her arrangement might be better. He'd been positively grumpy when his Chinese evergreen had produced its first flowers ever, three weeks later.

"I did my best to keep it as authentic-looking as possible." Heart pounding with renewed fury, the words left her in a rush. "If you don't like anything I can put it back the way it was." Hell, she'd even scuff dirt into the floorboards again if he insisted.

"Linnet, hush."

His lips were awfully close to hers, his brown eyes darkening with something she wasn't sure she recognized. Maybe didn't even want to identify. At least it didn't seem dangerous in the sense he meant to hurt her. Mint came to her again, warm and cool at the same time, as she took in the physical sensations. A strong arm encircled her back, and a large hand cupped her cheek, fingers stroking the edge of her hair ever so gently and non-threateningly. Warmth. From his body, eyes and hands, filling in the cold empty places inside her. Places she hadn't even realized were cold and empty.

"You did a beautiful job. The repairs needed to be made. The improvements make it more comfortable. Thank you." Spoken quietly, the words as much as the gruff rumble of his voice contributed to the weak feeling invading her entire body. Flight and fight were both impossible at this point.

His hand tilted her head back and she barely had time to suck in a deep breath before his lips lowered and brushed against hers. Blood pounding in her ears, she barely heard the kettle go quiet the way that meant it would begin to whistle in another minute. Opening her mouth to say she needed to get it, she never got the chance. Amazingly soft lips pressed against hers as he took her unintended invitation and fit his mouth to hers. Like a perfectly cut dovetail, their lips and tongues melded and the need to deal with the kettle faded.

Dizzy with never before encountered heat, Linnet wrapped her arms around the only solid thing handy. Hard muscles pressed against her body as her fingers sought handholds on his back. His shirt slid over rippling planes of steel and she held tight. Instead of pushing her away, he pulled her closer, his tongue probing deeply into her mouth, one strong arm holding her upright.

*Oh. My. God.* The power of the kiss swept her along faster than the current of the river and she gave herself up to it. No kiss had ever touched her like this and it made her head spin. Thankfully, he still held her head or she feared it might have fallen off. If not for his arm around her shoulders and her death grip on his back, she would have fallen when he abruptly broke the kiss.

"Manley, down," Creed ordered the dog. His gruff tone cleared enough of the haze surrounding her; she heard the kettle screaming and felt Manley head-butting their legs.

"The kettle," she whispered and shook her head. What was wrong with her? Kissing a stranger? Pulling back from Creed, relief and disappointment fought an epic battle in Linnet's heart when he let her go. Glad she had a task, Linnet turned to the small stove and turned it off. The whistle began to soften immediately and it accompanied the cooling of the lust that had overcome her.

Out of habit, she reached for her mug and the jar of tea bags on the newly installed shelf over the counter that served as part of the kitchen. Just one of the improvements she'd made over the last few weeks.

Living alone in the middle of the wilderness left one with plenty of spare time. Always good with her hands, she'd filled the non-working hours by organizing this one little corner of the world. It wasn't that she'd done anything big—the windows had been her most radical change—really, she'd just taken what was available and rearranged it.

A few nails, a little wood glue, and old wobbly furniture became solid once more. A thrift-store cushion or two and a mosquito net around her bunk and life couldn't get much more comfortable out here.

Creed's body heat warmed her back when he moved up behind her. She watched as he set his mug next to hers and reached for the glass jar holding packets of cocoa.

"Good idea to use glass for storage." His voice was a soft warm rumble in her ear.

She needed to move away from him, wanted to move away. Couldn't make her legs react to orders.

"Keeps the smell in and hopefully the bears out," she said with a shrug and took the jar from him. Weakness swamped her again when his other hand settled on her shoulder. His thumb stroked her neck as he reached for the kettle.

Opening the jar to select an envelope of the powdered drink was almost an impossible task. Only with great concentration was she able to open the paper packet and empty the contents into his stainless steel mug. It looked solid and sleek next to her tin mug covered with blue speckled enamel. He poured the steaming water while she closed the jar and returned it to the shelf. Teabag followed water into her mug and that jar returned to its home.

"Spoons?" His breath whispered over her ear and a shiver followed.

Not trusting her voice she pointed. Another series of glass jars held mismatched flatware.

Without releasing her, he selected a spoon to stir his cocoa. "Do you need one?"

She shook her head and lifted her mug. Already the fruity fragrance of blueberries perfumed the steam.

"Shall we go sit at the table?" Creed suggested and nodded to where she'd arranged what looked like an old, scarred, dining table under the front window. Furniture polish had cleaned the wood and made it shine like a fine antique. Mismatched woven placemats protected the top while showing off the wood beneath.

"Sure." She moved to her favorite seat. The best place to view the river, the spot was marked by her laptop and a stack of notebooks. Pencils and pens stood in a paper cup and further defined her workspace.

Creed pulled out the chair for her and then sat down next to her.

"Thanks." The automatic word popped from her lips before she could find something else to say. He acknowledged it with a smile.

"Quite the little office here," he teased her.

"Beats one in town."

"Good point."

Now what? What was there to say without babbling? The more she thought about it, the more the kiss scared her. Staring out the window she held the cup of tea before her and blew across the surface. A masculine groan made her look back at Creed.

"Women have no idea how their most innocent movements and gestures affect a man," he chuckled.

Linnet set her cup down on the table and folded her hands in her lap.

"I didn't mean to make you feel self-conscious." His hand settled gently over the back of her neck and she felt trapped.

She'd walked into this one all by herself. Cornered by the cabin and the furniture, she found herself blocked from her escape route by Creed. *Stupid, Linnet, just plain stupid.* Always placing herself in the corner was a bad habit. Hell, even the bunk she'd chosen was in the corner. *Dumb, dumb, dumb!* She never left herself an escape route.

Clearing her throat she decided to avoid topics that could easily grow too personal. "You were going to tell me your history," she reminded him. "How did you come to own this place? Is it a family homestead?"

His deep chuckle told her the redirection effort was obvious. "I'd rather keep doing what we were doing when the kettle whistled. It illustrated our condition rather well."

Linnet closed her eyes and turned her head toward the window. Maybe she should make this one open and screen it as well? The breeze from the river would feel great on her scorched face right about now. She never blushed! What was going on here?

Beside her, Creed sighed. "Right. Moving too fast. Sorry, was a long stretch on the Slope this time. Guess I was lonelier than I thought."

Linnet pursed her lips and turned her head even further. *Great, just great.* Probably looked good because she was the first civilized woman he'd seen in how many weeks? She knew women worked up in oilfields, mostly in the offices, but if he had any kind of ethics at all he didn't mix with them *socially*. The oil companies frowned on that sort of fraternization in the camps.

"Uh, that didn't come out right." His attempt to laugh it off didn't do much to convince her of his sincerity.

"Don't worry about it." She pushed her chair back and would have stood, but his hand gripped her arm.

"I'm sorry. I really am. I don't spend much time around women and was never the best student when it came to social graces."

She still refused to look at him. "Well, maybe you can dig up some of those old lessons. I'm going to get my evening bath." Shaking off his arm, she stood. His arm around her waist stopped her again and he pulled her close, until his head rested against her stomach and both arms held her gently.

Heart beating wildly again, she curled her hands to keep from using violence to push him away. He wasn't actually threatening her, wasn't hurting her and she could have stepped away if she'd really wanted to. The fact was, the embrace felt far too *right*. That alone scared her into standing still.

When he spoke, his voice was muffled against her stomach. "Linnet, I'm sorry. I keep saying the wrong things."

"Please." She pushed at his shoulders, finding strength at last. "Keep your hands to yourself. I'm here to work and not provide entertainment for lonely oilfield workers on leave. I'm a biologist, not a good-time girl."

Like stones, his arms dropped away and the expression on his face made her nearly regret her words. Determined not to give in and become a doormat—yet again—she stalked away from him. Agitated, her gaze fell on her plastic bucket of bath supplies at the foot of her bunk. A long-handled brush, wash cloth and bottle of castile soap were nestled in beside her comb and razor. Yeah, a good long soak sounded great right now.

The thought of clean clothes made her gaze fly to the laundry line behind the woodstove and she strode that direction. *Of all the displays...!* Plucking her towel from the laundry line, she also pulled down clean sets of lacy lingerie dangling from the line after yesterday afternoon's washing session.

With a burning face and jerky movements, she gathered them and rushed to stuff the pile in her duffel. The socks, jeans and tees weren't quite dry enough yet. At least she had one more clean set of dry clothing. Normally she would have undressed and just worn a long shirt and sandals to the stream, but not with him here.

Clothes, towel and bucket in hand, she hurried to the cabin door.

"Linnet..."

"Help yourself to anything you need," she cut him off and pushed the screen door outward.

Laughing at himself, and feeling like ten different kinds of an ass, the words left Creed before he could censor them. "What if I need you?"

His voice stopped her but she didn't turn around. "I'm not on the list of items available for public use."

The extra loud slap of the door closing, sounded like a shot propelling her forward as she rushed off, taking her sweet scent with her. Citronella, fresh air, and woman, what a combination, he chuckled to himself. Add a little gun oil and he'd probably combust on the spot.

Creed flinched and dropped his head back to stare at the ceiling. The cleaned ceiling.

Hardly able to believe what he was looking at, he sat up straight. She'd cleaned the peeled-log rafters and rough-cut cedar-planked ceiling? When the woman cleaned, she didn't leave anything untouched. Amazed, he turned to look over the interior of the cabin more carefully.

It had been easy to see the big differences at first glance, especially her lacy underthings on the line, but the details were astounding. The old large wooden bunks had never looked better. The cooking area was organized with dishes stacked neatly on new shelves, pots and pans stored under the counters. Glass jars of all sizes held basic staples of sugar, flour, coffee, tea and cocoa. The sitting area was comfortably arranged around the woodstove scrubbed and freshly blacked.

Even the indoor woodpile looked swept and sorted. Kindling on top, dried and split logs below. Old newspapers stacked off to the side along with a full box of matches and a pile of fire starters made from egg cartons filled with paraffin and sawdust. Sanding had brightened the wooden plank floor that probably hadn't been sanded since it had been laid down more than fifty years ago. Probably hadn't even been sanded then.

Well-thumbed paperback books, old board games, and miscellaneous supplies crowded a shelving unit made of old wooden liquor crates. Left over from when Great-Uncle George had worked for the local liquor distributor. More crates provided storage at the foot of and between each bunk. A good place to stash gear.

Manley whined then yelped at the door.

Creed stood to let him out. "Follow the lady, boy. Keep her safe." For a moment, he watched the dog run down the trail off to the right. Smart of George to send him along. Raking fingers through overly long hair, Creed turned back to the cabin to finish taking in the changes. *Had George tried to call? Probably should have checked the answering machine before taking off.* It had never occurred to him George wouldn't be here and there was no one else he wanted to talk to. Why hadn't George emailed him on the Slope? Why hadn't anyone else?

Creed pondered the implications of not checking for messages at home as he inspected the sturdy government surplus chairs that had looked worse for the wear with torn vinyl seats. Freshly painted in gunmetal gray, the seat cushions were reupholstered with thick canvas that had been hand-painted green. Good choice actually. The deep, deep winter cold and countless butts plopping down at the table had cracked the vinyl over the past thirty years and they'd been repaired with liberal use of duct tape.

And the laundry line. While not new, it had certainly never held delicate lacy items like she'd pulled off just a few minutes ago. He wanted to dig through her bag and get a closer look at them. *Pervert*, he snorted to himself. In his experience, wilderness women didn't usually wear such delicate clothing.

Actually, he wanted to look at them closer on her body. If he moved quietly he could spy on her bathing at the creek fed by a spring of hot mineral water. Now that would make him a pervert. He groaned. God, it had been so long since he'd held and kissed a woman. And never one as perfectly warm, curvy and delicious as this one. The memory of her breasts against his chest made him pace hoping to ease his iron-hard erection. Her whole body, hidden under the baggy shirt, had come alive under his touch. Trim waist, sleek lines, curved hips and sweetly rounded ass were perfect playing fields for his hands. Freshly washed, she'd be perfect for his mouth too.

*Sheee-at.* Four weeks of no privacy and now too much privacy. He had only himself to police his actions with her. While Manley seemed to obey her well enough, and he wasn't shy about tangling with village dogs when warranted, it was doubtful he'd get in the way. The only reason he'd interrupted this evening was because the piercing whistle of the kettle had probably hurt his ears. Creed almost wished a large group of tourists would come along right now.

The box against the wall, under the table, bleeped and Creed checked his watch. Thirty minutes she'd said. He wandered to the box and checked the dials. Yup, the battery was charged. Her laptop probably as well. He looked at her keys lying on the table. The least he could do was put the tools away and turn off the generator. And if he went for a little stroll through the woods to wash up at the creek, could you blame a guy for practicing good hygiene?

# Chapter 4

Stomping down the trail wasn't very mature, but it made her feel better. Linnet had to laugh at herself. The stunned look on his face must have been priceless.

Still trembling, she paused for a moment then continued along the trail. She'd been unfair, she knew it. Plain and simple—she was scared. Frightened to death. Terrified of being used and humiliated again. Pushing away with anger was her outlet, her test. If he pushed back now, she'd pack up and leave tonight. If he left her alone and respected her distance, she might be willing to share a meal or two, maybe even invite him in for coffee in the mornings. Might even welcome more kisses. Eventually.

Men. The biggest problems of her life. She loved her job and was good at it. Almost too good. Better than most men felt she should be.

California had been the worst as far as chauvinism went. Two years ago, one assignment had involved backpacking into the Sierras. She had the skills required for checking on the high mountain lake where it had been reported fish were dying for no apparent reason and no other women had been available to go along.

Refusing to let her go alone, her supervisor had picked the man he considered the least threatening as her hiking partner. When they'd returned, mission accomplished, the very same supervisor had refused to listen when she told him how sweet Billy James had doctored her tea, pulled her out of her sleeping bag and raped her. Repeatedly. All night long.

They'd been a three day hike away from anywhere and she'd had nowhere to go. Hiking out by herself would have foolhardy. Unable to sleep and suspicious of their food and water supplies after that, she'd been an incoherent, dehydrated, hysterical wreck when they'd gotten back, her condition making her story more unbelievable.

Billy hadn't been violent about it. Hadn't hit her or physically hurt her—at least not that she could remember. He'd just taken advantage of the situation. The pieces she'd eventually put together were fairly simple.

The night they'd arrived at the lake, debilitating exhaustion had overcome her after dinner. She remembered thinking it odd that only three days of hiking and the altitude could have sucked so much energy from her. Supposing it was her period coming on, she'd downed the last of the tea Billy had made for her and crawled into her sleeping bag in everything but her boots, just as she'd been sleeping every night of the trip.

Hindsight now told her he'd put a date-rape drug in her tea. What memories she had were vague and disturbingly erotic. The next morning she'd awakened groggy and sore... wrapped only in Billy's arms. According to him, she'd come to him naked and needy, begging him to fuck her. All he'd done, he said, was take care of a lady's needs. It didn't feel right, and of course, he denied drugging her.

Upon returning to Sacramento, she'd driven herself to the hospital, shaking from lack of food, water and cramping from the start of her period. They'd run the tests but more than seventy-two hours had passed and they could find no signs she'd been forced or drugged.

Her fiancé at the time, Henry, had taken her home after a night of IV rehydration and reluctantly held her as she'd tried to tell him what had happened, or what she thought had happened. Though he'd said the right words, the look in his eyes and the tone of his voice had been doubtful, his hold reluctant and cold rather than comforting.

If only it had stopped there. But no, Billy'd had to open his mouth. Whispers had followed her around the office until Linnet learned he'd bragged about how he'd made her come over and over again. As the story went, he'd been only too happy to play stud service and make the frigid bitch scream. Convinced he'd unearthed the fiery vixen within her, he'd continued to pursue her, making her life hell in the office.

Unable to sleep, she'd suffered from sheer exhaustion until one day she'd fallen asleep at her desk despite several cups of coffee. Several hours later, she'd awakened on the sofa in her boss's office. Though her boss was sitting in his chair behind his desk, he'd been watching her with an odd look on his face.

After telling her he'd brought her there for her own safety, he'd told her one more incident like that and he'd insist on drug testing. As it was, she was to consider herself on probation and he'd be watching her. Her work performance had been slipping and she was in danger of losing her job. Confused and groggy, she'd felt ashamed and extremely uncomfortable as she'd stumbled from the office and home to revive herself in a hot shower.

The next day she'd begun making appointments. A handful of lawyers had each sympathized, then advised her to quit and move. Taking it to court was risky at best. A case of he said-she said. No witnesses, no evidence. Nobody up the chain of command believed her or would listen.

Billy had gotten a slap on the wrist for fraternization and she got a warning in her file for insubordination along with a reputation for being a snooty, but lively and exciting, lay. Everyone had hit on her then and it was either endure the comments and pawing or move on. No other option left, six months later, her engagement a memory, she'd quit and found the job in Alaska.

She stopped her march at the creek and looked around. All was quiet and she set her supplies on a large dry rock. Manley's yelp came through the trees and, as expected, a moment later, he bounded down the slope behind her and danced to a stop at her feet.

"Well, hello, there. I thought you'd forgotten all about me." *Great, pouting to the dog now.* Contrite, she bent and spent a moment petting him. "I'm sorry Manley. I know you like him, but not all men are honorable. They'll take advantage of a woman every single time." A tear of self pity slid down her cheek. Angry with herself, she wiped it away and stood. A long hot soak would feel great.

One of the true prizes of this bit of land was the narrow creek before her. Now stripped of every flake of gold that had ever dreamed of settling there, the main attraction was the hot spring up the hill that fed into it. A remnant of mining days, a sluice funneled water from up the hill and allowed a bather to direct the water into an old cast-iron claw-foot tub. A genuine antique that made Linnet sigh with happiness.

Countless times she'd blessed the woman who had most likely insisted on it. How it got there, she hadn't a clue and didn't care. What she cared about was it straddled a small stream feeding the creek that drained into the Yukon a hundred yards away and could be filled with the most delicious hot mineral water she'd ever come across.

The spring wasn't much more than a steady trickle, so she'd come here before dinner, plugged the tub and started filling it with the steaming water. A perfect one-hundred-five degrees when it came out of the ground, it usually hovered around a hundred-three when the tub was full. Completely full, right up to the brim until it overflowed. Like an infinity pool, the sluice poured the water over the side of the tub, continually refreshing it. When she was done, all she had to do was pull the plug, move the sluice away and let the tub drain. No icky, slimy growths allowed. To keep it clean, she had a bear-proof bucket nearby with baking soda and a sponge for scrubbing. The perfect system for cleansing and renewing her spirit.

Listening to the woods, Linnet looked around again. Only a narrow strip of the river could be seen through the trees. Doubtful anyone could look up and see her as they floated past. A rocky cliff, about eight-feet high, that the creek tumbled over, provided a wall behind the tub. Once in the water, she had a clear view side to side and down hill. No one could sneak up on her. With shaking fingers, she began unbuttoning her shirt.

The reasonable side of her, the one that hated confrontations, reminded her she'd have to face Creed. Maybe even explain.

How could she? It wasn't any of his business. She didn't even know him. Only knew she was living in his cabin. What was to stop him from leaving his tent and moving inside? Her? Manley? What a mess. She was supposed to be out here alone.

Sleeping in the truck again was always a short term option. An older Norwegian gentleman had stopped one night to sleep out of the rain. She'd waited until he'd turned in, loaded the woodstove to keep him warm through the chilly night, then bundled up on the back seat of her truck with Manley to sleep. Heinrick had never even known she'd left the cabin. Pretending she was coming back from the outhouse the next morning, she'd merely set about making a fresh pot of coffee. They'd shared breakfast and she'd urged him on his way.

Still listening to the woods, she folded the shirt and removed her jeans. Each item of clothing was rolled together. With the bath bucket in reach, she removed the tie holding up her hair and carefully slipped into the tub. How long would Creed give her before he came looking? If this was his land, then he knew about the tub. Would he appreciate her improvements here as well?

She'd been somewhat dismayed when she'd first spotted the tub. George had left the water spilling into it and some type of algae had been growing along the edges. Happily, he'd warned her and she'd arrived armed with baking soda. All natural cleanser. Not as fast as Comet, but with elbow grease she'd been able to get the tub clean without polluting the creek. Bothered by the rust under the chipped enamel, she'd picked up several cans of enamel spray paint on her one trip back to Fairbanks. Not as good as professional refinishing, nevertheless the inside of the tub was evenly coated with the white paint. Outside, she'd let her creative streak break free.

Starting with a base of moss green paint to match the forest, she'd then embellished it with hand-painted, free-form wild flowers and trees on the sides. It was quite pretty in a rustic, handcrafted sort of way, if she did say so herself. Overall, the little spot had a very natural, garden bath feel to it. A few of the wildflower seeds she'd scattered were growing nicely and she hoped there'd be flowers in a few weeks. Heaven on earth. Surely both Creed and George would appreciate the more sanitary tub.

Linnet had a vision of Creed lounging in it with her, and felt a spike of heat ignite in her center and flash outward.

The double ended tub was the largest of its kind she'd ever seen. Six feet from end to end and nearly three-feet wide. Big enough for her to lie along the bottom and completely submerge. Certainly big enough for the two of them to sit face to face, or back to chest. What was it about him? After only a few hours, how could he intrude on her thoughts this way?

Annoyed with her fantasy and the longing it created in her, despite reliving her hike-of-horror memory, she splashed both away and reached for her bottle of castile soap. Nothing to harm the environment here. In the woods, she made an effort to be as natural as possible and the tea-tree oil in the soap helped soothe the small scratches and insect bites she picked up on a daily basis.

Usually she enjoyed the ritual of lathering her hair then standing to let the soap bubbles run down her body while she scrubbed with the brush. She wasn't so off men that she never thought of them, but her fantasy man had never had a face to distract her. Tonight the image of Creed, with genuine warmth in his eyes, intruded on the experience.

It was too easy to imagine him using the cloth and brush to cover every inch of her skin, washing away the day's dirt and aches from work, building new aches of desire. The bristles of her brush became his rough palms in her mind and she whimpered at the sensation of them scraping over her nipples, teasing between her legs. If she was a tad more thorough about scrubbing herself, there was no one to know.

Knees quaking with the need for release, she sank back down into the water, sliding under the surface to rinse. Thinking it would wash him from her system, she allowed herself to imagine his hands in her hair, loosening the strands, combing the soap into the water.

She felt like a nymph, her hands skimming across her skin. After writhing under the surface as long as she could, she broke the surface with a gasp. Cool air touched her needy nipples and she indulged, pinching and rolling them, in her fantasy begging her fantasy lover to pull harder.

Creed, how easily his name came to her lips, how effortlessly it rolled off the tongue.

\* \* \* \*

At the sound of his name, Creed nearly broke into a run. It was the tone of the cry that stopped him. Breathless and... what was that timbre? Passion?

"Yes!" her soft cry carried through the woods. *Ah. Passion.* A moment of self pleasure while thinking of him? He was ready to make it mutual pleasure. *Now. Five minutes ago.* He moved to step forward then stopped again.

He didn't want to repeat his last several attempts at relations with the female half of the species. There were several positives where women were concerned—they looked compatible to men, and he loved their structural design just for a start. Enough of the baffling creatures came on to him that satisfaction was relatively easy to maintain.

What happened the next day was another matter. And with Linnet, there would be a next day. And a few more. Plenty of good reasons to think before instigating a merger.

It had been at least a year since his last local liaison, and with good reason. Usually he didn't want to see them past the first time he returned to the Slope. By then they clung to him, wanting him to call nightly, pressing for more and more from him as the weeks went on until they exploded in frustration. The harder they pushed, the faster he withdrew. Once past the explosion he rarely saw them again. Or if he did, they'd warned the others of their pack he was afraid of commitment.

Yeah, he was afraid of being committed to the mental institute if they didn't leave him alone. He didn't understand their subtle signals. Much like wolves, they had their own language and most of the men he knew didn't understand it either. Those who'd married into the pack seemed the most confused.

Except George. For some reason he always seemed to understand his wife and daughter well enough. Would George understand this situation, though?

The sound of splashing came to him and he crept forward. He had to see what she was doing. All he could see from this angle was her head. There was another path... Manley's head swung his direction and Creed gave him the hand signal to stay.

A few minutes later, he lay on his stomach and inched toward the edge of the rock over the tub. Bushes growing along the edge provided enough cover she probably wouldn't see him unless she knew where to look, and the sound of the waterfall should cover his movements.

Perfect. He looked directly down through the clear water and had an eagle's eye view of the most beautiful sight he'd ever seen. She had the body of a goddess. His hands had already told him that, now his eyes confirmed it.

Lying back in the tub, dark lashes rested against her cheeks like tiny fans. One hand pinched and pulled at her nipples, light mocha against her creamy skin. *Not tanned all over*. The other hand combed its fingers through the triangle of dark curls between her thighs. If only she would push her hips up toward the surface so he could see better.

"Yes!" she moaned and he watched her mouth open, like a bird looking for a meal. The point of her pink tongue darted out to lick a drop of water from her upper lip and he imagined her licking him.

Biting his lip was the only way he could keep from groaning out loud. Unlikely as it was that she'd hear him, he didn't want to take the chance. She'd given him more than a handful of mixed signals and he didn't want to get it wrong this time, since they'd be sharing the cabin for a couple of weeks. Friendly relations on all levels would make life easier and she might even let him move into his own cabin.

A tent. He was sleeping in a tent tonight. Something he hadn't done out here since he was ten and had wanted to prove how brave he was. Okay, so it had been Solstice, a time when the sun didn't go down at all and Dad had spent the night in a chair beside the fire pit. Still, Creed was a grown man now and deserved a rock-hard bunk in a warm cabin over a tight sleeping bag on rocky ground.

Below him, she rocked her hips against the fingers between her legs. A hand shoved against his mouth muffled his heavy breathing but it didn't do much for the erection pressed between his stomach and the rock on the other side of his hard metal-toothed zipper.

"Oh, yes, yes… just… like… that!" she squealed, water splashing wildly from the tub with her gyrations. "Oh… God… Yes!" she cried out again, and his teeth nearly broke skin.

Good grief. Here he was, a thirty-two-year-old man, spying on a woman in her bath. The sexiest woman alive. It made a difference. This wasn't an ordinary case of Peeping-Tom-itis and definitely more than a plain case of full-blown, cock-aching lust.

It was guard duty. A woman out in the Alaskan Bush on her own. Who knew what kind of terrible beast could burst from the trees and try to devour her? Probably a beast like himself. A beast rock hard and deprived of blood to his brain.

*Stop. Think. She stormed out of the cabin to be alone. Just because she's getting off using your name doesn't mean she's thinking of you. Might know another Creed, however unlikely the possibility. He'd only ever heard of one other with the name, and the rock band didn't count.*

Calm for the moment, he looked down again. The waves had subsided and she rested. A goddess. A water nymph. She was perfect and he meant to have her. She stirred below and he watched as she reached for her razor. Moving with graceful languor, she made what he considered a tedious task an erotic episode.

One at a time, she raised long slender legs from the water and tested the smoothness of her skin with long fingers. Sleek muscles rippled under the pale skin. Visions of those legs wrapped around him stole another half pint of blood from his brain. The higher her razor moved, the dizzier he grew.

The true test of his control came when she sat on the far side of the tub and spread her legs wide. She reached for the bottle of soap and lathered thoroughly. Presumably to avoid nicking her most tender skin. Each pull of the razor was agony for Creed watching from above. Tantalizing glimpses kept him pinned to the ground as he maintained surveillance, eyes straining to see each hint of sweet flesh.

At last she rinsed away the soap and used her fingers to test for lingering traces of hair. Not clean shaven, she'd come very close. Well trimmed. Creed wiped a trail of drool from his chin.

A little dental floss was no big deal, the important thing was she was clean. Couldn't get those secret crevices any cleaner. He'd happily perform quality control if she needed a second opinion. He'd volunteer to be not only her personal inspector but to be in charge of cleanliness as well. Keeping her clean would be a dream job.

Fingers between her legs again, she moaned and slid into the water once more. Creed nearly fell over the cliff and into the tub with her. Deciding he was too close to doing that very thing, he inched backward until he could stand without her seeing him. A flash of bright yellow caught his eye and he peered toward the river.

Rafters, and they were close enough to shore they most likely meant to pull off the river for the night. Could he convince them to use the gravel bar another quarter mile downstream? A glance at the sky told him sunset was near. Another hour at the most. His watch confirmed it—ten o'clock—and it was time to get back. If Linnet wasn't back at the cabin in twenty minutes, he'd make a show of calling for Manley to get her attention.

"What is it, Manley?" Her soft voice made him stop. "Do you hear something? Okay, keep watch. I'll get dressed."

Damn. Creed had been looking forward to pulling her out of the tub. Undercover of her splashing, he circled through the woods and returned to camp just in time to greet four men climbing from the raft.

# Chapter 5

Linnet cleared the rise in time to see a raft with four men push away from the small gravel shingle she called a beach. Creed waved as they paddled for the gravel bar downstream. Good. She didn't want to deal with travelers this late at night. All she wanted was to dry her hair and fall into her bunk. Morning came early with the sun rising at four-thirty. Wouldn't it be something to be here the two weeks the sun didn't set at all?

Manley trotted at her heels and she opened the door to let him into the cabin. Spying her laptop as the door shut, she paused for a moment and realized the generator was silent. Had Creed shut it off or had it run out of gas? One more chore to complete before bed.

Cups still sat on the table and her towel needed to be hung. She kicked off her shoes and slid her feet into warm sheepskin slippers. The sound of the screen door opening made her tense, but she forced herself to go about her business and started by hanging up her wet towel.

"Linnet, I'm sorry," Creed said and stopped by the door. "I don't know how to explain myself. You're not just the first pretty woman I've seen in a long time. You're the most beautiful woman I've ever seen in my entire life."

Shaking hands dropped the clothes pin she'd been trying to attach to the line. Before she could move, he was there, crouching at her feet to pick it up. He stood slowly and she stared at the wooden clip in his hand. It was easier than looking him in the eye.

"Thank you," she said, then grimaced. Were they doomed to politeness?

When she didn't take the pin, didn't move at all, he secured the towel on the line for her.

"You've done a great job here. The cabin and the area around it look so much better."

Determined not to thank him again, she shrugged and turned away to put the rest of her things away. "Just something to keep my hands busy."

"George fishes to keep busy. But you don't like fish."

"I don't like salmon. No point in torturing the poor things just to amuse myself. People who don't eat fish shouldn't catch them for fun."

"Do you want more tea? Yours is probably cold by now."

"No. Did you shut off the generator?"

"Yes, and filled it with gas, too. It's ready to go the next time you need it. I also locked up the back of your truck."

He walked over to her and his hand slid into view, holding her keys.

"Appreciate it," she said, took them and dropped them on top of her duffel. "Anyhow, it's been a long day and I need to get some sleep. The sun always wakes me up." The body heat he radiated so close to her wouldn't let her go to sleep anyway.

"Do you want me to light the woodstove for you?"

She shook her head. "Don't need it."

"It's supposed to rain tomorrow. I'll lay it out so all you have to do is touch a match to it."

"I'm quite capable of building a fire." She glared up at him.

"I'm sure you are. I'm trying to find little excuses to stay nearby longer." His unrepentant grin reminded her of her fantasy in the tub and she felt a flush burn away any lingering chill from her damp hair. Would probably help if she put on a sweatshirt over the tank top and workout pants she wore to bed.

"I'm hoping to ingratiate myself with you by doing little chores so as to become indispensable in your life," he added.

There was something warm behind the laughter in his eyes that made her want to shiver. She clamped down on the urge but couldn't control her nipples perking up into tight peaks.

The way he stared at her chest for a long moment told her he noticed the tank and pants were the only things she wore. To put on a shirt now would make it obvious she was covering up from him.

"You'll catch a chill if you go to bed with all that wet hair. Let me stay and keep you company while it dries." His touch was slow and gentle when he reached out to finger a lock of hair. "I won't kiss you until you come to me. Fair enough?"

"Then you won't be touching me again, because I won't come to you looking for kisses. Or anything else." She stepped away from him and walked to the table. Sitting on the side closest to the door, she debated for a long moment before standing again.

Linnet picked up her tea and carried it to the sink area. Staring at it for a long time, she continued the internal debate of whether or not he might have tampered with it. A distrust she carried to this day and never let anyone hand her a beverage without a sealed lid. It was tiresome to always be on guard, which made being alone so much easier. Two weeks? Would he really stay for two whole weeks?

"I don't think you hate men, not the way you kiss, but it isn't just me who makes you jumpy, is it?"

She turned from the sink to watch him select kindling and logs from the woodpile. "I don't want to talk about my personality quirks. I asked you earlier about your family story."

It was like watching a moving piece of art as he arranged the wood, carefully stacking it over a fire starter. The satisfaction from her fantasy evaporated and she wanted to live the moment live. Unable to tear her eyes away, she watched until he stood, then she focused on the cold tea in her hands. Using great self control, she chose to keep the tea and returned to her seat to drink it.

"Do you always blush so much?" He chuckled and sat on the other side of the table from her.

Determined to get their earlier conversation back on track, she ignored the question. "So, Russian and Aleut? I guess I can understand that, but how did you get to the Interior?"

"Well." He leaned back in his chair and crossed an ankle over a knee. "My great-great grandmother was the product of a Russian sailor and an Aleut woman. Being half-blood anything in those days wasn't a good thing, especially since the sailor didn't stick around." He held up a hand and used his fingers to keep track of his ancestors.

"So, she signed on as a cook aboard a fishing vessel where she met a hopeful Swede. When they reached the Yukon Delta, they jumped ship and hiked up the river hoping to gather up handfuls of gold. They staked a claim here and later gathered up claims as they were abandoned, turning them into homestead land until we own from basically here back to what is now the highway. They had a daughter who grew up to marry another Swede. She and her husband moved into Fairbanks and homesteaded there. They had two daughters—one who grew up to marry an Irishman by the name of Willis and the other who married back into the Native world. That aunt is George's grandmother. His father married another Athabascan, so he's not anywhere near as handsome as I am."

She watched him wink as he ticked off the generations on his long fingers.

"So those were your grandparents, right?"

"Right. They homesteaded as well, right alongside her parents and had my dad, the first male child. He married my mother, a good girl of Swedish descent as well, and here I am. I have a younger sister who's living in Anchorage and trying to forget she was raised in Fairbanks. She has a seven-year-old boy the size of a yearling moose, or a large King salmon, take your pick."

The sparkle of affection in his eye eased her nervousness a little. He seemed to have good relations with his family. "And George, the one I'm replacing, is your cousin?"

"Couple times removed and such, but yeah. We're family and that's all that counts. What about you? Where's your family?"

"California," she said with a grimace and stuck out her tongue when he laughed. "Sierras, more or less. Lake Tahoe to be exact."

"Brothers? Sisters? Parents?"

"One brother, two parents."

"Names?" he coaxed.

"I didn't ask you for names."

"I need to know who to contact in the event you get eaten out here." His gaze drifted down her body again before reluctantly returning to her face.

She gave him a narrowed eye glare. "Eaten by what?"

He merely grinned at her and waved for her to continue. "Come on. Tell me about your family. You have an interesting name. It's a sure bet they do as well."

Linnet heaved a sigh and sipped her tea. "My brother's name is Hawk." She snuck a glance to see him biting his lip. "Good, don't laugh. He makes you look small."

Creed glanced around. "Is big brother nearby, waiting to pound me into bear bait?"

"No, *little* brother is in the Persian Gulf playing SEAL. He may be twice my size, but he's fourteen months younger. People thought we were twins growing up."

"Navy SEAL? I'm impressed."

Satisfied he was sincere, she nodded. "I'm proud of him too. He's been gone a long time and should be home soon. I… I really miss him." A sip of tea hid the act of swallowing the lump in her throat.

It had been all she could do not to tell Hawk what had happened with Billy and the following ugliness in general. Hawk had just left, and he would have come home if he'd known. She didn't want him distracted and worried, so she'd made her mother swear on a stack of Bibles and Farmer's Almanacs to not tell either Dad or Hawk. Linnet may have wanted to hurt Billy, but she didn't want him dead. He wasn't worth anyone going to prison over.

"What about Mom and Dad?"

"Dad is retired Navy. A helicopter pilot. These days he flies fire crews in the summers and does the occasional Flight for Life. There's always a chance he could get called up here if the fire season is bad enough. In the winter, he putters with Mom. He does handyman stuff for elderly neighbors and such. They live simply."

"So that explains the proficiency in firearms. And Mom?" Creed prompted. "What does she do?"

"She was a nurse at the local VA hospital when they met. The old injured hero and the nurse story." The grin came naturally. "Dad swore it was love the moment he heard her voice and when she told him her name it was merely Fate confirming it. Now she performs as domestic diva, goddess of all things pertaining to garden, hearth, and home."

"Oh? And what is her name?"

"She goes by Missy to the rest of the world, but her real name is *White Dove Who Sings in the Nettles*. Dad calls her Dove or Dovie." Linnet couldn't help the smile. "Those who call us a bird-brained family don't live long enough to regret it," she laughed.

"So you have a touch of Native American in you as well?"

"A faint whiff of Cherokee. One-thirty-second or some such. Way back. The rest is good old stubborn German and English."

"So we have Linnet, a sweet little finch-like bird, fierce brother Hawk, nurturing mother White Dove… where does Father Greenbriar fit in?"

Linnet sipped from her tea again. There was no escape. "Perry."

A confused look clouded his eyes for a moment and then it cleared. "Peregrine. As in the falcon."

She nodded. "But *no*-one uses that name. Perry. Or Falcon from his military days."

"I'm sure he wouldn't get upset at being called Mr. Greenbriar the first time I meet him."

"Who says you'll get to meet him?" She cocked an eyebrow at him. Damned presumptuous of him. "And that would be Captain. In the Navy, that's the same as an Army Colonel."

Caught unawares, she was claimed completely by a yawn. Her chest expanded and her mouth stretched open as she drew in a deep breath. Tears filled her eyes and tired muscles clenched from head to toe. Able to snap her mouth shut, she was still caught in the exquisite stretch and extended her arms. Blood rushed into her head and a red haze gathered under tightly closed eyelids. With a final exhale, she released the pent-up air and sagged in her chair. That ought to impress him. Real lady-like.

"Well. I guess that's my cue to bed down," Creed chuckled. "Give me your cup and I'll wash it out in the creek while I clean up."

Relaxed, Linnet stared at him through hooded eyes still filled with water. Slowly she blinked them clear and another yawn, less intense, followed. "You win. I'll let you do the dishes." She sighed and pushed to her feet. Unconsciously she reached to scratch an itch on the back of her neck.

"Where's the calamine?"

"Hmmm?" She looked up to see Creed standing close to her. "Oh, it's over there on the counter." She pointed toward the kitchen.

A moment later he stood behind her gently dotting soothing antihistamine cream on her bug bites.

"Any on your back?" he asked.

"I… I don't…"

"I won't attack you, so lift the back of your top. I promise, only the finger with lotion will touch you."

She hesitated then felt a familiar skin irritation—right where she couldn't reach and knew it would bug her all night. With a sigh she lifted the back of the top, careful to keep her breasts covered.

"Jesus," he swore softly. "You have a least ten in various stages of infection back here. You can't scratch them."

"They itch, I scratch." She let him hear her annoyance. Only because the cream felt good, she didn't step away.

"I just appointed myself your caretaker. I'll check them again in the morning. If they don't look better we'll need to dose each spot with antiseptic."

Even though he couldn't see, she rolled her eyes. He was right about not scratching, but it was hard.

Continuing his gentle work, he tsked. "You wear bug dope, I smelled it on you earlier. Doesn't it work?"

"It helps, but no, it doesn't really work. I've never had such a problem before and I grew up camping. There's something different about Alaskan mosquitoes. They don't react the same way. I've tried everything. That bath oil people rave about, pure deet, citronella—you name it, I've tried it. The coils in the cabin help." She nodded toward one on a little metal stand with a paper plate under it to catch the ash. "I wear the colors everyone says they ignore. I've changed my shampoo and my soap. I've even tried adding more garlic to my diet. It hasn't helped."

"There," he said and tugged on the back of her shirt. "That part's done. There's a couple on your arms and then I'll get the ones on your face."

He worked in silence and it felt comfortable enough that she relaxed— until he turned her around. With great care he touched a dot of the cream to the bites on her cheeks, neck and above the neckline of her top. Then with ever-slowing touches, he rubbed the cream into each red mark. The cream was cool, but his touch was hot. By the time he'd rubbed the last bite, her breathing was labored, but no less than his. Reluctance was clear in each movement as he stepped back and attached the cap to the tube.

"That should help tonight. I'll check again in the morning."

Because of the dry spot in her throat, she nodded to avoid speaking. "Good night," she finally managed to whisper. "I'll try not to make too much noise when I get up. I'm sure you'd appreciate a chance to sleep in."

"Sleep? In the summer? That's what winter is for," he chuckled. "I wouldn't be adverse to a cup of coffee in the morning." A hopeful note added to his half smile.

"I usually only make a cup for myself, but I'll put a pot on if you knock on the wall to let me know when you're moving."

"Thanks."

They shared a smile, his wide and friendly, hers faint and somewhat shy, and then he turned.

"Do you usually bar the door at night?" He pointed to the two-by-four near the door.

"Yes. When I'm alone. Should I tonight?"

He turned back to look at her and gave her a self-conscious smile. "Oh yeah. Definitely."

Mouth dry again she just nodded and watched him close the wooden door behind him.

# Chapter 6

Creed shook the rain off under the roof overhang before knocking on the door. It felt damn funny knocking to enter his own cabin. Even funnier sleeping in the tent next to it. Especially a cold and damp tent. Dammit, he was moving into the cabin tonight.

Manley barked a greeting, so he tried to open the door only to find it still barred. Really didn't trust him, did she? A moment later he heard Linnet mumble and guessed she'd said she was on her way. Stepping sideways to peek through the window, he watched her bat away the netting hanging around her bunk. Still asleep? She looked adorable with wisps of hair escaping from her braid to fly around her head like a dark halo.

Obviously groggy, she slipped her feet into slippers then staggered to the door just long enough to lift away the bar.

"Come!"

Since Manley was inside, Creed assumed she meant the order for him. He opened the screen and then slipped through the wooden door after Manley dashed out. Looking around he saw her crouched in front of the woodstove with a lit match that she touched to the fire starter and kindling.

Briefly, a thought about teasing her crossed his mind and just as quickly disappeared. Didn't look like she was much of a morning person as she shuffled across the cabin to light the burner under the percolator.

"Coffee in ten," she mumbled, shaking out the flame on the match.

Amusement kept at bay, he had one weapon that might get her attention. "I brought fresh eggs. Would you like an omelet for breakfast?"

Bingo. That opened her eyes. He used the moment to walk to her side.

"Real eggs?"

She turned to him and almost smiled as she looked up at him, so he gave her one of his smiles and nodded. "Fresh from the Lower Forty-Eight."

The joy didn't last long as her eyes narrowed with suspicion. As he'd noted the night before, not very trusting. He stepped closer, making her look up at him. Sleepy and very sexy. He could enjoy this face every morning for a long time. Too bad these looks didn't usually last.

"What do you put in your omelets?" she asked warily.

"Cheese, bacon, and tomato. Onion if you like that too."

"Caramelized sweet onion or just plain sautéed yellow onion?"

Her scrunched up nose proved too irresistible and he bent down to kiss it. "Sweet Maui onions, caramelized in butter to a gooey brown mess, crisp bacon, sharp cheddar, and ripe, red tomato. All wrapped in a fluffy egg blanket and topped with a sprinkling of cheese."

That earned him a sigh and eyes closed in bliss for just a second. "Sounds delish. I'll get out of your way and let you cook." She sidestepped him. "What time is it anyway?"

"Nearly eight." He grinned as first she yawned, covering her mouth with her hand, then hung her head.

"I'm so late," she groaned. "George will be disappointed. Oh. Shit." She stood up straight, green eyes open even wider.

"What?"

"I didn't call him last night."

"Call?"

"He sent me out here with a satellite phone. I'm supposed to check in every other night around nine. Last night was the other. I completely forgot."

"He's awake by now. Give him a call. I need to get the food. I'll be right back."

Manley stood waiting to come back in, when he opened the door. The dog had just lifted a foot to step in when he froze. Creed froze as well, listening. "What is it, boy?" *Moose? Bear? Boaters?*

A familiar, sharp whistle cut through the air from the direction of the trucks. *George? Here?*

"What is it?" Linnet asked from behind him as Manley streaked away.

"I think George is here. I'd better go see what's up. What's he doing out here if he broke his leg?"

"I can't imagine. He was in a fiberglass and plaster cast when I saw him three weeks ago. The wet ground will be murder on it."

"Hmm, I'll go see what he wants and try to buy you a few minutes to get dressed in peace."

He smiled when she nodded and turned back toward her bunk. Because he suspected most of her curves would be hidden when he got back, he watched her walk away. The way her stretch pants hugged her ass brought instant drool to his mouth. His hands twitched wanting to feel the span of her waist between them.

Leaving the cabin last night, knowing she wore only the tight pants and tank top, had been agony. Each curve was superbly defined and enhanced by the fabric stretched over her body like a second skin. Touching her to apply the cream to her bug bites had been its own torment and test of his self-control. Sleeping had been erotic torture, each dream reliving her bath but with his hands touching her, inventing new ways to have clean dirty fun.

Linnet reached the bunk and glanced back at him. A single raised brow sent him out the door with a sigh of longing.

Another whistle rent the air and he glowered at the rain-gray sky. What was up with George? Pulling the hood of his raincoat up and over his head, he trudged into the rain to find out.

\* \* \* \*

"What the hell do you mean by leaving town without answering your messages?" George growled at Creed.

Approaching his cousin's truck, Creed avoided growling back. Instead he shrugged. "The extra two weeks on the Slope were tough. All I could think about was getting away, so that's what I did. What wild hair crawled up your butt to send you out here?"

"I left you an urgent message, which you didn't return. Climb in the truck," George ordered then rolled up his window.

Creed yanked open the door of the rusty old truck crowding the now-filled-to-capacity clearing for parking. The metallic squeal of protest shattered the peace of the morning. "I have email up on the Slope, you know," he said, and slammed the door behind him. He had to shove Manley out of the way to get comfortable on the bench seat. "I even have a phone up there and you have the number. You didn't tell me about your leg."

George shrugged in his casual way. "I don't like bugging you at work."

"But at home you don't mind."

"Nope."

Creed shook his head at George's wide grin. "What's the urgent message?"

"I broke my leg and there's a prickly woman taking my place. Oh, and she's staying in the cabin and cleaning it up a bit."

"I know all that now. So why did you drive out here? And so early?" George would have had to have left Fairbanks around four this morning.

# Chapter 13

At the touch of Creed's lips, Linnet sucked in a lungful of air. That must be what made her feel dizzy. The aftermath of her nightmare dissipated like the morning mist, so it had to be the sudden infusion of sweet oxygen over her tender membranes. It didn't explain her suddenly thundering pulse, but one thing at a time. Her foggy brain couldn't quite take it all in.

"Sleep, sweet bird," Creed whispered, his voice taking on a new gruffness.

"Creed..." How could she say it? What had he heard? Did she shout out in her sleep as Henry had mentioned the few times they'd been together between the attack and their break up? Her nightmares had kept him awake, sending him home in the wee hours of the morning in an attempt to find a few hours of rest.

"Hush, baby."

Linnet flinched at the use of the endearment. Billy had called her 'baby' all during the rape, during the rest of their hike, and every time they came face to face in the office.

"You don't like that?"

"No, please, don't use that... nickname with me."

"I won't," Creed promised and lightly kissed her forehead. "Off the list, I swear."

"Thank you." Relief swamped her again and she slumped against him.

"Want to tell me about the dream?"

"No. Not now. Not tonight." The images were already as ephemeral as mist. But the nightmare had changed... she just couldn't figure out how. Not by the campfire. Indoors, but not a bedroom... she blew out a frustrated sigh. The details were gone.

"S'okay. I won't push. When you're ready, I'll listen. I'm a good listener. You wouldn't believe some of the stuff I have to listen to up north."

"I'll tell you… someday. I don't want to talk about it now."

"Fair enough. Want me to sing you to sleep?"

Matching groans came from the bunk above and the center lower one. Even Manley groaned. Linnet buried her face against Creed's chest in an effort to smother the snort that stung her sinuses.

"Very funny," Creed said in a normal voice. "I actually have a very good singing voice."

"Sure you do," George answered. "You just have a limited repertoire. Either go fishing or go back to sleep."

She couldn't stop the giggle even though it stung.

"Fine, laugh all you want. Just wait until we're fishing and you'll see." Creed's sniff made her laugh out loud. The bunk frame shook and soon he chuckled too. "I'll show you." He whispered the promise and lightly kissed her nose.

"Show her later," Hawk yawned above them. "Quit making her laugh now or we'll never get any sleep."

"Yeah," Linnet giggled, "stop making me laugh."

"I only know one way to do that," Creed whispered, his eyes dark and hot looking all at once.

She had a good idea what he had in mind, and she was eager for a demonstration. "I dare you. Show me."

"Remember, you invited me…"

Moving slowly, his eyes staring into hers, she could have pulled away at any moment. But she didn't want to. She wanted to kiss him, as much as he apparently wanted to kiss her. If what she felt against her thigh was a good indication, anyway. Two heartbeats passed. Three. His breath was warm across her lips. Four heartbeats melted into five, six and seven…

No mistake this time, his lips touched hers and Linnet's heart raced. Counting heartbeats became a useless occupation. Slow and gentle, his lips brushed over hers, still allowing her room to turn away. Impatient for more, she added pressure to the contact.

He pulled back a little, just long enough to ask, "Are you sure?"

"Yes." *Oh God, yes.* "Kiss me, Creed. Just like you did…"

With his arms wrapped around her, hard body firm against hers, warm lips brushed hers again. There was that dizzy feeling. Heat, delicious and welcome filled her from the inside out, chasing away the final clinging threads of the chilling dream.

The arm supporting her head curled around her, his hand warm and secure on her shoulder. The hand attached to his free arm settled on her waist. Hungry for more, she wrapped her free arm around his shoulder, pulling him closer. Tangling with his hair, her fingers sought out the softness in contrast to the granite of his body.

Not quite silent, his soft groan vibrated through her as their lips parted to deepen the kiss. Still tender and numb at the same time, she was grateful for his soft exploration. Gentle touches of his tongue tested just inside her lips, allowing her to set the pace, the intensity. His patience increased her impatience.

Wanting him, wanting reassurance, she rolled backward, dragging him with her. He landed naturally in the cradle of her legs, fitting perfectly. The fabric of her stretch pants was thin, the fabric of his sweats was worn and she could feel the weight and size of him nestled against her. Her hand on his hip urged him even closer and he thrust forward in response.

The bunk shook as Hawk rolled from the upper level and dropped to the floor with a loud thump. Pretty noisy for a guy trained to be silent.

"That's it. Willis, we're going fishing. Get dressed."

Both she and Creed groaned and separated, taking in great gulps of air.

"You just developed a case of performance anxiety, Willis," Hawk persisted while pulling on his own jeans.

"What do you mean?" Linnet gasped, even though Creed chuckled softly.

"He can't perform with me, George and Manley here. So I'm hauling his ass out of here before you try to make him. The poor man needs rescuing and I'm just the guy to do it. Move your butt, Willis. The fish are waiting."

"Fine," Linnet exhaled. "*You* go fishing."

"I'm not leaving George here to witness the entire sordid spectacle. And I'm not hauling a man with a cast out on the river at three in the morning. That leaves pretty boy here. He just volunteered."

A pair of jeans landed on Creed's back and he groaned, rolling away in surrender. "All right, you made your point. Truth is, it's cold out there and it's about to rain. I'm warm and comfortable right where I am."

"Too comfortable. Suffering in the elements does a man good." Boots thumped on the floor next to the bed.

Linnet made one last desperate reach for Creed, only to have him yanked from her arms.

"Good God, man, I'm trying to save you!" Hawk's agitation was beginning to creep through and with a grunt of frustration Linnet rolled to the back side of the bed. Hawk wouldn't let up, as she very well knew. "She's turned into a succubus. She'll steal your very soul. There's a time to run, far and fast, and this is it, I'm telling you."

Creed muttered a few choice words but changed clothes just the same. "Fine, we'll take George's boat. All the gear is there. One hour, tops, though. Just a small rainbow for breakfast."

"Hawk! I'll get you for this!" she called after them as her brother nagged Creed into his hip wader boots, raincoat and out the door. The wooden door closed softly, followed by the twang and slap of the screen door. Several minutes later the outboard jet motor of the boat fired, revved up, then slowly faded away as the boat moved upstream.

How embarrassing. She'd have to face George soon and then Hawk and Creed when they returned. To say nothing of their campers. Thankfully the Roys slept in their own tent and hadn't witnessed the drama. Wanting nothing more than to crawl into the woods and hide under a rock rather than face all those men, Linnet pulled her quilt over her head and, a long time later, drifted off to sleep.

* * * *

Creed maneuvered the boat over a hole mid-river, a mile or so upstream from the cabin, dropped an anchor then cut the engine. Silence fell like a brick and he turned to his unwanted guest. "All right, you pulled me out of the warmest bed I've had in months and dumped my ass in the middle of a cold wet river on a cold wet boat." A rain drop hit the aluminum roof of the cockpit. "And it's about to get a whole lot wetter real soon. Happy?"

Hawk had the nerve to grin back at him. "Now I am. My sister was about to do something in reaction to her nightmare, which I'm assuming was a replay of the time she got raped, and I didn't want her to regret it later. Not to mention I didn't want to witness it and I'm guessing George would agree."

"George is used to the village way. Bedrooms don't always have doors or insulated walls, so if you waited for everyone in the house to be asleep you'd never have sex." Creed snorted and reached for his tackle box. "Since we're here, might as well toss a line or two out."

"Yeah and I'm used to hearing guys jack off in their bunks, but it doesn't mean I have to be an unwilling bystander while my sister does it right below me."

"I wasn't going to let it go that far. I realize she was reacting to her nightmare. No matter what you may think, I'm not that big an ass."

"I didn't say you were, but now that you do..." Hawk gave him a wide grin and Creed felt like dumping him overboard. SEAL boy could probably make it back into the boat, but the waters of the Yukon weren't for playing.

"Take that pole and use this bait. We're a little far out from shore to be catching rainbows, but what the hell, let's see what's biting this time of day."

Soon they sat on the astroturf-covered engine cowling in the middle of the boat, their poles cast to opposite sides. Since Hawk had mentioned the rape first, Creed decided he could ask about it.

"Tell me what you know of her rape," he ordered calmly.

"Didn't get it all while eavesdropping yesterday?"

Figured that out had he? The man had good ears or eyes in the back of his head. Creed refused to feel guilty. "I got the gist of it. Asshole took advantage of a remote location. Even bigger asshole dumped her because of it."

"And she ran off to hide out here at the end of the world. From what I hear, she's been bugging her boss for the most remote assignments he's got on the docket."

"And George getting hurt was the perfect answer. Somewhat close to transportation routes, with enough traffic going by to make sure someone saw her every few days, but out of the boss's hair." Creed adjusted his line.

"Exactly."

"So, what happens now?"

"Dad wants me to bring her home. He wants to lock her up, fix her, and protect her. My gut reaction is to do the same, but realistically, she's doing what she can to put it behind her. Judging by her boss's reaction and her landlord's, she holds everyone at arm's length, which is why I'm baffled she let you crawl into her bunk last night."

"She dragged me there. I'm nothing but a weak mortal, and couldn't say no. Didn't want to either."

Hawk snorted. "Weak mortal, my ass. The latter is more likely."

"Guilty as charged. I want her, I won't lie about that, but I'll do my damndest not to hurt her either. On the flip-side, don't forget she's an adult who can make her own choices."

"For all her independence, she's still basically ignorant of men. Henry was her one and only long-term relationship and he treated her like a dress-up doll. I'll give him credit for improving her fashion sense, but he was a shallow bastard. In my experience, politicians usually are and he's working his way up the ranks damn fast. He's a game player and she was the perfect pawn for him. I'm surprised he didn't take her rape and turn her into the poster girl for STAR. That would have shot his political star into the stratosphere."

"STAR?"

"Stand Together Against Rape. Victim's recovery and advocate group."

"Ah." Creed felt a tug on his line and played with it a little, not really wanting to pull in a catch. They still had several pounds of salmon left from the night before. Hope George got the leftovers put away. "Damn, you hauled me out here without any coffee."

"Sorry, dude. Will a Dew work instead?" Hawk pulled a can of Mountain Dew from the pocket of his raincoat and held it out.

Creed eyed it suspiciously. "Nah, I'll wait for something hot when we get back. I'm trying to cut back on sugar. Getting old is a real pain."

"Sucks to be you," Hawk snickered and popped the top of the can. "I'll run this off when I get back from leave. For now I intend to spend a few days getting fat and lazy."

"How long do you have?"

"Four weeks. Just long enough to get really out of shape. And into trouble."

"You're not spending all of it here are you?"

"Been thinking about it."

"Shit." If he wasn't careful, Creed could find himself on the wrong end of a shotgun wedding. Then again, if the man needed something to do… "I've got it. You can stay, as long as you build a cabin."

He didn't even try to hold back his grin when Hawk choked on his soda.

"What?" Hawk spluttered.

"Your sister suggested adding a small bunk cabin off to the side. You can handle it. There are some trees that need to come down and they'll work just fine. There's a book in the stack on how to build an honest-to-God, genuine Alaskan bush log cabin. The tools to do it are there as well. Everything used to build the existing one. George knows a few things about it as well. Linnet does her biologist stuff and you can keep an eye on her while doing something constructive when I have to go back to work for a couple weeks."

"You want me to build a cabin from scratch, using timber from the area? Doesn't it have to be dried or seasoned first?"

"The intrepid pioneers and gold diggers didn't have time to season the logs. They chopped 'em down, notched them out, stacked them up, stuffed moss between them for chinking, tossed some sod on the roof then fell to prospecting."

"You're nuts."

"Once we make a list of the supplies we don't have here, I'll run into town and pick up some lumber and nails. We can also make furniture from that."

"Furniture?"

"Okay, a bed. A nice big bed. A perfect little private retreat."

"For Linnet, and only Linnet, right?"

That's what Creed liked about men. They were so damn clueless. "Sure, Hawk, just for Linnet."

"Liar."

# Chapter 14

Quiet as he tried to be with it, George's cast hitting the cabin floor still woke Linnet. Pretending to sleep, she kept her back to the room. It was all the privacy she could give him and once more she thought about the little sleeping cabin she'd suggested to Creed. How had his parents managed? Probably much like she did when others used the cabin: by either changing in the outhouse or out by the tub.

Unable to judge the time by the light level, Linnet carefully looked at her watch. A few minutes before six. So she'd gotten a couple more hours of sleep. The sod roof was too thick to let the sound of the rain through, but she heard it dripping from the eaves and trees. A good downpour then. Sore muscles spoke to her as she shifted on the mattress. Not only the work on the river, but the coughing and sneezing had taken their toll and the antihistamine grogginess clung to her limbs. Creed had been right about her being sore today. It was a good day to hibernate and input yesterday's data.

Clanking from the woodstove told her George had just put a few fresh logs on. He'd probably put the kettle on next. What was George's usual morning routine out here? She was the intruder even though it felt as if all the men were. She'd established herself and set up house. For an outdoors girl she had a strong nesting instinct. Henry had commented on it one time. Back when he thought it was cute. Utterly inconvenient when he'd left a stack of boxes full of her stuff outside his apartment door.

Good riddance. Hawk was right about him after all; self-serving and dull as dirt. Much as he claimed to love the outdoors, he'd never gone camping with her. Always had an excuse. A fundraiser here. A dinner there. Political rally of some sort. Possibly another woman on the side. Wonder how he'd explained her clothes in the closet?

Linnet rolled to her back and stifled her groan of pain with a grimace. Maybe a little more sleep would be a good thing. Searching for a comfortable spot, she rolled to her stomach and hugged Creed's pillow close.

It couldn't have been much later when Manley's cold nose slipped under her hand hanging over the edge of the bed and flipped it. A common system that worked for the two of them. If she didn't wake up soon enough to suit Manley, he let her know about it.

"Okay, Manley, okay. I'm getting up. I promise."

The pillow swallowed the last of her words but the dog was having none of it. A cold wet nose in the eye was his next level of assault. If that didn't work he'd move to the foot of the bed and drag the covers off, followed by her socks. He was a persistent cuss who'd learned how to get under her netting.

Before she could move to crawl out of bed, a weight threw itself across her lower legs and her socks were ripped off.

"Hawk!" she screeched, and was answered by his evil laugh. Kicking was futile since he weighed roughly the same as a cement mixer and was just as immoveable as dry concrete. Cruel fingers well remembered from when they were kids danced across the bottoms of her feet and she screamed out every insult she could think of.

Though the torture felt hours long, it probably lasted less than a minute. Reaching backward, she tried to grab his hair but it was too short to do any good. She settled for slapping the back of his head and he retaliated by twisting around to slap her butt.

"You'd better run, 'cause I'm going to roast your ass!" she shrieked.

"Tsk tsk, dear sister." He laughed at her. "I already found, and hid your weapons. You don't get them back until I'm far away, then I'll call you and tell you where they are." He landed one last stinging spank on her bottom then pushed off her and out from under the upper bunk. "Coffee's ready, but I'm pretty sure you're awake now and don't really need it."

Free, Linnet bolted from the bed and flew at her sibling. "You are so dead." The taunts of their childhood came back easily and, just as easily as he always had, he caught her wrists and flipped her around until he held her, back to his front, hands crossed in front of her. Frustrated, she raised a leg to stomp on his feet. Quick as a cat he lifted her bodily, rendering her efforts impotent. "Arrgh!"

"Still a wee thing, you are."

"If we were outside I'd flip you over so fast you wouldn't know what hit you," she growled. "I just don't feel like breaking the furniture today."

"Good thing for me." Hawk kissed her cheek and slowly lowered her to the floor. Once he thought she was calm enough he slowly released her.

She meant to turn and punch him, but Creed was there with a cup of fresh coffee. Spilling it seemed wasteful since the water had to be carried out from town in plastic jugs. Fresh drinking water was precious and not to be carelessly tossed away.

"Playtime is over, children. Breakfast will be ready soon."

Linnet glared at his overly cheerful face. Considering he'd only had a few hours sleep, he looked remarkably awake. And clean.

With twinkling eyes he answered her unspoken question. "I took a bath while you were sleeping. Hawk's fish was a little messy. Your clothes, all of the newly washed ones, are hanging on the line."

With a grunt, Linnet turned to see her jeans and last night's sleeping clothes hanging behind the woodstove. She blew on her coffee to cool it. "Where's the cream? Hawk, you know I drink it with cream of some kind. What's with this black stuff?"

Hawk's hands embraced her shoulders and steered her toward the table. "Creamer is on the table, right where you left it. I didn't have a chance to order it up just right for you."

Not quite ready to make peace and play nice, she grunted again and settled in the chair Hawk held for her. Creed pushed a small jar filled with ivory-colored powder and a spoon across the table.

"Is she always this grumpy in the morning?" Creed directed the question to her brother, right over her head.

"Depends, but more often than not, I'd suspect. She does better when she's had adequate amounts of sleep, and judging by the circles under her eyes, she hasn't slept so well the last few nights."

"Enough," she muttered. "I'm sitting right here, if you don't mind."

"Are you going to be nice?"

"Are you?" She glared right back at Hawk.

"Oh, all right. I suppose I will."

"Good. Now go away and let me enjoy my coffee in peace." Linnet set the mug down and pulled her computer across the table. Half a cup of tasteless coffee later and the machine had booted up. She connected the sat-phone and started her email download. Knowing the slow data transfer could take five minutes or more depending on volume, she opened her data spreadsheet and blinked.

Cutting her eyes toward George, she found him looking at her from across the table.

"Hope you don't mind, it was quiet, so I input the data from yesterday."

"Oh. No. That's fine. Thanks." Now what she supposed to do all day?

"Are you upset I used your computer?"

"Huh? Oh. No. That's fine." Well, yeah, she was a little upset, but it looked as if he hadn't messed with her email. Messages were downloading at a prodigious rate. Who had a bee in their bonnet? Most likely Mom trying to tell her Hawk was on his way.

Sipping the rest of the weak brew she watched the emails stack up. Mom. Newbauer. Mom. Spam - Viagra no less. Mom. George. Mom. Mom. Newbauer. George. Henry. Mom.

*Henry?* "Hawk? How did Henry get my email address? You didn't give it to him, did you?" Would he have called Mom to get it?

"What?" Hawk came to look over her shoulder. "What's it say?"

"First of all, he's using my work email." Rubbing a hand over her face, she hoped it would make the threatening headache disappear. "I haven't opened it yet." Downloading complete, she disconnected the satellite link. At nearly a dollar per minute, she only connected for fast email up and down loads. Surfing was saved for trips to town.

"Since you're government, he probably got it that way because he's government too."

"Is he?" The return address seemed to indicate so. Was that a step up or step down from lobbying? "I suppose…" She closed her eyes and wished for the email to disappear.

"Want me to read it for you?"

Shaking her head she opened her eyes to see Hawk's intense eyes trained on her face. "No. I'm a big girl. But before I do open it, just what did you say to him when you saw him?"

The heavy chair next to her scraped against the floor as Hawk pulled it out to sit down. "I grilled him about the break up, but he wasn't real forthcoming at first. Said differences of opinion caused the split. Such as you wanted to move and he didn't. Made it sound like you left him crying in his chardonnay. I doubt that."

"Why? Why did you doubt it then?"

Hawk cleared his throat and looked away. "He'd moved out of the mid-level condo he was living in when you two were together."

"So?"

"He's living... with somebody."

Considering it had been more than a year and a half since she'd seen or talked to Henry, there was no logical explanation for the uneasy feeling churning the coffee on her empty stomach.

"Who? This is going to be brutal isn't it? I don't really want to know, do I?"

"Let me read it first."

"Why? What are you afraid of?"

"Please, Linnie? Let me spare you, if I can. He's out of your life. You don't need to reconnect with him in any way. It's not like you left him pregnant or anything."

Intently focused on Hawk, Linnet jumped when the screen door spring stretched with its signature twang. The Roys, she guessed, when a knock fell on the door a moment later.

"Let them in," she murmured.

"Don't open that email," Hawk warned her before standing to get the door.

Deciding Henry could wait for a moment, or more, she opened the most recent one from Mom. Great. Dad was in state and, as of this morning, because of the rain, he was standing down from the fire to the west. Even though it wasn't close enough to be a threat, Mom still worried and begged for an email update.

"Miss Linnet?"

Impatient with the interruption, she looked up to see a contrite Junior. "Yes?"

Acting like a nine-year old, he had his hands behind his back and shuffled his feet. "I'm sorry about the rice and beans last night. I didn't think they were hot at all. I tend to forget not everyone has cauterized their taste buds like we have."

"I forgive you," she said wearily and waved him off. "Just next time someone asks, please do them the courtesy of full disclosure. I'm not sure when I'll be able to taste anything again."

"I will, ma'am, I promise."

She nodded. Anything to get the man out of her face. "Is there anything you need?"

"We'd appreciate the chance to make breakfast out of the rain."

"It's up to Creed. This is his place. If you'll excuse me? I need to answer some of these emails before I run down the power much more."

"Yes, ma'am. Pardon us. You won't even know we're here."

She gave him the best smile she could at the moment, pitiful at best, and glanced at Creed. He merely winked at her then turned to deal with the Roys. That left her free to soothe maternal feathers. Since most of Mom's messages were pretty much of the same thread—how was Linnet doing—she decided to draft a general update note.

> *Dear Mom,*
> *Hawk arrived yesterday. Is the offer to come home*

*still good? Just joking.*

*Hawk wasn't the only one to arrive yesterday. In roughly twenty-four hours I went from just a dog and a river full of fish for company to the addition of five men. I'm not lonely at all. I do, however, expect to go stark raving mad soon.*

*I think the only other female in the area is the yearling moose who wanted to share my bath last night. No, she didn't really try to climb in with me, but Manley barked and that brought Creed (who owns the cabin I told you about – oh he likes the improvements!) and Hawk running. Talk about a little over-exposure.*

*Anyhow, Creed arrived night before last. His cousin, who I'm filling in for, (the George I told you about), arrived yesterday morning - cast and all. Hawk was waiting for us when we came in from a day of data gathering and soon after two river travelers stopped for the night.*

*It's raining very hard now, probably the same storm grounding Dad, so I don't expect anyone will move far from the cabin today. The fire is far enough away we aren't even aware of it, so don't worry I'm about to be over-run by it. I'll get Hawk to take some pictures so you can see I'm still one piece. Everything is fine, really. Please tell Dad he's welcome to visit, but I'm not leaving... unless it's to jump in the boat and find someplace to camp until they all leave.*

*Love you lots,*
*Linnet*

"Everything okay?"

Linnet saved the email and looked up to see Creed filling her coffee cup. *Eww*, she was going to have to teach these guys how to make coffee, or take over the task herself. "Just answered Mom so she doesn't send out the National Guard."

"Good. Keep Mom happy." Creed grinned. "Any word on your Dad?"

"Standing down. The rain. Who knows if he'll show up here or not? Everyone else seems to be making his way here."

"Hey, does your computer have AutoCAD on it?"

"What?" The change of topic took her by surprise.

"AutoCAD. Computer Aided…"

Waving impatiently, she cut Creed off. "I know what AutoCAD is, but why do you think I'd have it on my laptop?"

"It was just a question." He held up his hands signaling peace.

Was it the rain or the over abundance of company making her touchy? In an effort to curb her impulse to be sarcastic, she pretended she was in a boardroom meeting and spoke with an exaggerated polite tone. "Fine. No, I don't. But why do you need AutoCAD?"

"I want to draw up some plans so I can write out a supply list."

"For what?"

"Does it matter?"

"No, I guess not. It's your place, not mine. I have desktop publishing, a paint program and the usual office stuff."

"I just need a simple structure. Those will work. Mind if I borrow your machine after breakfast? We're sorta pinned down by the weather."

Starting to look like a good day to read. "Sure, you can use it. I'll shut it down now to preserve the battery power."

"Finish your emails. I'll cook breakfast. The biscuits are nearly done anyway. Then we can turn on the generator if we need to. I have one in my truck along with extra gas."

"Biscuits?" Come to think of it, the aroma was making her stomach growl.

He pointed behind her. "Dutch oven on the woodstove. More reliable than the old camper oven." A tilt of his head toward the kitchen indicated the tiny and finicky oven designed for a small RV kitchen.

"I'm impressed."

"You should be," he whispered and kissed her nose.

Creed's warm smile, twinkling eyes and the promise of hot kisses melted all the bad feelings inside of her. Even the coffee didn't seem so bad now, and Hawk's playfulness was his way of cheering her up. She could live with that, as long as Creed made soft food for breakfast, but even the irritation in her mouth and sinuses was fading. More water and she'd flush the last of it away.

Feeling strong enough to face anything, she opened Henry's email.

> *Linnet,*
>
> *Hawk's visit the other day took me completely by surprise. Just when I felt I was at last getting over you and the pain of our breakup, I was thrust into the maelstrom again. I'm not sure who was hurt more, you*

*or me. For awhile I wondered if it was you by the way you took off.*

*The rumors flying about the incident weren't pretty at all before you left and grew worse afterward. I spent some time hanging out at the bar where the guys from your office go and overheard more than enough to suspect maybe you were right. They weren't kind in how they spoke of you. Every last one of them is a low class jackal.*

*I'm sorry I doubted you. I was sure you were trying to find a way to break up with me and a story of being raped made it seem like you were trying to give me a way out. I even wondered if you and Billy had something going on behind my back. Hell, from the way your boss looked at you, I even suspected him. I realize now I was probably wrong. Can you forgive me?*

Probably wrong? Leave it to Henry the politician to never come out and directly admit anything. But her boss? Jack Weston? The mere thought of standing close to him was enough to make her shiver. Ugh. Never in a million years would she have an affair with him. Especially after the way he'd treated her demands for support after the rape. Shaking off that horrible thought she returned to the email.

*Anyhow, on the rebound, I believe I did something even more foolish. Hurt, I was stumbling through life, barely existing, and one day I stumbled into your friend Cyndi. She didn't know where you were and was feeling pretty put-out herself about you abandoning her as well.*

*Long story short, one thing led to another and we're now living together. She expects a proposal any day and now I realize I may have wronged you. I'm not sure I can give it to her.*

*I have some vacation time coming and I'm looking into flights north. Exactly where are you and how do I get to you? Hawk said you were someplace fairly remote and indicated it might take a couple days to locate you. He did mention you had access to email, so how remote can you be?*

*I found your email through the State website. Good*

*picture they have of you. Seeing your face again brought
it all back to me. I even dug out the photo of you I kept
in my wallet. It's there again, but even more so, I want
to see you in person. I want to beg your forgiveness and
see if we still have the spark.*

    *Please reply as soon as you get this. I need to know
you're safe and willing to at least meet me for dinner.
In case you don't have it anymore, my cell is (916) 555-
5375. It might be best to call during the day. Call me
soon.*

    *All the best of my love,*
    Henry


Stunned, Linnet didn't know whether to laugh, cry or go throw up.

He'd *stumbled* into Cyndi? Cyndi circulated nowhere near Henry's path. Linnet's *best*—cough—friend had lain in wait and ambushed her ex-boyfriend. Yeah, Cyndi was so cut up about being *abandoned*, she'd spread most of the rumors about Billy and the rape. Yep, that was friendship for you.

Cyndi had also been the one to loan what Linnet now realized was the most hideous and unflattering dress ever made, for her first date with Henry. Old *Cyn* must have been furious when that backfired. So. He was living with the woman who'd never made it a secret she felt Henry was wasted on Linnet.

Call during the day.

Right. Catch him at work so Cyndi wouldn't know they were talking. Nothing like keeping everything above board and out in the open.

And he wanted to get back together with her.

Now what?

# Chapter 15

"You opened it, didn't you?"

Creed turned around to see Hawk standing over his sister, hands on his hips and dark scowl on his face.

"Yeah, well, it is my email after all," she snapped back at him.

Not good news then. An email from the ex. So much for everyone's good moods.

"I told you not to open it."

"Well, I figured he couldn't say anything to hurt me."

"You were wrong, weren't you?"

"No, I wasn't. I'm pissed, but I'm not hurt. I'm also glad he was stupid and narrow-minded because otherwise I'd probably be stuck with the idiot for good by now. Instead he actually did me a favor."

Funny, Creed glanced her way, she didn't sound like she believed her own words. She'd been looking soft and relaxed, quite beautiful in fact, before she'd opened the email. Now she was tense, with a pinched look around her mouth and eyes.

Sizzling sausage recalled his attention to the camp stove. The onions and potatoes were already browned nicely, the sausage was about done, and it was almost time for eggs, followed by shredded cheese. Nothing like a pan of classic Camp Slop, the official dish of the cabin. Might be a good idea to skip the green Tabasco this time and let everyone add their own.

"So," Hawk pressed her. "What did he say?"

"I don't want to talk about it. Nothing important."

Sure, Creed really believed it too. About like he believed ice worms tripped skiers. He heard the sound of the laptop being slammed shut.

"Let me read it." Hawk nagged at her like a dog with a bone.

"No. I promised Creed I wouldn't wear out the battery."

"Where's the generator? I'll go start it up."

"No. I'm almost out of gas for it."

"Creed said he had more."

"Let it go, Hawk!"

The only sound heard in the cabin for a few moments was the sizzling from the pan in front of him and the crackle of dried wood burning in the woodstove. He glanced over his shoulder to see Linnet shoving her feet into her sneakers. As she straightened and grabbed her coat from a hook by the door, his gaze met hers. She paused for a moment, then shoved her arms into the sleeves and pulled the door open. Two steps and she was out of the cabin. Judging by the sound of her footsteps, she was headed for the outhouse. At least it wasn't the boats.

Creed looked sideways and caught George's eye. He glanced at the Roys next. They appeared entirely too interested in Linnet's business, not to mention the sheer awkwardness of the situation.

"I'll be done here in a few minutes," he said to Roy Sr. and turned back to the stove. "Why don't you pour yourselves a cup of coffee and relax until then?" He gave the older man a brief smile, then stirred the eggs one more time before pouring them into the pan. If timing worked out right, he'd have the plates on the table when Linnet came back.

"Damn, she's got her email passworded," Hawk complained.

"You're spying on her computer? Pretty brave." Better if Hawk got caught. Creed had been planning on snooping while working on the plans for the sleeping cabin.

"Yeah, I want to read that email. Think, what would Linnie use for a password?" It sounded as if he muttered to himself.

Creed snorted and stirred the mixture in the pan. "You got me. I don't know her well enough. Did you ever have a dog growing up?"

"Yeah, Abel... nope, too short anyway."

"Any other pets?"

"A rabbit that ate Mom's garden one year. He made a great stew." Hawk typed again, presumably the name of the stew. "Nope, not Patrick."

"A combination of family names?"

"Hmmm, PerryDoveHawk... Nope."

"Falcondove?"

"Nope."

Creed heard the screen door opening as he sprinkled shredded cheese on top of the slop in the pan. They were about to be busted.

"Why don't you try 'treasonous rat bastard'?" Linnet snapped. "Close my computer. Now." She slammed the wooden door for emphasis.

Hawk was busted.

"Keep your big nose out of my business. Because you just had to go and play investigator, terminator style, all this got stirred up again. Now back off and mind your own business. If you can't do that, then pack your bag and hike out. You SEALs like doing stuff like that and the twenty-odd miles into Circle should take you only a few hours. Then go explain to Dad why Henry wants to come chasing after me."

"A-ha! So that's what all this is about. What about where he's living?" Hawk challenged.

"Not your business, and not mine either. I won't contact him. At. All. You read me, Lieutenant?"

"Ma'am, yes, ma'am!" Hawk jumped up and gave her a snappy salute. All that earned him was a solid punch on the arm.

So the ex wanted to reconcile? Too bad for him. He'd have to find her first, and then explain his callousness from before. And Creed was on his home turf. No one could beat him here. Grinning to himself, he served up four plates and stepped aside, gesturing to the Roys the stove was theirs.

* * * *

Linnet looked up from her book. All the men, all five of them, had their heads together over the computer. What could be so interesting?

Rain continued to pound down and the Roys had laid out their tent and sleeping bags in front of the fire, draping them over the chairs to dry. Seemed the tent couldn't take one more ounce of rain and had collapsed on them. Good thing they could make Circle in a day, but it wasn't going to be today. Looked like they were sleeping inside tonight.

Rolling over onto her back, head at the foot of her bed to take advantage of the meager light from the window, Linnet held up her book again. At least the book was good enough to drown out the discussion of trees and cabin building. She'd agreed Hawk could stay as long as he kept busy and out of her hair. Might even be able to send George back to town.

No, the book wasn't good enough to distract her after all. With a sigh, she slid her bookmark between the pages and twisted her wrist to glance at her watch. Twelve-sixteen. Breakfast had been late enough no one was interested in lunch so there wasn't even that to break the monotony. At this rate she'd be old and gray before this day passed.

Determined to do something useful, she decided to make that trip down river. She'd been planning on going today as it was and, if Hawk was staying, they'd need more supplies. Rolling to the side, she tossed her pillow and book back to the head. Glancing toward the men, she saw that only George looked her way, his expression neutral. Ignoring him, she bent and dug through her duffel to find her keys and wallet. Even out on the Yukon, cash was needed for gas and food.

The key's jangled as she tucked them into her pocket. Silence fell and the men watched her shove her wallet into her hip pocket. Hawk had teased her for years over her men's-style wallet, but hey, it worked better than carrying a purse.

"Where are you going?" Creed asked.

"Shopping."

"Thought you said you didn't need to?"

"I changed my mind." She didn't feel like arguing or explaining herself.

George reached for his crutches. "I'll go with you."

"Honestly, I've made the run several times with only Manley for company, I can make it. Anyone who wants to toss some cash in the kitty is welcome." Striding to the front of the cabin she kept her eye on her goal. Getting out the door. The extra coats were an annoyance as she dug for her rain pants, life jacket and coat. Irritation propelled her to forego the pants and stomp into her hip boots. She pulled the rest on as she headed out the door with Manley on her heels.

"Hold up!" George called and Linnet slowed. "Creed gave us a list. I've got money, too."

What kind of list did Creed have? The store in Circle had very little in the way of hardware.

"All right," she sighed. "I'll push us off once you get settled."

George was surprisingly nimble as he hefted himself up over the bow. Linnet handed up his crutches then lifted Manley. Within a matter of minutes they were racing down the river, George at the controls, driving several knots faster than Linnet would have.

"What's the hurry?" she asked as he swung around a gravel bar. The turn was sharp enough she had to brace her feet on the deck and grab the dashboard for stability.

"Creed said to hurry back." George shrugged and gave her a small wink.

"So when you going to drop the dumb Indian act?"

"The what?" George's face went suspiciously blank. Too fast.

Time to share a little lore of her own. "Once upon a time there was an old Indian chief. This chief, Fierce Hawk, had a beautiful daughter he named *White Dove Who Sings Among the Nettles*. To the world she was known simply as Missy." A glance showed George's impassive face, but she knew he was listening. "Fierce Hawk was brave and much like his name, fiercely proud and protective of his small dove. One day she met a man named for the peregrine falcon. Like her father, he was a fierce warrior and decorated for bravery in battle. When they met, he was wounded and she nursed him back to health. One day, she decided it was time for her father to meet her hero. Fierce Hawk was not pleased with this warrior, for he was not one of The People. However, Missy had her heart set and soon the dove married the falcon. In time, they had two children. The children remembered their grandfather as being stern and silent, always speaking slowly in a quiet voice wise, with many years. The children never understood why their father rolled his eyes when their grandfather spoke of mysteries and ancient ways." Linnet glanced sideways to see George still trying to look disinterested, but the set of his shoulders told a different story. He was practically leaning toward her to catch every word.

"One day, the wise grandfather was teaching his grandchildren how to throw the tomahawk the way he'd been taught. The youngest, a boy of seven, grasped the handle as instructed, lifted the tomahawk, and threw it with accuracy that made the old man cry silent tears of pride. When his sister, a delicate flower, the apple of his eye, pulled the tomahawk from the target, it stuck and she gave it a mighty pull. So mighty a pull it flew backwards and landed on the grandfather's toe. Blunt end down of course."

George winced and Linnet looked aside to hide her smile.

"And what do you suppose that wise old Cherokee grandfather said when that heavy weapon landed on his foot?"

George didn't answer her, but he did look at her with raised brow.

"The delicate little flower and her brother watched in amazement as their stern and proud grandfather danced a jig and cursed like a sailor. Of course they didn't know the words, but they weren't spoken slowly or with great gravity as usual. Later, Missy and her falcon laughed quietly and pronounced his dancing worthy of Grandfather's Irish grandmother, his cursing worthy of the best of the sailors in the Navy."

George chuckled. "So Grandfather wasn't an old Indian Chief?"

"There may have been one back in the family tree, but history doesn't tell us. Instead, the children later learned it was an act their grandfather used to annoy their father more than anything else. Worked pretty good on nosy neighbors as well."

Crinkled, George's eyes twinkled as he let out a snort of laughter. "You got me."

"Glad to know my gut instinct still works."

"You're one sharp squaw, Miss Greenbriar."

"And you're one wily old coot, Mr. Nyuchuk. Now, tell me why you put on the act?"

"I think you have that figured out already," he chuckled.

"So what did you pick up on our guests? The Roys, that is."

"They aren't what they seem, but they don't feel criminal either. Just hiding something."

"I agree. Plan on running their names through the data banks when we reach Circle?"

George glanced her way then shook his head with a smile. "You're reading my mind, little missy."

"Missy is my mother." She laughed back.

"Is that why you let me come along?"

"You're the actual officer. I'm just a biologist. I'd have to run it past Newbauer; you can go straight to the Troopers. Your way is faster."

"Is that why you wanted to go to town in the rain?"

"Not really. It's a good excuse though. I really just wanted away from all those men." She looked out the side window with a sigh. "I'm not used to the crowds and I'm feeling put out."

"Got settled in, did you?"

"Yeah, and I know it isn't my place to settle into." Another bank around a corner and she held on again. George took it easier this time. Probably no longer trying to impress her. Already he seemed more relaxed, his accent softer, less guttural. More white.

"Don't worry about it. The place is happier for you being there."

Linnet cut her eyes toward him again, but the neutral, blank face was already in place.

"So tell me how you really broke your leg," she challenged him.

George winced. "I slipped in the mud."

"How?"

"Why do you ask?"

"George, have you ever slipped in the mud and broken anything before this?"

"No."

"Then why this time?"

George's hand inched toward the throttle and Linnet stared him down with a glare. "Trying to drown me out with the motor won't work. I'll just strand you in Circle until you 'fess up."

"You're a hard-headed woman, Linnet." His hand moved back from the throttle.

"You say that like it's a bad thing. Too bad I don't believe you."

"Okay, I give. Only Newbauer knows this since he asked the same questions as you. I was trying to help a lady bring in a big king. Her reel was coming apart and she'd snagged a big one. Too bad she had to let it go... was really huge, probably eighty pounds, maybe more. Was a real hard fight, but at the last minute she got excited and dropped her pole too soon. The damn fish smacked me in the leg and the mud caught my foot just right. One foot gave way, the other didn't and I ended up with a spiral fracture on the small bone, a complete break on the ankle bone."

Linnet winced in sympathy. "What happened next?"

"They had to set the king free, since snagging doesn't count. Then they helped me to the truck and promised to close up the cabin. Manley and I drove into town and Creed's folks met me at the hospital."

Damn, that was a long drive to make in pain. Her truck was covered and filled with dust kicked up the last fifty miles of the road that steadily narrowed. Once past Central, the track was rarely much wider than two cars with several soft spots where dirt had been dumped after rain washed away small sections. The road wasn't so bad four-wheel drive was required, but who could call a narrow dirt road a highway and keep a straight face? She watched as George slowed the boat, maneuvered into a wide channel and pulled up to the landing. In a matter of minutes life vests were shed, the boat was tied up and they stood on shore with Manley.

Eyeing the village for signs of activity, she saw very little. Two blocks to the store over dirt roads wasn't bad with empty cans. Usually there was someone around with a truck willing to give her a lift. With the rain, no one was out at the moment. "You have Creed's list?" she asked. With George along, maybe help would be easier to find. Not that she generally had a problem. When strangers showed up in town people got curious. As far as she knew, she was still a stranger.

"Yeah." George pulled a piece of paper from his shirt pocket. Next he extracted some cash and passed it along as well. "Your brother kicked in for some food and gas, Creed wants some nails and simple tools if they have 'em. I'll round up someone to meet you at the store with a truck to haul it all back here."

The list looked reasonable when she scanned it. Nails, rope, string, engine oil and gas. A few extra large nails, spikes, to help hold logs together. Yeah, they'd need help hauling the stuff. "Will you get someone to help haul the fuel cans as well?"

George glanced at the water and gas cans on the ground beside them. Four red two-gallon plastic gas containers and four blue five-gallon water jugs. Definitely needed wheels. Gas could be bought at the store. Good thing the water jugs could be filled for free at the washeteria where one could also do laundry and take a shower. Since most of the village didn't have running water, it was a common gathering spot. A place where she spent as little time as possible. Seemed every time she showed up there, so did half the village.

"I can haul them up empty, but will need help getting them back. I usually only fill one at a time," she explained.

"Yeah, me too." George's grin was rueful. "Yeah, I'll get Bobby to help out. I'm heading to the Council building first."

"Right. Meet you either there or at the trading post."

Linnet hauled the cans to the trading post and left them outside for Bobby to fill. When he tipped his baseball cap to her and started singing that awful song, she resisted the urge to deck him. Tempting as it was to rearrange his neglected teeth, knocking two more out wouldn't help him much. The old codger needed every one of them, tobacco stained and crooked as they were. Straightening her shoulders, she marched to the store leaving the cackling old man behind.

# Chapter 16

Linnet counted out the bills and slapped them down on the counter. Wes Hall had picked up the song and hummed it behind the register as he counted out her change. A few snickers came from behind the row of shelves forming just two aisles in the long narrow store.

"You'll send everything down to the boat, right?" she asked again. Ignoring the song and the peanut gallery, she resisted the urge to sigh in resignation. Instead she spoke with her best get-down-to-business voice.

"Yup. As soon as I can get Bobby to help me load up his truck. If you're not there we'll just leave everything stacked up on shore." Wes may have been decades younger than Bobby, but his teeth were in nearly as bad shape, showing a need of preventative care. If he didn't smile, he wasn't half bad looking with his mixed white and Athabascan heritage. The village was about half and half, with the natives slightly more predominant, and had more than a few half breeds mixed in. Even though Wes had offered at various times to take her fishing and hunting, she'd declined. She wasn't sure, but somehow felt he was too young for her anyway and used that excuse often.

"I'll be watching for you. With George on crutches, I need help loading."

She picked up her smaller purchases, a treasured bottle of Starbucks mocha and a pack of Starbursts, turned and left the store as Wes broke into full out song. "...*the squaws along the Yukon, are good enough for me!*"

The door slammed shut on his final words and she stood on the steps in the shade of the building a moment with her eyes closed, reining in her temper.

"Well, lookee here, if that ain't the prettiest little bird I've ever seen."

Linnet's eyes flew open. Even though he stood a step down from her, she still had to look up a little to meet his eyes. Too happy to see his familiar, care-worn face, she forgot to be annoyed.

"Daddy!" She threw her arms around his neck and hugged him tight. His arms were tight enough he lifted her off the step and swung her around.

"Baby bird, you are a sight for sore eyes." If she didn't know better, she'd almost swear he choked back tears. Daddy never cried.

"Well you can't look at me when you're squeezing the stuffin's out of me." She laughed. "But it feels good to hug you too." She gave him a final squeeze then wiggled out of his arms.

"Well, this is a fortuitous event. You just saved me hours of chasing you down. Nobody around here was willing to tell me where you were. How long will it take to pack up your gear and get your brother? Is he here with you?"

"A couple of years. Actually, a couple hours to get back to Hawk, then maybe half an hour to get him packed up, longer to convince him to leave with you. If you're in a hurry, anyway. As for me, I'm scheduled to be out here until the end of August. After that it's back to Anchorage unless I can get a transfer to Fairbanks."

"Wrong direction, baby bird."

Linnet stared up at her father's lined face. He had a few more gray hairs and the forehead was slightly higher, but the stormy gray eyes she remembered stared back at her. She knew that look. The Captain was in charge and meant to see his orders followed.

Not this time. She glared back as good as she got. She wasn't the Falcon's daughter for nothing.

"I'm not leaving. I'll try to bring Hawk down river, but I think he has it in mind to spend his leave here."

"Here?"

"Yes. The guys have an idea about building a sleeping cabin. It'll keep Hawk busy for a few weeks."

Linnet let her father take her arm and steer her away from the door. People were starting to gather, staring at the two of them with small-town curiosity. Most people ended up in the village by accident, thinking they would reach the actual Arctic Circle. In reality, the Arctic Circle was fifty-eight miles farther north. If you wanted the circle, this was the wrong road to follow as it ended at the river.

"No good. It's time for you and Hawk to come home."

"What about your fire? How'd you get here?"

"The chopper is out at the airstrip. The rain brought the fire under control, so extra crews aren't needed."

"Well you can hop right back in your whirly bird and take a kiss home to Mom for me."

"You can kiss her yourself, baby bird."

"Sorry, Captain. I'm not one of your flight crew. I'm a working adult and have a job to do." Linnet folded her arms and faced her father with a scowl, matching his stance.

"Miss Linnie? This man bothering you?"

Blinking in surprise, she looked down to see gnarled old Bobby tugging on her sleeve and glaring up at her father. Unbelievable.

"I'll make him leave you alone if you like."

"Thanks, Bobby." Linnet relaxed her posture and put a hand on her father's arm. "But I need you too much to do that to you. Wes is piling up the groceries and hardware inside. I need you to haul it down to the boat along with the gas cans and water jugs. Forty dollars enough to make it worth your while?"

"Ah, ma'am," Bobby still glared up at her father, "I'd do it for the pleasure of whupping this man who's buggin' ya."

"I appreciate the chivalry, Bobby, but this is my father. I... um... I don't want him hurt, okay?" More to the point, she needed Bobby ambulatory enough to haul her supplies and not trundled off to the health clinic. "I'll see you down at the landing just as soon as I can round up George and Manley."

"Okay, if you say so." Bobby backed off with a good show of being reluctant. "George is over at the Council building."

Like that would intimidate her father. Though his face remained stony, Linnet felt him trembling with suppressed laughter.

"Thanks, Bobby. Would you coordinate with Wes about the supplies? I'll watch for your truck and we'll meet you there."

"K-O, Miss Linnie." With a final narrow-eyed glare at her father, Bobby mounted the steps into the Trading Post.

"Whew, feared for my life for a moment there," her father joked once the door shut.

"Yeah, well, they may annoy the crap out of me, but nice to know they're willing to stand up to Outsiders. Must mean I'm not such a Cheechako anymore." She considered her father for a long moment then shook her head. "Hawk already told me what you want, but I'm not going home. Maybe for a visit this Christmas, but I'm staying in Alaska. I like it here."

"We'll talk. But first, why don't we tour this town and find George and Manley. Manley is the dog, right?"

"Oh, so you do read the emails I send." Linnet took his arm and steered him toward the Tribal Council building—a grand name for a small annex off the school. It served double duty as the police station when the itinerant trooper or magistrate was here. Occasionally did triple duty as the clinic. Or a gathering spot for the elders to sit and chew the fat.

They met George on his way out, Manley at his side, stepping carefully to avoid the crutches. Linnet could almost see the relief in Manley's eyes when he caught sight of her.

"Manley, go get Linnet," George ordered gruffly. A look of amused disgust crossed his face and he shook his head as Linnet knelt to greet the dog who ran to her. "I think he likes you better."

"Sure he does. I pamper him," Linnet laughed. "But he listens to you first."

"He's just a gullible male. Kind of like a few young bucks I know," George chuckled and swung to a stop. "This one doesn't look so gullible." George extended his hand. "George Nyuchuk. Pleased to meet you, Captain Greenbriar."

"Ah, I see my reputation precedes me." He returned the handshake. "I go by either Perry or Falcon, George."

George nodded then cast a sideways glance at Linnet. "I have my ways of finding out what's new in town."

"In other words, one of the elders was gossiping like an old woman," Linnet muttered.

"It's called sharing news." George chuckled again, then hitched his chin toward the landing. "Not to mention the family resemblance. Let's mosey along. Bobby and Wes have the truck nearly loaded."

Arguing with her father didn't slow the loading process. In the end, Bobby gave him a ride back to the airstrip. Following the river, the helicopter caught up with them five miles upstream and stayed with them until George pulled the boat up at a large sandbar a hundred yards downstream from the cabin.

"George," Linnet growled. "Let him swim. I don't want him at the cabin."

Typically, George ignored her and waited until her father had the helicopter tied down securely and had vaulted onto the boat. Even Manley sided with the male conspiracy by greeting the Captain enthusiastically.

"From zero to six men in forty-eight hours. Has to be a record."

"Nah, just your lucky day, baby bird."

\* \* \* \*

"Lieutenant."

A hard, parade-ground, officious voice barked out the single word before Creed caught up to Hawk who secured the boat. The distinctive sound of the helicopter had gained everyone's attention and Creed had jogged down the bank to Linnet's favorite spot to watch the aircraft land and the older man tie up while George waited to ferry him to shore.

Even though he wasn't military, Creed nearly followed Hawk's example of saluting the man who jumped from the boat before turning to lift Linnet to the ground.

"Captain." Hawk stood at attention with his hand raised in a perfectly straight salute.

Ah. This must be Papa Greenbriar. The closer Creed drew, the more obvious the family features. Even down to the crispness of the returned salute.

"I thought I sent you on a simple mission, son. Does it always take you longer than twenty-four hours to extract a damsel in distress?" The twinkle in the old man's eye softened the rebuke. Was this the Greenbriar version of a family joke?

"No, sir, Captain, sir. The damsel showed a disturbing lack of distress, sir." An impudent grin hovered at the edge of Hawk's mouth but he managed to keep it under wraps.

"Son, you're never going to understand women, so don't even try. When you're sent to extract them, just toss 'em over your shoulder and high tail it out."

Creed had to grin as the Captain delivered the last bit of advice with his arm around his daughter and a wide grin on his face. The grin merely widened at Linnet's gasp of outrage.

Hawk's face twitched, but he never broke attention. "Yes, sir."

"At ease, Lieutenant."

The moment the old man's gaze found him, Creed stepped forward, hand out. "Welcome to Alaska, Captain Greenbriar. I'm Creed Willis."

"Daddy, Creed owns the cabin. He's George's cousin," Linnet said.

The old man's gaze never wavered as he returned the handshake with a firm grip. No lack of strength there, Creed noted. Direct gray eyes bored into him like a laser and Creed glared back. A moment later, once again a grin split the Captain's face. "Both my daughter and your cousin speak highly of you. Thanks for letting my children move in on you."

"My pleasure, sir."

The Captain cast a glance at the darkening sky still heavy with gray clouds. "I'm guessing you all will tell me it's too late to pull out of here tonight."

"Daddy, I'm not leaving." Linnet removed herself from his side and faced him, hands on hips. "I'm a State employee and I have a job I love. You will not ruin this for me. Besides, I already told you, Hawk has a job for the next few weeks as well."

"Grab the grub, girl and feed me. I'm grouchy on an empty stomach, you know that."

Creed felt Linnet's sigh nearly to his toes and despite the twinkle in her father's eye was about to step in when she waved at the boat. "Unload it, boys, if you want to see food anytime soon. No eating until the provisions are put away."

He wasn't all that surprised when a few minutes later he was trudging up the rise to the cabin with a crate of fresh vegetables and other food supplies. Over his arm hung plastic bags filled with a mix of nails, saw blades and other tool parts. The Roys followed with water jugs while the Greenbriars carried the fuel. A good run. No wonder it had taken them so long. Normally the run into town shouldn't have taken five hours.

Linnet met him at the counter in the kitchen. "Sorry, Daddy insisted on coming along. I'm hoping to send him and Hawk away tomorrow."

"But you just told your father Hawk has a job here."

"If he can get one of us home, Hawk makes the most sense."

"You want my help?"

"I might need it," she whispered as the outer door swung open.

Creed could feel the eyes on his back as he and Linnet stood side by side unloading the groceries. The intensity grew as she stepped closer to him to put a canister of oatmeal on the shelf.

"We need some more glass jars," she said.

"Hmm?" What did glass jars have to do with anything right now when her old man wanted to kill him?

"Next time you go into town, see if you can get a hold of some large gallon sized glass jars. You know, the kind the warehouse stores sell pickles in."

"I don't eat enough pickles to get jars like that."

"Don't you know any of the restaurant people?"

"I'll ask my mom to keep an eye out. Will that be good enough?"

"Sure."

"Nice set up here, Willis." The old man's voice boomed out behind them.

Creed turned, letting Linnet finish with the few remaining items. "Thank you, sir. Been in the family awhile. Guess we should find you a bunk and spare sleeping bag."

"Just a bunk will do. It isn't below zero around here yet, is it?"

"No, sir. We only drop into the high forties at night these days."

"Balmy."

Creed merely nodded at the crusty old guy.

"I'll toss something together for dinner if you want to look around, Dad." Linnet kept her attention on putting the groceries away.

"Sure. Willis, show me around."

Creed grimaced and leaned close enough to Linnet to whisper, "Thanks a lot."

The little wink she gave him was cute enough he wanted to kiss her, but with the old man watching it probably wasn't wise. "Sure, Captain, I'd be happy to give you the tour."

# Chapter 17

Linnet busied herself making salmon salad sandwiches while the men, she used the term loosely, scouted out the building site. Watching from the window over the kitchen counter it appeared they were all getting along just fine. Predictably, Hawk and her father had their opinions. Judging by how Creed nodded, he agreed with their comments. Survey tape was tied around trees to be downed and stakes were pounded into the ground where the corners of the cabin would be. Soon the men were meandering from sight, more trees being marked to form the walls of the cabin. To her it looked like little boys playing lumberjack as they measured and sized up each spruce marked to come down.

By the time she asked George to yell out the door that dinner was ready, they all looked like drowned rats. The Roys took longer to appear, apparently they'd found something else to do other than play with trees.

After she placed bowls of food on the table, Linnet plunked down a large pot of coffee and jug of water. Feet stomped on the porch, boots were kicked off at the door, coats were hung on the pegs. At least the Roys' gear had dried and was folded on the chairs. Rain still dripped from the sodden clouds and Linnet staked her claim on her usual chair.

Creed wasted no time securing the chair next to her, leaving George near the end closest to the kitchen. If only they could have banished her father to the other end. Instead Linnet felt his stare as he took the chair directly across from her.

"What's this?" her father lifted a bowl and used the spoon to poke at it.

"Salmon salad. Like tuna salad, only with salmon caught and cooked yesterday. I made a few modifications." Linnet took a slice of bread, shaking her head at Creed's offer of leftover rice and beans.

"You took good Yukon River salmon and mixed it with mayonnaise?"

"Sort of. Try it, you'll like it."

The men all gave her sideways glances. Didn't trust her, did they? She grabbed the bowl from her father and scooped out a spoonful. Seconds later she had an open faced sandwich and bit into it. Not her favorite, but with Creed's tzatziki sauce, a little onion, and extra diced cucumbers it passed. Fresh tomatoes, dearly bought and thinly sliced to spread around a little further, added to the treat. Well, if you could call salmon a treat. She'd rather have a hunk of beef, ribeye steak to be exact, but this would have to do.

Thankfully, Creed followed her example and bit into his sandwich. Before his mouth was empty enough to speak, he moaned as he chewed, head nodding. At last he swallowed and leaned over to kiss her on the cheek. "Awesome improvisation."

She stared at him. No one had ever praised her for making up a recipe. Their gazes locked, she barely heard the appreciative noises as man after man tried the dish. Only a foot kicking her under the table interrupted the stare. Judging by her father's scowl, it must have been his foot.

Creed pushed back his chair. "This deserves a celebration."

"A celebration?" Linnet looked over her shoulder to see him digging in one of the ice chests.

"This is so good, it deserves a good wine." He came back to the table with a corkscrew and a bottle of white wine in one hand. A finger from the other was hooked through the handles of a selection of clean mugs. "We'll skip the fancy crystal this time."

Linnet's cheeks heated at his wink. To hide her confusion and embarrassment, she turned her attention to her dinner. Flirting wasn't one of her better skills, and doing it in front of her father, brother and strangers didn't make it easier. She took a mug from Creed, a simple stainless mug, and stared down into the golden depths. An odd feeling pushed at her and she glanced up to join in the toast Creed was poised to make.

"To our visitors. We hope you like Alaska."

Nice and simple. Worked for her. Linnet lifted the cup. Before sipping, she sniffed the bouquet. The action was second nature to a well-trained California girl, raised on Napa's finest. The delicate aroma was familiar somehow. Mild. Flowery… without sipping, she could taste the wine… it reminded her…

The room around her faded, and the rushing of blood filled her ears as she stared into the cup, unable to move. The flames from the woodstove flickered at the corner of her eye as blackness closed in, the horror washed over her, stealing all her composure.

The tea. The wine smelled just like the chamomile tea she'd drunk the night Billy had raped her. With one whiff of the wine she was there, on that mountain, camped beside the lake, sitting across the campfire. As if he were there, she could see Billy watching her from the far side of the flames, a predatory look in his eyes, belying his relaxed posture as he sipped from his own cup, leisurely puffing on a joint.

"Linnet?" The voice came from far away, a whisper on the wind. Like another voice... another vision assaulted her. The office. Jack Weston leaning over her, his face drawing closer, a weight pressing her down... leather sticking to her back...

"*Oh. My. God.*" With a shriek, she blindly thrust the cup away from her. Dizzy, her ears filled with buzzing, glitter danced before her eyes, and yet she couldn't take in the vision. Hallucination. It had to be a hallucination because it just couldn't be real. Never would she have had sex with her boss on the sofa in his office. Never.

The implication of the vision was too much to take in. She reached for the edge of the table. Something to stop the sensation of falling. Something solid to hold onto in the world now spinning madly out of control.

Creed watched Linnet's face lose all color as she stared into the standard issue camping mug. It wasn't the cup entrancing her, she'd drunk from it before. "Linnet?" he said again and set down the bottle beside his own cup.

"Linnet!" Her father called from across the table but it seemed as if she didn't hear him.

Linnet dropped the cup and it tipped over, the pale gold liquid spreading across the table like water released from a dam. All color bleached from her face and, visibly trembling, she gripped the edge of the table, her knuckles white. She pushed back from the table and stood, her chair falling with a crash to the floor behind her.

"No," she moaned, and would have tripped over the chair if Creed hadn't grabbed her by the upper arms.

"No, don't," she cried, swaying on her feet. "Get off me!" She tried to wrench herself away, but Creed held on to her to keep her from falling.

"Linnet. It's Creed. Linnet, you're in Alaska. On the Yukon. In a cabin," he spoke softly, urgently.

"Get away, Jack! You can't do this!" she screeched, while trying to push Creed away. Oddly enough, there was no force to her struggles.

*Jack? Who was Jack?* Creed's heart raced as he tried to calm her by keeping himself calm. A glance at Hawk earned a shrug even as the SEAL's face filled with thunder clouds.

"I thought it was Billy...?" Creed let the question fade away as he continued to grip her shoulders.

"First Billy... then Jack..." Linnet moaned. "Oh, God."

"What's going on?" Junior asked.

"Flashback," the Captain said sharply. A moment later he was around the table. "Linnet, Daddy's here, baby bird. Daddy and Hawk are both here, honey."

"Daddy?" Glazed eyes turned to her father and Creed felt her body softening. She blinked rapidly and, with each blink, the shadow of her memories seemed to fade from her terrified face.

"Daddy?"

"Yes, baby bird. I'm here." The Captain reached out a hand to grasp her arm, but hesitated when she flinched and cast her gaze about the room.

At last her eyes settled on Creed and a flush bloomed across her pallid cheeks. Relief flooded Creed and he started shaking in reaction as recognition lit her eyes.

"Oh. My. God!" Linnet raised a hand to her lips even as the other gripped Creed's forearm. "Creed," she whispered, her face now red.

The next moment he pulled her into his arms, shushing her and murmuring soft words in her ear. "It's okay, Linnet, I've got you. I won't hurt you. No one will hurt you, I promise. You're safe, sweet bird." It was hard to tell who trembled more in the aftermath, him or her.

Face burrowed against his chest, Linnet flinched the first time her father touched her, then relaxed, letting the extra touch soothe her. But, Creed noted, she didn't try to pull away from him. Instead, she snuggled closer.

"Uh, maybe we'll just take our plates outside," Roy Sr. mumbled and Creed heard George agree. Soon it was just Creed, Linnet, her father and brother left in the cabin. Even Manley had stepped out.

"I... I'm so... sorry." Linnet shook, a small sob wracking her frame.

"Shhh, it's okay, don't worry about it, Linnie. You're safe here. We only want you to feel safe," he crooned. "Let's sit down, my legs are shaking so badly I just might fall."

That earned him a small sobbing laugh. A step in the right direction.

He backed into the chair Hawk held for him. Linnet followed and curled up on his lap, her arms tight around his neck, her warm tears sliding down his throat to wet the collar of his flannel shirt. One of his arms slid across her back, the other curved around her waist and she felt warm and right in his embrace. As right as it had felt to lie beside her in the bunk.

"I've got you, Linnet." His murmurs seemed to be working, so he kept talking to her. The Captain picked up Linnet's chair and sat in it.

The man looked distinctly put out that his little girl was clinging to a man other than him. Had Hawk been holding her, Creed had no doubt the Captain would have pulled her into his own arms. As it was, he merely rubbed Linnet's shoulder while Hawk crouched beside the two chairs.

"That's the second time," Hawk said quietly, "in as many days, sissy. You're not as over it as you want us to believe. Was there more than once? Who is Jack?"

Linnet trembled. "Jack Weston. My boss…"

"In California?" Her father's voice was a low rumble of angry thunder.

"Yes. I… I… think… in the office. There was an afternoon I fell asleep at my desk and woke up on the sofa in his office…" The tremors in her body increased and Creed had to wonder if his trembling was adding to hers.

Her boss, too? Had he given Billy the original drug then used it himself to follow up in the office? Creed's grip around Linnet increased until she squealed in protest. Loosening his hold he cradled her in his arms. "Ah, Linnie, we'll get him. He'll pay. They both will," he murmured against her temple.

"I'm fine. It was just…" She sniffed and tightened her grip.

"The wine? Was it the wine?" Creed asked.

"It… it smelled… looked… like the tea."

"The tea?" Her father asked.

"The tea Billy drugged?" Creed asked, and she answered by nodding her head against him. "It's okay, no more white wine. Only red from here on out, deal?"

"Deal," she sighed against him. The sigh seemed to deflate her and she relaxed completely in his arms. "I like red wine."

"There's my girl." Creed kissed the top of her head, her hair soft, the scent fresh. All he wanted was to hold her close and had her relatives not been there, he would have carried her to a chair by the woodstove or directly to the bunk. Instead he looked up to see the male Greenbriars staring at him. "Now tell your father and brother you're all better. Otherwise I'm afraid they'll want to rescue you from me."

Linnet sniffed, her tears coming to a halt. "I want to stay right where I am for the moment. I'm too embarrassed to see anyone else."

"Oh, baby," the Captain started to say, but found his hand flung off her shoulder.

"Baby isn't a good nickname, sir." Creed felt it only fair to clue him in.

"We've always called her that." The Captain sat back in surprise.

"And so did her attacker." Attackers? Had both of them used the endearment, turning it into something far more sinister?

"Ah." Understanding dawned on both faces. "I'm sorry, Linnet, I won't use that name again. Promise."

"Me neither." Hawk added his promise.

Linnet shuddered and raised her head. "Looks like I ruined dinner yet again." Eyes closed, she rested her head against Creed's and he chuckled.

"No worries, sweet bird. We'll wipe up the offending liquid and take our plates out to eat on the porch. A little fresh air, the river, a change of scenery and we'll pretend like nothing happened. Later, if you want to, we'll talk it through. But only if you want to."

"Okay. I'd like that."

"I'll clean up, sissy." Hawk stood. "Starting with a cold towel for your face."

\* \* \* \*

Linnet made it through dinner with pure bravado. Ignoring the questioning looks, the false cheer, and sideways glances, might have been more difficult were she not surrounded by the two most important men in her life and one fast joining their ranks. Tucked in between Creed and her father, with Hawk and George across from her, she felt protected. Safe. Most especially, she felt warm where her thigh, hip and arm touched Creed's.

Seeking more warmth, she leaned closer to him as dinner wound down. As food was finished, Creed's arm slid behind her until his large hand rested on her waist. Braced and embraced, he held her close and his shoulder made the perfect resting place for her head.

Two nights ago she'd nearly bitten his head off, and now... he was like a talisman that kept the nightmare away. She'd tried thinking through the event and the back-to-back flashbacks she'd just experienced, but the thoughts faded away each time Creed's fingers lightly rubbed her hip, or the muscles in his arm bunched at a slight movement. Even his breath brushing against her temple was enough to drive away the paralyzing terror. Longing to lie beside him, secure in his arms as she had lain last night, became a physical ache.

How had he crept under her skin this quickly? Three days, well, two really. The third night was just beginning. Just the third night. And they had a very limited number of nights to go. Suddenly it felt as if time was running at warp speed and she had to grasp and hold on to every moment available. No one had ever become so important so fast to her before.

His voice was a soft rumble as he answered George. The words didn't matter, she'd long ago ceased to follow the conversation, but she felt him. Could hear his breath move in and out. If she moved her head just a little, might she hear his very heartbeat? What would that heartbeat sound like with her ear pressed to his skin? His chest?

Creed's hand rubbed her waist, slipped to her hip, and she scooted closer yet. His warmth banished the last of her tension and her eyelids felt impossibly heavy.

"Time to tuck someone in, I think." Daddy's voice repeated the words she'd heard nearly every night for most of her childhood and well into her teens.

"Come on, Linnet." Creed nuzzled the top of her head. "You're exhausted."

"Only if you come with me," she murmured.

The reactions were subtle, yet immediate. To her right, Daddy stiffened. To her left, Creed's breath hitched and his arm tightened. Across the table, just before her eyes blinked shut for a long moment, Hawk's eyes narrowed ever so slightly. Conversation paused, then George spoke to Manley, and the Roys stood with offers to clear the table. In short order, Linnet found herself alone again with Creed, her father and brother.

"Dad," Linnet said without opening her eyes. "I mean to sleep, in the literal sense. Creed's right..." a yawn interrupted her. "I'm exhausted. I just want to sleep. If I were little still, I'd want to sleep in my Daddy's arms, but I'm not a little girl."

"That's the point," her father said dryly. "You're a beautiful woman and I've seen the way Willis looks at you."

"I doubt he's the kind of creep who attacks weak women. Especially when there's a cabin full of men around including male relatives..." Another yawn made her eyes water.

"You're absolutely correct, Linnet. I've never forced a woman in my life and I'm not about to start. The very presence of your father in the cabin is a definite mood killer as far as making love goes. Not to mention I only got a few hours of sleep last night. Seems to me I was on the river before the sun rose."

"See, Daddy? I'm safe. Besides, someone will have to double up in the bunks."

Silence stretched out and Linnet listened to the sounds of dishes clanking inside the cabin, the quiet rush of the river and the wind sighing through the tree tops. Birds flitted about the branches of the nearby trees, chirping and calling to each other. From somewhere far overhead came the drone of a small airplane.

"Willis," her father used his command voice, the one he saved for misdemeanors. "If you harm one hair…"

"Excuse me, Captain," Creed interrupted. "Don't make any sudden moves, but slowly turn your head and look off to your right."

Linnet lifted her head and forced her eyes open. "My moose." For some reason she smiled. Not five yards off, the yearling stood on the trail at the edge of the woods. Head tilted curiously, Linnet thought she looked surprisingly child-like. How something so big could look so much like a toddler was one of the mysteries of the universe, she decided.

"Linnet's moose. The same one that took a peep at her in the bath last night," Creed confirmed. Remembering how Creed and Hawk had also had a peep brought a flush of warmth to Linnet's cheeks. Did she have the energy for her bath tonight? What would Daddy think if Linnet invited Creed to join her?

"I thought we scared her off?" Hawk shot the question at Creed in an undertone.

"Apparently she's feeling lonely." Linnet could feel Creed smile against her temple. "They do that sometimes. Find sympathetic people and hang out nearby. After all, she spent a year with her mother then was cut off for no good reason that she can think of."

"A pet moose?" her father said with a note of disbelief in his voice. "That beats everything you two ever tried to drag home as kids. Wait 'til I tell your mother about this one. Anyone got a camera on them?"

"Inside." Linnet, Creed and Hawk all spoke at the same time.

"Some tourists you are," her dad growled back. "Good thing I bought this little toy." Moving slowly, he extracted a small camera from his shirt pocket. Hardly bigger than a credit card and about four times as thick, the camera was easily turned on and pointed toward the animal. "You say this is a yearling?"

"Not done growing yet. She should reach full growth by the end of the season."

The camera whirred quietly as her father snapped off a few photos. "We can load these on your laptop. Are moose solitary creatures or do they travel in herds?"

"Mostly solitary," Linnet murmured. "Caribou travel in herds."

"So there aren't likely to be many others hanging about, right?"

"There are a few in the area, but no, they tend to travel alone except during rutting season and of course the young ones stick close to Mom until she's ready to give birth to the siblings. Then she sends the yearlings away."

"So this one has a mother and siblings probably not too far off?"

"Somewhere in a twenty mile radius, most likely." Creed shrugged, gently lifting Linnet's head then lowering it again.

"How dangerous are they?"

"When riled, plenty dangerous. They've been known to stomp people and dogs to death."

"So... are we reasonably safe just sitting here?"

"Yes. Reasonably so." Creed's amusement made Linnet smile. Had she been alone she would have eased herself into the cabin and watched through the window. But Creed had his arm around her. Instead of nervous, she felt safe. And nearly as curious as the moose.

"Can we feed her?" Hawk asked.

"Not a good idea. We want her to be independent."

"Good point."

The humans and the moose spent several minutes just watching each other. Someone dropped a pan inside and the moose flinched. With a twitch of her long ears, she ambled across the front of the cabin and on to the path leading downstream. A few minutes later, not even the swaying of the branches gave away the fact she'd been there.

Creed watched as Hawk and the Captain bent over the hoof prints left behind in the mud.

"Creed?" Linnet whispered.

"Yeah?"

"Please? Sleep with me tonight. Like last night. Please?"

"Anything you want, sweet bird. Anything you want."

# Chapter 18

Linnet slept like an angel. Snuggled close in his arms, her face was peaceful, a slight smile on her gorgeous lips. Dark lashes rested against her cheeks and her soft hair brushed against his face. She smelled sweet and womanly and oh-so-right.

Creed didn't sleep much at all.

The bed was narrow, not much wider than Linnet's full-size air mattress. Until this trip, the bunks had always been comfortable enough, if a little hard. To accommodate his height, he'd always slept a little diagonally. Since Linnet was tall for a woman, the bed didn't quite fit her height either, and the most comfortable position was for Creed to spoon up behind her. She liked that well enough, judging by how she wiggled her bottom against his aching groin. His right arm under her head curved around so his hand naturally came to rest over her left breast. She made sure it stayed there by hugging his arm. His left arm rested over the indent of her waist.

That hand had trouble deciding where it wanted to rest. It would have preferred to slip under the waistband of her stretchy sleep pants far enough his fingers could rest warmly between her legs, but with snores from the cabin's extra inhabitants rattling the windows, he deemed it inappropriate. Instead, he splayed his fingers across her soft abdomen to keep her from wiggling more than necessary.

As much as he loved the feel of her body against his, it was the equivalent of being on a hot Mexican beach, mouth burning from a spicy burrito, while a pitcher of sweet, tangy cold margaritas, super-glued to a nearby table, sat mocking him. Complete with condensation sliding down the glass of the pitcher in big, fat, wet, salty drops. He could embrace the pitcher, but he couldn't drink from it. A lick wouldn't satisfy, but would rather drive him to madness from wanting more than the taste of the salty rim.

*Morgan Q. O'Reilly*

He could kiss her, but he couldn't truly taste her. Which led him to ponder a parody of the saying: '*It is better to have loved and lost than to never have loved at all*'. Was it truly better to kiss and dream of more, than to never touch in any way?

Oh damn. Now he was hungry for Mexican food. An image of Linnet's breast over him popped into his fantasy screening room. Freshly dipped into a *grande* glass, precious liquid dripping into his mouth, bits of salt clinging to her skin, the desire to lick and suckle...

That was *not* the way to chase away his erection or get to sleep. Sleep. Needed sleep. How to bring it on? Right, Linnet's flashback. Her brother. Her father. There it was, the topic to chase away lust.

Once more he played the sequence of this evening's events through his mind in an effort to bring sleep. The Captain had not-so-subtly grilled him during the tour of the property. Creed had to admit Linnet's father had contributed plenty of ideas to the cabin building project. Hawk had studied the few books available on the subject and added what he knew from his own experience. Tomorrow, land clearing would begin. That situation was under control, as much as it could be. He had a feeling Father Greenbriar would stick around at least another day. No problem.

That situation out of the way, he turned his attention to pondering the Roys. Those two seemed in no hurry to meander down the river. They'd taken off after unloading the boat, presumably to try some fishing, but had returned for dinner without a catch, though their pants legs were damp from more than just rain, their hands red as if they'd been held in icy water for a long time. Gold panning? If so, why would they bother to hide it?

The creeks had been tapped out decades before. A few flakes occasionally appeared, but only after many hours of hard work. Digging, emptying bucket after bucket of gravel and sand into the sluice box nestled in the gravel bed of the creek. Many hours spent standing in the cold water watching it wash the lighter weight dirt away, only to spend a few minutes swirling water around a pan to find a few flakes of color. It was back-breaking work and rarely worth the effort. All the big nuggets had been mined out by his great-grandfather, and never enough to make his family obscenely rich. Barely able to scrape by each winter was more like it.

The cabin had been built more for recreation than working. They'd joked about someday opening up a road house like Slaven's to mine from the boaters who floated and canoed down the river in hopes of finding the Great Alaskan Adventure in seven days. One day's leisurely float upriver from Circle, they probably could have made some money providing a hot bath, warm food and a dry bed for travelers weary of six nights in mosquito infested tents.

The idea had been abandoned each time it was mentioned as being too much work. Too hard to bring in supplies, and no one wanted to clean up after travelers who felt their money earned them gold star treatment. No, it was better to offer good old-fashioned Alaskan hospitality from time to time. Although the Roys, staying over for a second night, had begun to wear out their welcome.

Creed didn't like the way Junior watched Linnet with hungry eyes, or the way the older Roy watched everyone else. Friendly enough, Creed supposed, but their Texan accents slipped from time to time.

George hadn't discovered anything about them during his brief search using the Public Safety Officer's computer in Circle. No wanted posters, no records under those names, no hint of mischief attached to either man at all. A quick phone call up to Slaven's hadn't produced anything more than a few words of distrust. Nothing anyone could exactly put their finger on. Just slightly shifty eyes and undue attention paid to the people around them. Little information that sounded genuine about who they were or where they came from.

Couldn't arrest a man for a fake accent or the movement of his eyes. With luck the two men would move on downstream in the morning.

His right arm began to burn from lack of blood and movement. Shifting a little brought a touch of relief, but it also made the air mattress squeak, a sound that for a moment drowned out the snores.

In the bunk above, Hawk shifted, making the entire bunk frame tremble. A few of the snores ceased as well and an air of waiting, watching, listening fell over the cabin. When silence had reigned for a few minutes, the tension around him relaxed. Creed already knew Hawk was a light sleeper. Apparently Perry was as well.

It was probably his imagination working overtime, nonetheless, Creed felt he could sense sharp eyes staring at his back from the upper level of the middle bunk. On the far side of the room, the Roys were sprawled on the third set of bunks, Junior on the upper level, the old man snoring loud enough to compete with a sawmill on the lower.

Needles of sensation stung his fingers as blood moved back into them. In an effort to speed the process, he flexed the fingers of his hand, inadvertently massaging Linnet's full breast at the same time. Yeah, like that was a mistake to avoid. Against his palm, her nipple immediately puckered up, begging for attention. Linnet shifted, pushing her breast against his hand, her arms pulling him closer at the same time. Her sleepy moan caused another spell of silence to fall.

The bed frame vibrated once more and Creed prepared to be pulled from bed again. Had he been so protective of his sister? Had he ever noticed Aaron trying to feel Terri up at family gatherings? What a waste of a brother he must have been.

"Go to sleep, Willis." Hawk's whisper still managed to sound threatening.

There were a dozen responses he wanted to make, but Linnet's hand stopped them all. Under Creed's hand, he felt as her heartbeat hitched before speeding up. But then she reached behind her, her hand expertly and immediately sliding between their bodies to wrap around the length of his cock, which already pressing uncomfortably against the fly of his jeans.

"Not now, Linnet," he murmured against her ear and tried to dislodge her hand.

Much to his dismay, she only gripped harder—just the perfect pressure, actually—and moaned louder.

"Linnet, don't," Creed groaned. "This isn't the time, sweetheart." One more squeeze and he'd go back in time to prepubescent hell. He'd been turned on for so long, with no relief in sight, it wouldn't take anything at all for him to come in his jeans. The jeans he'd slept in to avoid this very situation.

Instead of making enough noise to wake the dead, this time when Hawk landed on the floor beside the bunk, only air movement gave him away. Linnet's netting was pulled open and Creed moved his hand off Linnet's breast a second before Hawk's hand landed on his shoulder.

"I'm not doing anything," Creed whispered over his shoulder. "She's got a hold of me."

Hawk ducked and leaned over Creed to look things over. "Yeah, she's got you, buddy." The chuckle that followed ignited a need to punch the other man. And Creed didn't consider himself the violent type. "Need me to extract you from danger, again?"

"Creed," Linnet's soft voice moaned his name in a way worthy of Marilyn.

Teeth clenched, he finally managed to uncurl her fingers from the front of his pants. "I'm here, but you need to go back to sleep, Linnet."

Her response was to roll toward him until she faced him and snuggled against his chest. Now he had her sweet breath puffing against the base of his throat. No good. Worse, in fact. All he'd have to do was roll them both until he lay between her legs. With great disgust, he could see himself dry humping her, so desperate he was to make love.

"Hold me, Creed," Linnet murmured against his throat.

"Uh, Linnet, I need to, um, get up... for just a minute. I'll be right back, I promise."

"Okay," she sighed and rolled to her back, one hand flung out on her pillow.

Groaning, he let Hawk pull him from the bed.

"That's two you owe me, Willis. I've extracted your ass from temptation twice." Hawk practically held Creed by the scruff of the neck and pulled him to the front of the cabin. "Quit your moaning or you'll wake everyone up."

Creed shrugged him off and crouched in front of the woodstove hoping to hide, and decrease, his major boner. Moving with years of practice at being quiet, he tossed on a few more pieces of wood, just enough to keep the fire going another few hours. A glance at his watch confirmed it was three in the morning. Hints of lightening showed outside. Another rainy day or would the dense cloud cover break?

Soft noises from the kitchen indicated Hawk was making coffee. Fine. Might as well get an early start, then find time for a nap in the afternoon. Creed could still pull about forty-eight hours with only cat naps, but it was getting harder each year. Sometimes work on the Slope demanded it. Sometimes insomnia forced it. A woman and her family, now that was a whole new angle. At least he liked the men folk of her family. The Captain was a little scary. Creed hadn't grown up in a military atmosphere even though he'd known plenty of the Air Force and Army kids stationed near Fairbanks with their families.

Finally, his erection eased and Creed was able to stand. Damn. He hadn't had that strong of a reaction in... years? Or ever? Still a tad unsteady, he made his way to the table where he plopped into a chair and waited for the coffee to finish perking. Only the wavering flames from behind the glass door of the woodstove lit the dark cabin. It was the best kind of mood lighting as far as he was concerned. Too bad it was wasted with a cabin full of unwanted men and an untouchable woman.

He lay his head back and stared at the ceiling. Damn. To be honest, had the other men not been in the cabin he wasn't sure he'd have made love to Linnet just yet. Okay, so maybe with her hand wrapped around him as it had been he might have been convinced. However, with a touch of distance from that situation, the scare of her flashback was too close, too frightening.

He didn't want to be a rebound guy. He wanted… oh shit. Nope, that thought had never entered his mind before. A long way from the M word, he found himself easing toward the R word. *Relationship*. He flinched. *Ouch*.

But there it was. Out in the open and from his mind first, which was still a very long way from the word coming out of his lips. And it would just have to stay that way. One more trip to the Slope, one more trip here and then it was time to shut down the cabin for the season. She'd go back to Anchorage and he'd go back to his steady routine. Two weeks on the Slope, two weeks in Fairbanks.

Anchorage was too far away to keep up a steady… association. There. Association. That was a good word. He could do a short term association and then it would fade away naturally without the mess and fuss of his usual associations with women. Heck, he might even look her up when he went to Anchorage for Thanksgiving. Wonder how she'd feel about spending time together then? Probably better to cut if off clean.

Yeah, that was a good thought. Except he started wondering about her house. Or apartment. What did her personal space look like? Was it as homey and comfortable as she'd made the cabin? Great. Now he was wondering about her domestic situation. This was bad, bad news.

When he groaned, Hawk chuckled and set a cup of coffee down on the table. "You're so lost, sucker."

"I am not. I'm just suffering from look-but-don't-touch syndrome. I'll get over it once all you guys clear out."

"Then you're screwed, cuz I'm not leaving for the next few weeks." Hawk settled into a chair and Creed glared across the rim of his cup.

"I have ways of making even little SEAL boys disappear out here. You're on my home turf, and don't forget it." A glance out the window showed a large dark brown hump where he didn't ever remember seeing one before. Great. The moose had decided to sleep over. Or was it a grizzly? Hard to tell in this low light. Either way, no one was going outside until it moved.

Creed nodded toward the small brown hillock. "There, I'll feed you to the moose. No one would ever know."

"Unless that's a grizzly, it won't eat me," Hawk retorted.

"Yeah, well swimming with the fishes takes on a whole new meaning up here. We don't even need to add the concrete boots. The silt in that water will drag you down in two minutes flat."

"And if I'm lucky, my body will wash up when it reaches the delta. Yeah, I know all about your Alaskan tricks. Did a winter survival course just out of Fairbanks one year." Hawk's eyes laughed back at Creed. "Have to give you points for creativity."

"Were it not for the fact that I'm too lazy to build a cabin by myself, especially since George is incapacitated, I'd be tossing you in that boat to head downstream. Otherwise, don't need you, don't want you, don't even like you much."

Hawk laughed quietly and sipped his coffee.

"And on top of all that, you make lousy coffee," Creed added. "You could stand to take lessons from your sister."

"Speak for yourself." Hawk reached for the coffee pot in the middle of the table and held it out, offering Creed a refill.

With a grimace, he held out his cup and let Hawk fill it with the hot battery acid. Yeah, with a touch of the evil white powder, maybe, just maybe it would be drinkable.

# Chapter 19

"There." Linnet noted Creed's satisfied tone. "See, everything will stay dry while we go play upstream for a while." He patted the covered pile of clean clothing and towels.

"Play. You mean gold panning."

"Yes. Panning, play, same difference." He held out a hand to her and she took it without thinking. "There isn't much left in the stream, but seeing the Roys packing a gold pan reminded me that every once in a while something pops out of the ground and makes the effort worthwhile."

"I've done some panning already this summer." She carried an old laundry detergent bucket holding a small shovel and two black plastic gold pans. Pail swinging from her hand, she followed him around the outcropping of rock and let him pull her up the steep faded trail alongside the waterfall that created the stream beneath the tub. In his other hand, Creed also carried a large plastic bucket, his holding a small modern sluice in it, a small camp shovel and bottles of water.

"Did you find anything?"

"No." She hated admitting that, but still returned the smile he shot at her.

"You didn't go with an honest to God Alaskan prospector. If nothing else, you'll have a few flakes at the end of the day. If we're really lucky, you'll have enough to make a pair of earrings as a souvenir."

"I can hardly wait," she said dryly.

Actually, today promised to be a fun break from taking care of the camp. Even though the men pitched in, six of them created an awful lot of extra work. And since they were the ones cutting down trees, digging out the foundations of the cabin, hauling gravel to fill it in, and refusing to let her help beyond dragging the scrub to the fire pit, she'd taken on most of the cooking duties. The last two days had been lots of hard work but had produced amazing results. The first two courses of logs were in place and several logs stood by, ready to be notched and hoisted onto the rising walls.

Still, Dad was talking about heading home, Creed was making noises about the Roys moving on down the river, and George watched everything with his alert eyes. Right now George was playing river guide and had Dad and Hawk out on the boat for a spot of fishing. They needed something for dinner and Dad wanted to take a fish home to Mom. Linnet already planned to pick a couple gallons of blueberries to send with him. Tomorrow, God willing, Dad would fire up his whirly bird and start making his way south.

Just before leaving the tub behind, Linnet looked back to assure herself that their clean clothes would remain protected from the rain. Creed had wrapped everything in a sturdy waterproof duffle and Linnet's bath bucket sat in its usual spot. Assured they'd be cold, wet and muddy after panning, the bath would be hot and ready when they finished. Whether she'd bathe alone was still up for discussion.

"I never would have pegged you as such a worrywart." Creed looked back to tease her. His eyes twinkled with good humor that did funny things to her stomach and warmed her in ways she now associated with him. She couldn't remember ever knowing a man who always wore such a ready smile on his face. Just looking at him cheered her up and made her wonder if she'd always been so gloomy. Where Creed was, the sun shined. Even on the darkest, dripping day. Fortunately, it looked like the light drizzle was easing. Maybe they could cast off the rain gear when they got to their destination.

"I'm not a worrywart," she protested. Actually, she was envisioning Creed in the tub with her...

As if he read her mind, Creed waggled his eyebrows and pulled her closer. "Later. When you're ready, I have this fantasy about soaping you up and rinsing you off."

Damn, there went her heart again. Hope she wasn't developing an arrhythmia or anything dangerous. Did heart murmurs make one's heartbeat feel like a native drum?

"Oh, no you don't. I love that look in your eyes, but not right now," he groaned. "Let's go find you a nugget the size of a fifty cent piece and then maybe I'll have earned enough hero points to deserve that look and what goes with it."

"Hero points?" Linnet laughed and followed him along the bank of the stream. Only a few feet across, the stream carried water clear enough she could see underwater islands of gravel. The tailings of long ago mining activity. How many flakes hid beneath the sand? Had the miners let the smallest bits through while concentrating on the search for nuggets?

"Yeah, hero points. See, I've got this worked out in my mind. I find you a nugget so big you can barely hold it, thereby proving to your male relations that I'm worthy so they'll leave. We drop the Roys into their canoes, and send George back to Fairbanks leaving just the two of us, the dog and the moose. The last two don't count, by the way." Creed ducked under a low-hanging birch branch and watched to be sure she did the same. "Then, because I've earned so many hero points, I'll have earned the right to explore a certain landscape to my satisfaction. Along the way, of course, you'll be completely satisfied." He gave her a quick wink before turning back to pay attention to the uneven trail.

The promises he made her with his words, wink and squeeze of the hand had Linnet weak in the knees. Her blood running both hot and cold, her poor confused body couldn't seem to make up its mind.

Ever since her flashback, she'd been spinning with so many conflicting emotions, desires and dreads she didn't know which side was up anymore. In just over a week Creed would leave for two weeks. Maybe that would allow her time to figure out just exactly where her head was. She wanted Creed, in the worst way. Moments like now, when he held her hand, filled her with the desire to climb right under his skin. She loved the way she felt in his arms. He made her feel small, delicate, feminine in the right way. And yet, that very feeling also terrified her.

What if he used his power to hurt her as Billy had? The other she refused to think about and shut it away with a grimace. Most likely a bad dream and not reality anyway. Her heart knew Creed would never treat her the same way, but a small dark corner of her mind wouldn't let go.

What if she was as wrong about him as she'd been about Billy? What if he was more like Henry, happy to have her tucked away in private, not so happy when things became public and embarrassing? What if all that was nonsense and he was just as wonderful as he seemed? What if he really did wave her goodbye at the end of summer? What if she found herself back here next year? What if… a powerful question that kept her from completely relaxing. Ever.

"How far are we hiking anyway?" she asked after ducking under the branch he held up for her.

"Not too much farther. It's fairly well hidden…" Creed rounded a boulder and stopped. Linnet ran smack into the middle of his back.

"What?"

"I guess it isn't hidden so well after all."

Linnet moved to his side to see him frowning and then looked to see what caused it. Up ahead, it was obvious someone had recently been digging into the side of the hill. Fresh scars indicated as recently as minutes ago. She followed Creed as he closed the last ten yards and stopped between the dig and the stream. Fresh, wet, footprints crossed the stream and disappeared into the trees in the direction of the cabin.

"Modern day claim jumpers," Creed finally chuckled. "So that's what those two have been up to."

"The Roys?"

"Yeah. Prospecting their way down the river. Well, they'll be moving on now, after I search their gear."

"You're not…" Was their outing over before it started?

"What?" Creed turned to look at her, and something of her dismay must have showed in her face because he dropped the bucket and pulled her into his arms. "We're here to prospect. I'm not going to cut that short, but if they're still at the cabin when we get back, I have a right to pat them down. Any gold they take from here is legally mine." Creed dropped his forehead to hers and rubbed their noses together. "If they're smart, they'll light out before we get back."

"Let's hope they're smarter than they look."

"Mmmm."

She didn't resist when his lips lightly brushed hers. It was even more natural to lean into him, increasing the pressure until he groaned and deepened the kiss just enough she could answer or pull back. No need to think about that, she opened to him and teased her tongue into his mouth. So gentle. She loved the way he kissed, gradually pushing them both higher. The bucket, shovel and pans didn't make much noise when she dropped them to wrap both arms around his neck. Or at least she didn't think they did.

Untold minutes later, breath desperately rushed, Creed eased back, reclaiming his tongue enough to murmur against her lips. "Don't jump, but we're being watched." He didn't let her respond other than to dive back into the kiss.

Who cared who watched? Right now the USC football team could be cheering them on and she wouldn't care. Finally she was able to gasp, "Who?"

"Your moose." She could feel Creed's smile and shared his soft chuckle.

"Ah, some children just don't want to leave home."

"She's latched on to you as the only other female around for twenty miles."

"My sweet little girl."

That did it. Creed's chuckle started soft but quickly escalated into shaking shoulders and full out laughing. With a quick peck on the nose he released her. "We'd better get digging if we want to see color by dinner time."

Sighing to herself, Linnet cast a glance toward the moose and saw she was several yards back in the trees. A safe enough distance. Turning her attention to mining, Linnet bent to pick up the fallen tools. "Color. Why do they use that word? Why not just say gold or nuggets?"

Creed shrugged. "Gold comes in all sizes. Color pretty much covers the spectrum." He stepped into the stream, the water level with the ankles of his knee high rubber boots. It only took him a minute to snug the three feet long aluminum sluice box into the gravel, securing it in the fastest running part of the water with a big rock. A length of astroturf rested in the bottom, beneath the riffle grid. Earlier he'd told her the fake grass would catch the smallest flakes of the heavy metal, forcing it to the bottom of the sluice while the rocks and sand washed away.

"Ready for your first bucket of dirt?" He straightened and Linnet lost a moment staring at him. A stained wide-brimmed red felt hat protected his head and his rain coat gaped to show his red plaid flannel shirt. Practically threadbare jeans and the black rubber boots made him look like a prospector right out of the eighteen nineties gold rush. All he needed was a scruffy beard to make the picture complete. His three day shadow put him well on the way.

"Um, yeah." She swallowed a fantasy of him mushing into town with a huge sack of gold. Now wouldn't it be fun to play the saloon girl waiting to bathe and shave him, then find ways to lure him and his bag of gold up to her room? She could almost hear the tinny sound of a poorly-tuned upright piano playing in the bar.

"Earth to Linnet," Creed's joking broke up the instant fantasy and she felt herself blushing as she turned away to look at the fresh digging scars in the rise of the bank.

"So, we start by digging?"

"Fill the bucket and pull the big rocks as you do it. On public lands, you're restricted to digging in the streambed, but here, obviously, we dig into the hill. The streambed was cleaned out long ago."

"Okay then."

Creed dropped the bucket between them, hefted his shovel and dug in. Because all was fair, she stabbed her shovel in and pulled it back loaded with a mixture of rocks, coarse sand and the so very fine glacier silt that worked its way into everything. Scoop after scoop filled the bucket until Creed set down his shovel and reached for the bucket handle.

"That should do us for our first run. Any fuller and I won't be able to lift the bucket. You probably could, but I don't want either of us to develop hernias just now."

The way his eyes twinkled as his gaze wandered down her body melted every ache from her muscles and started a new one.

"Ha." Using the back of her hand, she wiped away a thin layer of sweat. The rain had ceased and the work had warmed her up. "Just a good stretch of the muscles." A few mosquitoes buzzed around her head but veered off. Had Creed's cooking done something to change the chemistry of her sweat enough they left her alone now?

"So she says. Bring the small shovel." He waded into the stream and set the bucket down in the water, right next to the head of the sluice box. "In the old days, they used much bigger tools, but it was a much more serious business. If they didn't find gold, and large quantities of it, they could very well starve all winter."

"They relied solely on prospecting?"

"One of my ancestors put out trap lines and also traded furs, but there was little time for planting or tending gardens. Summer was for mining. Winter was for trapping and getting ready for mining. Or wintering over in town."

Creed sent her a sideways look as if he'd seen into her fantasy earlier. Wintering in town could mean that much of the time may have been spent in warm rooms over busy saloons.

"So, how does this work?" Time to move on from fantasies. In the middle of the cold stream was not the place to stage a seduction.

"Come over here. You need to be in a position to easily shovel the dirt from the bucket into the top of the sluice."

Maybe Creed thought this was the spot to stage a seduction. He stepped aside only long enough for Linnet to get in place before him. Long arms reached around her as if she needed help. It was on her lips to protest, when he kissed her neck. Maybe it was fun to play the fragile female every once in a while…

"Use your feet to help funnel water into the top of the sluice." Words that shouldn't have been sexy gave her goosebumps. "Now load a shovel and dump it into the top." Bent slightly, his body wrapped around hers, they watched as a puff of fine dirt clouded the water then drifted downstream.

"Are you sure...?"

"I'm sure the gold won't wash away." Soft warm air caressed her cheek as he chuckled. "I promise."

"Okay. If you say so."

"Trust me on this."

"So when do we find the gold?"

"After we pour many, many more of these buckets into the sluice."

Six buckets of dirt later Creed relented and filled one of the buckets half way with clear water. He showed her how to release the riffles mechanism, lift out the carpet, then dunk it into the bucket. "All the little stuff that was trapped in the carpet comes out here. After we wash it all out, we take this bucket and pour its contents into a gold pan. Then, if we're lucky, we'll find something other than black sand." He took her arm and led her over to a rock on the edge of the stream. "Might as well get comfortable."

"Yeah, yeah, just show me how to do this."

"Beginners," Creed sighed with mock resignation.

Crouching beside her, he emptied the pile of black sand into the gold pan.

"I saw some gold!" Linnet exclaimed and pointed.

That earned her another chuckle. The more childlike she acted, the more he grinned at her. "Yes, there's some in there." Calmly he swirled the water around the pan, deftly letting the sand settle on the side with the raised ridges. "You want to use the riffles, pretty much the same as the riffles in the sluice box work. Always pan over your bucket just in case too much dirt spills out." A trickle of sand washed over the side and splashed back into the bucket.

Creed must have seen her flinch because he grinned at her again. "There weren't any flakes in that batch."

"So you say."

Creed was close enough he leaned over and kissed her. "Oh ye of little faith."

Linnet wrinkled her nose at him. "I've seen the pros do this and they'd have cleaned out this pan already."

"You're right. I'm just teasing you." With a flick of his wrist, the black sand swirled away and Linnet saw a scattering of gold sparkling along the bottom of the pan.

"Oh!" Her heart skipped a beat and she drew in a breath. "They're so small..." But it didn't really matter. They'd struck gold.

# Chapter 20

Tired, dirty, yet happier than he could remember in a long time, Creed followed Linnet back down the trail at the end of the day. Spurred on by the flakes from the first bucket they'd panned, Linnet, laughing off all attempts to make out, had kept him shoveling gravel for hours. Long enough to make him wistfully consider making love to her, but all he really wanted was a long hot bath, a large hot meal, and a soft bed to go with his desire for silken dreams.

As they traveled the trail back to the tub, he argued with himself long and hard. He'd planned today right down to seducing her into the tub with him. The plan hadn't included four hours of hard manual labor. Today was supposed to have been a holiday after the previous days of hard manual labor. Rounding the last boulder and dropping down near the tub, a whiff of grilling salmon wafted by on a faint breeze. His stomach growled.

"That does it. I'm starved. You get your bath and I'll save you a plate."

Linnet turned to him, her smile wilting a little. "Food first, eh?"

Creed set down his bucket and pulled her close enough he could loop his arms around her waist and lace his fingers together at the small of her back. Good woman that she was, she rested her hands on his chest and he liked them there.

"As much as I want to lie in that tub with your very enticing curves pressed against me, I wouldn't be able to do justice to either of our expectations. When I seduce you, I want to be fully rested so I can devote every ounce of my attention to pleasuring you." He leaned forward to kiss her and smiled as her eyelids dropped in anticipation. The kiss stayed light and sweet. "Right now I fear falling asleep halfway through a kiss."

"Ah, poor man." Laughter made her eyes sparkle as she patted his cheek. "When I'm done I'll set the tub to refill. You can get a long soak in after dinner."

She hadn't argued with the seduction comment. She hadn't agreed either, but her body language leaned toward acceptance. "Thank you. Oh, and if I take too long, you get to come looking for me. Don't send your brother, please."

"Fair enough. Vice versa if I take too long in the bath."

"Whether you fall asleep or not, take too long anyway. I'll come get you." With some food in him, his energy might be revived. "Just wait until I get back before you do anything... interesting." That made her blush even though she pushed him away.

"Go on. I smell fish, and that's right up your alley.

With a last long look, Creed picked up both buckets and trudged up the trail. Just before the path would take him out of sight, he looked back to see Linnet watching him. He gave her a smile and turned away.

"'Bout time you got back," George greeted him a few minutes later from the campfire.

Creed ignored him long enough to return the buckets to the shed then sauntered down to the fire. A glance at the beach showed the two canoes missing.

George poked at the fish over the fire. "Yeah, they're gone."

"Did you see them leave?"

"Nah. We were fishing upstream."

"I figured they'd be gone."

"How's that?"

Creed reached into his shirt pocket and pulled out an object. Wordlessly he dropped it into George's hand.

The lump of gold, a little smaller than a marble, had a dull shine to it where it lay in George's hand.

George slowly rolled it around his palm. "Where did you find this?"

"It and several smaller nuggets tumbled out of the hillside while Linnet had her back turned. The rest are hardly bigger than flakes. But I'm guessing by the signs we found at the site, the Roys helped themselves to a few nuggets then skedaddled. I'm only hoping what they found was on the small side and not larger than this."

Creed stared into the flames. Sounds from inside the cabin indicated the male Greenbriars were fixing the side dishes for dinner. Good. Linnet deserved a break from KP.

"You want to go after them?" George finally asked.

Did he? Letting his head hang for several heartbeats he considered the time and trouble versus the value of what might have been taken. The chase, the law, charges, court... He finally shook his head.

"Nah. A minor bit of claim jumping. We'll call it in and put out a warning for others to be aware, but they couldn't have taken much. I hope." One big nugget would be all they'd need.

It wasn't the money that bothered Creed, it was the legacy. Three generations before him had scraped and dug and mined until their hands bled and their backs were bent, and not one of them had ever found the big one.

The hope, bred in the blood, was always there that instead of just eking out a few ounces of gold each year, one of them would find the vein and prove the original hunch successful in the face of derision. Everyone along the river had heard the story from countless others, not just the Willis's.

The huge boom in this area had lasted barely more than a year before petering out. Only the diehard hopefuls hung on, generation after generation. Wouldn't it be one for the history books to find the big one now?

"You're sure? If they found something significant, it doesn't seem right to let them keep it. After all, did they ask if they could pan?"

"No they didn't. But there's something that gives me hope." He reached into his pocket again and handed George a lump of rock. Waxy looking white quartz, streaked with lines of purple and yellow, edged by a rusty rim around one side.

George whistled low. "Listwanite. Where did you find it?"

"Linnet found it. She was whacking at the hillside and this chunk broke off."

"Did you mark the spot?"

A barely remembered spark of excitement lit George's eyes. Yeah, he knew what it meant. While valuable itself, listwanite often covered deposits of gold. The chunk George held was roughly two inches cubed. Creed had examined where it had been knocked off and he was sure this was the proverbial tip of the ice berg.

Just how big a tip and how big an iceberg they were looking at, he didn't know. His father the geologist would know. Creed's own geology was pretty much limited to getting black gold, North Slope crude, out of the ground.

"Yeah, I know where it is. Too late in the season to start a big dig on it now, but I have a feeling Linnet will be back there every spare moment. She's got half a vial full of flakes and a few small nuggets."

George raised a dark brow. "You didn't share the others with her?"

"I want to surprise her with them." That was the sticky part. His mind's eye kept seeing a ring with the nuggets across the top. The weird part was it looked an awful lot like a wedding ring.

"Uh huh."

Creed glanced at George and snorted. "Get that idea out of your head right now. I am not thinking of making a ring." Though who he was speaking to, he still wasn't sure. "Anyhow, I'm pretty sure we'll spend a few evenings out there. Linnet has gold fever."

\* \* \* \*

After dinner Creed chuckled into his coffee. Fresh and clean, Linnet glowed nearly as much as the few flakes of gold they'd managed to collect. The miniscule glass vial she picked up to stare at again held only a couple grams of gold, barely enough to fill it half way, but the few in there swirled around in the clear water, mesmerizing her and raising the spirits of the remaining inhabitants of the cabin.

Surprise filled Creed when Linnet leaned across the table and set the vial down in front of her father.

"Take that back for Mom," she told him.

"What? I can't do that." The Captain pushed the vial back but ran into Linnet's hand.

"No, serious. Creed says that's only about sixty dollars worth of gold. Mom will love it. I'll also pick some fresh blueberries in the morning. When you get to Fairbanks, you can have them packaged and frozen right alongside the fish you're taking back."

"I'd rather take you back with me."

Had to hand it to the old man, he wasn't giving up just yet. He was also beginning to recognize the inevitable. His arguments seemed more a matter of practice rather than conviction.

"I'm not going, Daddy."

"Hmph."

Creed sipped his coffee to hide his grin. Two down, three to go. "So, George, I know Hawk is hanging for another month. What about you?"

Emotionless black eyes stared back at him. "Trying to dump me too?"

"Yeah." Maybe he could send Hawk upstream for a night or two. "I didn't come out here to spend all my time catering to a cabin full of people. Linnet's staying, so that means you go. Don't need two fish counters. Besides, if you don't go home and assure them you're fine, they'll all come out here. Mom, Dad, Miry, Terri…" he let the threat fade away and bit his lip.

George nodded slowly. "Even a phone call wouldn't stop them," he sighed. "Yeah, I'll head back in a day or so."

That was something. Creed glanced at Hawk who faced him with folded arms, a grin and shook his head. "Nope. I'm not leaving until the already appointed date. After you get back from your next hitch."

"I figured that. Someone has to build the cabin. You might need to take a run up to Slaven's though. The boys up there like to whittle and sometimes they produce a bit of furniture."

"Good point. But day trips will cut into the construction schedule."

"I wasn't thinking a day trip."

Hawk slowly shook his head, his grin widening. "You are so transparent, man."

"I wasn't trying to hide my agenda."

Linnet snorted then reached for a napkin. Oops, caught her with a mouthful of tea. Creed grinned at her, not feeling the least bit repentant. One way or another, they'd find some time alone in the cabin. Day or night, he wanted several hours without interruptions. Her shy smile said she did too.

"So, Daddy, what time to you plan to take off tomorrow?"

Ignoring the Captain's glare, Creed leaned close enough to whisper in her ear, "That's my girl."

# Chapter 21

"Linnet."

She watched as Creed dried the last of the dinner dishes and stacked them on the counter beside her.

With all their cabin companions gone—Dad and George on their way back to town, Hawk upstream for some fishing and exploring—they'd enjoyed their first dinner alone. All evening, their eyes had met in long gazes, their hands touching while reaching for glasses, plates and utensils.

After a stretch of long hot days, the sky was unusually dark due to heavy cloud cover. They'd lit a few oil lamps and the woodstove, making the cabin cozy and as warm as the tension between them.

Barely louder than the rain dumping from overloaded clouds outside, she felt the word more than she heard it. A counterpoint to the fire crackling in the woodstove, Creed's warm breath on her neck fought the chills wracking her body. Try as she might, as hungry as she was to make love with him, the panic making her heart race didn't want to give way. It was time, she'd waited and wanted this all week. They were finally alone, and now her courage left her.

"Please," she begged softly. "Go slow... I'm trying..."

*It isn't the same! He's not going to hurt me... I want this... I need this...*

All the positive self talk wasn't helping. Memories of being forced to respond, the flicker of firelight... it didn't matter they stood in the kitchen area of the cabin, the panic was overwhelming and she bit her lip to keep from screaming. Only steps away from her bunk, hands curled into tight fists, she gripped her jeans to keep from flailing about and hitting Creed. She didn't want to hurt him. She wanted this. Really, she did.

"Easy, sweet bird, easy. No rush." Each word was a caressing puff of warm air against her skin, his lips surprisingly soft and gentle, like the down from dandelion gone to seed. His lips nibbling on her earlobe changed everything. Heat, blessed and bone melting, raced along each nerve, making her tense muscles feel as soft as jelly. "You can call it quits anytime."

She believed him. Creed had pulled away plenty of times for her to know he spoke the truth. Anticipation pushed the fear further away.

Standing behind her, his hands rested on her hips as he continued to tease her earlobe and nuzzle the soft spot just behind her right ear. Like it was the most natural thing in the world, she rested her head on his shoulder, tilting her head away to give him more access.

"I've got you, just relax." Creed's soft voice was seductive. Low and soft, the vibration of it rumbled across her skin. "You tell me when you're ready for more."

"Did you lock the door?"

Creed chuckled. "The door is barred and if there were any way to put out a *Do Not Disturb* sign, I would. But with the rain, I think all river travelers are pretty much buckled down for the night already." His lips traveled down her neck to the edge of her shirt collar.

"B... but it... would be so..."

"So typical of every time we've tried to do this..." he added.

"To have someone drop in." There, she got a sentence out. Or rather the rest of the sentence.

"I promise not to answer the door. There is no world beyond the cabin tonight. Just you and me."

Just how she wanted it. Needed it. The constant influx of visitors for the last several days had been on the edge of driving her batty. Each look between her and Creed had been witnessed and commented on by far too many people. She was amazed he still wanted her. A man with patience like that...

"Touch me."

"Where? Where do you want me to start?" His hands flexed, but didn't move from where they rested. He wanted to touch her, she knew it, but he wasn't going to rush off to just any body part.

"My... my..."

"What, pretty bird?" The trail he kissed toward her nape nearly stole the words from her.

"My... shoulders." The embarrassment of directing him burned across her skin. Why was it so hard to ask for what she wanted?

"Like this?" His hands cupped her shoulders and squeezed lightly

"Yes," she sighed, his fingers massaging even more tension away.

"Do you like to have your back rubbed?"

"Yes," she sighed. Maybe he did understand.

As his hands, his wonderful, large, warm, gentle hands, moved toward the center of her back, she made her hands relax and open.

"Drop your head forward," he murmured against her neck.

Slowly she rolled with the tender but insistent pressure of his thumbs. Needing an anchor, she reached back to grip his thighs, and pulled his hips against her backside.

"Mmmm." The vibrations of his lips sent more heat along her nerves. "You're the perfect height. I don't have to strain my neck to kiss you."

At last! A man who didn't complain she was too tall. But he had a point, and it was pressing up against her ass at precisely the right spot. Under her fingers, through the denim of his jeans, she could feel the hardness of his muscular legs. Remembering the view of him standing in the river, legs braced against the flow made her breath hitch, or was it the tip of his tongue now drawing designs on her neck? The man had a body she wanted to see naked, and painted by the flames dancing in the woodstove.

Creed's fingers continued to slowly rub her upper shoulders and neck, his skin warm where it touched her, making Linnet want her clothes to melt away.

"My shirt," she whispered.

"What about it?" His voice was gruff, as if he had as much trouble as she did speaking.

"I... I..." She'd never had to talk about it before.

Henry hadn't wanted talk during sex and Billy, well, he'd used her like a blow-up doll, paying no attention whatsoever to her complaints or screams. With the others she'd been too shy or too drunk to speak much... and so very, very young. Creed made her feel new, as if she'd never experienced good sex before. Maybe she hadn't—yet.

"Do you want me to take it off?"

"Yes." She'd already removed the flannel over-shirt. That was easy. Now it was just the form-fitting long-sleeved microfiber t-shirt she wore. Glancing down, she could clearly see her nipples, peaked and tight, pressing outward through her thin bra and shirt.

Still moving with the same deliberate pace, Creed worked his hands down her back, his hips slowly moving against her where they touched. Unlike any other experience in her life, she felt herself falling under a magic spell. If it felt like this with her clothes on, would she burn up with them off? Suddenly anxious to find out, she released his legs, reached for her own shirt and began tugging it from the waistband of her jeans.

"Easy, Linnet, easy," Creed crooned near her ear again. "Let me. I've been dreaming of it for days. Let me undress you. Please."

With a hitch in her breath, Linnet stilled. Could she let him do it? Did she have to direct each step? Wasn't making love about giving and taking? Sharing?

"Okay," she breathed out, barely able to control the quaver she felt building from inside.

"If you say stop, I will."

"Okay. I trust you."

"I'll continue to earn your trust, sweet bird."

Was she still withholding it? Did some part of her still feel threatened? A fresh wave of heat cleared her mind as Creed's hands slipped beneath her shirt. For a long moment he paused, his hands resting on the flat of her stomach. Did he feel the muscles fluttering there? The butterflies in her stomach beating against her insides with wings of steel?

"Soft. Smooth. Your skin is like silk."

"Creed, don't take all night." Oh Lord, hadn't she just told him to go slow?

"We have all night. I intend to touch and taste every inch of you, some parts more than once, before the clock strikes seven. I would say before dawn, but that still comes too soon at this time of year." Creed's chuckle chased the shiver through her.

A different kind of shiver from the chills she'd had a little earlier. One mass of quivering jelly, she wanted everything he promised. Everything. She wanted to experience everything he wanted to share with her. She just didn't know if she could raise a hand to join in. Drugged with pleasure, she wanted to lie in his arms and just feel the cleansing flames of passion lick into every frightened, lonely corner of her soul.

"Lift your arms." Apparently she was as limp as jelly, judging by his chuckle.

No, she wasn't going to sit by and make him do all the work. Fairness said she needed to participate, returning one caress for another. Putting it into play was something else again as his hands traveled up her ribs, slowly pushing the shirt upward then pulling it off over her head, the sleeves peeling away from her arms like a snake shedding its old skin. The black shirt drifted to the floor as his hand made a return journey down her arms, letting them lower to hang at her sides.

Still in no hurry, his hands once more covered her back, the skin to skin contact all she'd hoped for.

"Beautiful, Linnet. You're so beautiful."

Once more she gripped his thighs to steady herself.

"More." Her bra felt tight and constraining. A bird didn't wear clothing. She wanted to be naked and free. Birds needed to fly and the need was growing fast, deep inside her.

"In a few. My hands are in love with your skin, they want to worship."

Impatient with his slow study of her body, she released his thighs and bent her arms behind her back. If he wouldn't unhook her bra, then she would.

"Easy, sweet bird, easy." Once again his words were puffs of soft hot air against her neck, his hands firm but tender as he lowered her arms to her sides. "Hold on to me if you need to occupy your hands."

Good idea. Instead of his thighs, she reached behind her, fumbling for the button on his jeans. Two could tease. A smile of triumph was impossible to resist when he moaned at her touch. Behind the denim and the heavy zipper, she could feel the outline of his cock. Must be uncomfortable to be pressed that hard inside that stiff fabric.

By the time she had his zipper lowered, she felt the last hook on her bra release. Her own dark chuckle was followed by a hiss of pleasure as he pushed the straps of her bra down her arms until she had to release him to let the skimpy garment fall away from her body.

A cool breeze from the open window teased her torso, her skin gathering up into tiny goose-bumps, nipples hardening, almost painfully, into tight peaks. Creed rested his lips on the top of one shoulder and she had the sense he was looking down, watching her body react.

"Beautiful."

Damn, but the man knew how to seduce her. Without him touching more than her waist, she felt as if he'd caressed her entire body.

So slowly she barely felt him move, several minutes, or was it mere seconds, later he cupped her breasts. Not even brushing her nipples with his fingers, he just held her. It had happened so naturally, so gently, she didn't have to fight any panic back. Relaxed and yet tense with erotic anticipation, she let her head fall back on his shoulder and reached for him again. As a side benefit, she pressed her breasts deeper into his cradling hands.

"Ah, Linnet, you're perfect. You fill my hands just right."

"I... I..." Despite her new-found feelings of desire to please him, she still couldn't quite voice them. "I want to..."

She felt his breath catch as he waited for her to vocalize her wants. "I want to touch you." The words left her in a breathless rush. There, she'd said it.

"I want that too."

The light brush of his thumbs over her nipples acted like dynamite on a dam. So fast he barely had time to wrap his arms around her waist again, she spun in place and pulled his hips to her, hands gripping his incredible butt. Desperately her lips sought his and though she tried to rush the kiss, he held back. The soft cotton of his t-shirt warmed her nipples, but not like his skin would. The barrier had to go.

"Weren't you the one who said slow?" His amusement was warm, fueling the fire burning her.

"Forget that. Get naked. I need to feel you... your skin... against mine," she grunted each phrase between gasps for air while tugging on his shirt. A moment later it was off his body and they reached for each other again. For a long moment, they held each other and she savored the feel of his hands spread across her back, the smooth skin of his beneath her palms. Her breasts pressed against his chest, their warmth combining, scents blending. It was heady in a way that made her feel like the first woman to have ever experienced it.

"More," she ordered and slid her hands between them to the fastenings of his jeans.

"I agree," he groaned and let her pull his jeans open and push them down his lean hips. No tighty whities... or boxers. God, he had such a tight butt! Not an ounce of spare flesh on him, she could almost feel the fibers of his muscles through the skin covering them. She took care to protect him as she peeled his jeans away from the hard erection straining for freedom. It was only right she should cover him and that meant from tip to soft sack below. His groan brought a soft laugh to her throat as she slid down his body to do the job right.

"You're killing me, Linnet," he chuckled then sucked in his breath on a sharp hiss when she nuzzled his cock. Velvet over steel. The cliché description was too true. Overused, maybe. Accurate, dead on. From temple to jaw line, she felt him. Beneath the skin, his pulse danced against her cheek.

Feeling daring, she extended her tongue. Just a taste was all she had in mind. He smelled so good... warm, musky... a hint of fresh air. The tip of her tongue had barely touched the base of his cock when his hands cupped her face and drew her upward again. Tongue still extended, she drew an invisible line from the base of his cock, to the tip, over the line marking the center of his tight abs, his pecs, up his throat, ending at his mouth where he sucked her tongue in and pulled her body tight.

Restrained urgency made them both shake. She felt the force it took for him to control his hands, ordering them to move slowly as they left her face and traveled down her neck, stopping only a second to cup and rub her breasts before settling on the fastenings of her own jeans. Giving him room, she raised her arms to his neck and fed her passion into their kiss, hardly noticing him tugging her jeans over her hips.

So fast their lips created a popping sound at the release of the kiss, Creed pulled away and lifted her to the counter, sitting her bare ass on the sanded wood. Without stopping, he pulled her jeans down until they caught on her slippers. Air warmed by the fire in the woodstove touched her skin as slippers, socks, jeans and panties were all removed.

As palpable as a touch, Creed's gaze swept up her body as he rose to stand again, his own clothes gone as if he'd removed them by magic. "You're so beautiful. I've never seen a more perfect woman."

Linnet let her own gaze take in his body. "You're beautiful too." Suddenly dry lips demanded her tongue wet them again. When she looked into his eyes again, they'd darkened to nearly black, but they weren't flat. Ragged want, heated desire, all the phrases she'd read in her romance novels through the years came back to her. He wanted her... like no one else had ever wanted her. No one had ever looked at her with such naked need. Lust she'd seen, but not this swirling mixture of emotions. It was heady stuff and made her feel light and dizzy with anticipation.

"I'm doing my best to let you set the pace here, sweetheart, but I have to tell you..." Creed drew in a long ragged breath. "I want you. I need you. I'll die if I'm not in you soon."

"Then take me to bed," she gasped, as he wrapped his arms around her waist. Her own arms wrapped around his neck, her legs clinging around his waist as he lifted her from the counter. Between them, his hard length nestled against the soft folds of flesh guarding the core of her body. "I guess I don't need to say, 'now', do I?" She chuckled, as they reached the bed in a few long strides.

"You implied it clearly enough, sweet bird." One hand pushed aside the netting around her bunk . "Head room is a little low," he apologized then wrapped a hand around her head to keep from smacking it as he laid her down on the bed.

"Maybe we're just a little tall." She laughed, and scooted back to make room for him. She didn't even take time to push down the quilt. It was soft and added a layer of comfort to the sleeping bag and air mattress below.

"Once we get that little cabin done, I'm bringing in a king sized bed."

"Oh, yes," Linnet agreed, and pulled Creed down on top of her. "I need you... right now," she panted. "I feel so empty..."

Creed's lips cut off her words as he settled between her legs. When she tried to flex her hips to allow him to slide in, he shifted back a little.

"What?" she complained.

"I want to taste you first. Before we add things like condoms and other prophylactics. I want to drink from you... taste your natural sweetness."

"I'm on the pill, Creed." She reached for his shoulders even as he moved down her body, lips and tongue leaving behind a hot, wet trail of kisses.

"I was conceived on the pill, little bird. My sister was a failed condom with foam. The mighty Willis sperm is able to overcome most methods." He kissed her stomach now shaking with laughter.

"Oh, so we're using the gold plated version of a condom?"

"The best around," he agreed. "Fully loaded. But first..."

Linnet lost her ability to speak as his mouth closed over her nether lips in the most intimate of kisses. For a brief moment, panic closed tight around her heart and she tightened her thighs around his head.

Though he had to be suffocating, Creed didn't use his hands to force her thighs open. He merely cupped her bottom and gently suckled on her clit. A surge of heat burned the last of her panic away and she let her legs fall open. Creed didn't react, one way or the other, but continued to lick and suckle.

Emotion and exquisite pleasure carried her beyond any plateau ever visited before. When Creed hooked his arms around her thighs and used his fingers to stroke her, she tilted her hips and crossed her legs across his shoulders. Afraid to hurt him with her nails, she instead dug her fingers into the bedding below her.

Finally, what seemed like an eternity later, she reached that moment when the world stopped spinning and held its breath. Unable to breathe, speak, or move, she hovered in that space until Creed used just the right touch, the perfect pressure, and sent her shooting to the far reaches of the universe.

Burning air escaped her lungs as the shout left her. Wordless, it floated in the realm of ecstasy until she drew in another lungful of air, clinging to the bedding, her legs holding Creed hostage against her. She may have shouted his name. She may have prayed to her Creator. It didn't matter. Where before she'd ridden the wave of ecstasy as silently as possible, she didn't have that control now, especially since Creed didn't let up, didn't let her orgasm fade away, until she was nearly sobbing for him to stop. When he did let up, she lay limp as he kissed her mons and every inch of skin between her hipbones.

"Oh Creed," she sighed.

He didn't answer but continued to kiss his way up her body, finding each spot that made her quiver. Between her fingers, his soft hair tickled as she clutched his head to her, encouraging him as he nuzzled between her breasts. Finally he reached her mouth and she cupped his face, holding him tenderly as she kissed him, tasting the remnants of her tangy juice in his mouth.

"You taste wonderful, sweet bird," he murmured against her lips. "I warn you now, I'm going to spend a lot of time feasting on you."

"Later. Right now I want you inside me. I need to feel full, Creed."

"And I'm the man to do it."

She felt him reach beneath the pillow. A moment later he used his teeth to rip open a square packet then handed it to her.

"Hold this."

She took it and he reached in to pull out the latex barrier. Single handed, he put it on while still cradling her head with his other hand. She dropped the empty package over the side of the bed then pulled him back to kiss her.

"Now, Creed. I want you now," she said, her lips moving against his.

"Your command is my desire."

Before she could answer him, he slid into her with deliberate slowness, his deep brown eyes watching her closely. Had she flinched at all, she knew he would have stopped. Instead she lifted her hips to meet him, seating him that much sooner. With the last thrust, she felt her body stretching to accommodate him and she smiled to ease his worry.

"And you obey, so very well, my handsome prince." Oh lord, did she really purr? However she said it, he smiled the smile of a man confident in his ability to please a woman. The smile faded as he slowly pulled back. The passion filling his face was surely a mirror of the need in her heart.

"Don't tease me, Creed."

"I want to make this last, sweet bird. You're too wonderful to rush. I want to savor every thrust, every inch, every pulse of your sweet body. Even now I can feel the tremors inside you." His eyes closed as she exerted her control and squeezed him tight in her channel. "Oh good Lord, woman, don't do that... not yet." He emphasized his plea by plunging into her.

"I can... feel... you... so deep." The arch of her back came as naturally as breathing.

"Yes, enjoy it, Linnie. If I feel half as good to you as you do to me, then we're both in heaven."

"I've never... felt... better." She exercised her inner control again, softer this time and Creed fell down on her, his arms under her shoulders as he buried his face in the curve of her neck.

Instinct took over as they intertwined their bodies as closely as possible. Mouths and tongues, arms, hands and fingers. Linnet wrapped her legs around his and let him direct the rhythm, squeezing him only when he drifted into moving too slowly. The burn was building deep inside and her body reached for it, nurtured it, drawing him in to feed the growing inferno.

When they both needed air, they panted in each other's ear, fanning the flame from another angle until all control fled. Linnet let her body rise, pressing her chest to his as he drove her down into the mattress.

"Come with me, sweet bird, I want to feel you..."

Linnet didn't hear the rest of his plea as sensation overrode all else. Everything around her faded—the sound of the rain, the crackling of the fire, Creed's ponderous breathing, even the sound of her own voice crying out. In the very throes of release, she was vaguely conscious of her body convulsing and gripping Creed, her arms clutching at his back as his hands wrapped around her shoulders, pulling their bodies tighter together, on and on. It felt as if the universe swirled in a bright maelstrom with only the two of them at the very center.

And through it all, he held her safe within his strong arms. She closed her eyes and held him close.

Creed's heart pounded hard against his chest as he rested against Linnet's body. She seemed in no hurry for him to move off her. Indeed, she drew him in closer and he made sure to lift some of his weight and rest on his elbows. Words escaped him. Who knew sex could be so... so... whatever it was, who needed words? He closed his eyes and dropped his head to her shoulder. Soft skin met his lips and he kissed the spot. When his strength came back he'd kiss more. He still had at least sixty percent of her body left to kiss anyway.

Now what? Talk or sleep? He was voting for sleep, but most women wanted to talk afterwards. What about Linnet?

"Sweet bird?" he murmured.

"Hmmmm?" Her moan was barely audible. The breath she drew in filled her lungs, pressing up against him. She held it then let it out, her body relaxing completely, arms and legs falling limply to her sides.

Creed pushed up a little, just enough to look at her face. Lady Linnet appeared to be asleep. Carefully, he disengaged his body from hers and gently rolled to her side. His hand hung over the edge of the bunk and he felt a cloth. His or hers, it didn't matter; it would work for a temporary cleanup since he didn't feel like getting up from bed at the moment.

The last detail taken care of, he rolled to face Linnet, and pull her into his arms. With an adorable sigh, she snuggled closer, fitting perfectly against his body. Soft hair teased his nose, the scent clean and yet all Linnet. No sickly sweet perfume. No thick makeup to worry about smearing. Just clean, clear, smooth skin. Fresh air and natural living made for a wholesome, healthy woman. And for now, she was all his.

Not wanting to think beyond the rest of the week, he buried his face in her hair and let himself drift to sleep.

# Chapter 22

"Creed?"

He hated to hear that tone. Though she tried to cover it with briskness, Linnet's voice held a hint of wistfulness. A reluctance to let him go. Just like every woman he'd walked away from at the time he had to return to work. It was that tone that turned into constant phone calls and emails—subtly or, more often, not so subtly—begging for his devotion and constant attention.

Resisting the urge to sigh, he tossed the last pair of socks into his duffle and zipped it shut. Straightening, he put a smile on his face and turned to Linnet. She was close enough he pulled her into his arms.

"Yes, sweet bird?" With her close enough to kiss, he didn't have to look at her face and see the lost look he knew would be forming there.

"Stick this in your pocket." She kissed his chin then stepped back. "It's the list of supplies you made with Hawk last night."

"Ah yes, the supplies to bring back." The list went into his shirt pocket. "Got everything?"

"I believe I do. Anything you want me to bring back?"

"Just you." She cocked her head and gave him a silly grin. "Okay, maybe a thick steak. I'm missing red meat."

Playing along, Creed clucked his tongue and slowly shook his head. "There's a river full of fresh fish out there, and you want red meat?"

"Fine, then bring some shrimp and crab with you. And a loaf of really good sourdough bread." She gave him a smirk. "Along with the steak. Rib-eye is best. T-bone will do in a pinch. New York strip if nothing else looks good. Sirloin if that's all they have."

"The California girl speaks. Is that all?"

"That should do it, Alaska boy." She lightly punched his chin then stepped away. "Well, you have to hit the road and I have work to do. Hawk carried your cooler out to your truck already."

"You trying to get rid of me?" He cocked an eyebrow at her. Had he really heard the wistful tone in her voice or was it just his imagination hoping?

"Hate to burst your bubble, but I'm behind because of you. Good thing George knows the river well enough to make reasonable estimates. I need to dig in and catch up. As it is I still have to contend with the brother. Not to mention my pet moose."

She gestured toward the side window where they could see the yearling hovering in the woods watching Hawk. With even strokes he cut notches in the next set of logs to be stacked up to form the walls of the new sleeping cabin.

Creed shook his head. His peaceful cabin was now inhabited by a dog, a woman, her brother and the neighborhood moose, instead of George. And he had to leave for two weeks to go back to work. Who was the one bent out of shape this time?

"Well?"

"What?" Creed shook himself. "Well... what?"

"You looked spaced out for a moment there. Are you going or staying?"

"I'm going, I'm going. Sheesh, I've never had anyone trying to kick me out of town before."

"I'm kicking you back to town to send you back to work." She sighed, leaned close, kissed him lightly then tugged on his arm. "Get going already. You're the one who said you had things to do tonight before jumping on the plane tomorrow."

She was right. He did have things to do tonight, but damned if he could think of even one right now. The four-hour drive back to Fairbanks would give him plenty of time to figure it out. Tugging the strap of his duffle up over his shoulder, he resisted the urge to drop-kick it under the bunk again. More than anything he wanted to pull her back down into the bed and not get up again.

The familiar ache and reluctance pulled at him. He'd be fine once he got on the road, but leaving the river was always hard. A glance at his watch showed he'd make it just in time for dinner with the parents.

"All right. I'm out of here." He grabbed her arm and pressed a kiss on her lips. "Be safe."

"Yes, Creed. Don't forget I lived out here for four whole weeks by myself. I'll survive the next two quite easily. Now go." She stepped away and held the door open for him.

Where were the tears? The clinging, sad, meek woman? The woman begging him to call each night? This one handed him a shopping list and orders to bring back steak. She hadn't even tried to pin him down to a time.

"You have my email, right?"

"Yes, Creed, and you have mine. Try to remember to give me an ETA a day or so before you return, would you? Not that I expect you to show on the exact minute, but if you get held up I'd like to know. Otherwise I might worry."

"How long do you have left out here?" He was stalling; he knew it, but couldn't help it.

"I'll stay four more weeks." She folded her arms and gave him an impatient look, but it didn't show in the tone of her voice. "That takes us into September. I'll spend a couple days in Fairbanks to finalize the end of season reports with George and then head back to Anchorage. By then you'll be back on the Slope and we'll go our separate ways. I don't think I can get a transfer to Fairbanks. If we choose to keep seeing each other, we'll work it out when you get back. You know all this, Creed. What's up?"

"I don't want to leave," he sighed. Unable to resist touching her, he reached out a finger to touch her sleeve. Sure, he'd been reluctant to leave the river before, but never like this. This affair would end sooner or later, but right now he'd prefer later. What would two weeks apart do to them? Once they'd sent all the guests, except Hawk, on their way, it had been the best week of his life.

"I never would have guessed." Her droll tone made him smile.

Yeah, he was being obvious. "No need to be sarcastic." His finger traveled up her arm to her shoulder.

Linnet laughed, shook her head and tried to shrug him off. The effort was half hearted at best, he noticed.

"Get going will you? If you don't leave soon I'll drag that gorgeous ass of yours back to bed and you'll miss your plane. So get out of here so I don't get you fired."

"Being the brave one are you?" Intent on torturing her as much as he felt tortured, Creed's finger skimmed lightly over the skin of her throat until he reached her earlobe. If he was going to leave here aching, it was only fair she shared the agony.

Stepping away from him, Linnet's escape was foiled by the door at her back. "Being the practical one."

"Will you miss me?" A gentleman wouldn't take advantage of her like this. But then again, his father had failed to raise a gentleman. One step and he had her loosely trapped. If she really wanted to, she could still get away.

"Of course I'll miss you, but I'll live." The shrug she gave was indifferent, her eyes carefully amused as she hugged her folded arms closer to her body. Her nipples were visible beneath her thin shirt. The day was warm enough she only wore the long sleeved undershirt, and that only to keep the mosquitoes off. An image of Linnet at the creek, wearing shorts and a tight tank top while she worked the sluice box reminded him of one particularly fun afternoon where they'd ended up making love in the hot sun on a big flat rock at the edge of the stream.

"Hey, Willis. You still here?"

Creed scowled out the door to see Hawk pulling the screen door open.

"He's dragging his feet," Linnet told her brother.

Hawk wore a look of pity that said Creed was being a pussy. Yeah, maybe he was infatuated with Linnet, but wasn't that part of life? Lord knew enough women had accused him of playing with their feelings. Live the dream for a few weeks and then get cold feet. Well he wanted to ride the high of the infatuation a little longer. Break ups were enough of a bummer and he didn't want to rush this one. The affair would end naturally after his next off cycle, so why deal it a death blow now?

Hawk laughed at him as he spoke. "I promise I won't leave until you get back. You will be back in two weeks, right?"

"Two weeks from tomorrow," Creed confirmed.

"No worries. I still have three weeks of leave. I'll book my flight back to California for that Wednesday."

"You're letting the bugs in," Linnet complained to her brother and waved at a large black fly buzzing her.

"Sorry, thought Willis was on his way out. Why is he dragging his feet? You two should be ready for a rest from sucking face. In fact, he should be running for the Slope so he can get his stamina back. He's going to need it for his next furlough."

Creed rolled his eyes. "You can stop smirking anytime now. I'll have George gather the supplies we'll need to finish the cabin. Might want to make those reservations for Thursday."

"Nah, I'll have it done. The only thing missing will be the furnishings on your list. You can put in the windows and mount the door yourself."

"All right, I'm gone." Creed stopped in front of Linnet, kissed her on the nose, shook Hawk's hand, and forced himself out the door. Manley walked beside him, tail wagging. Without looking back, Creed lengthened his stride over the slight rise behind the cabin and down the back side to stop next to his truck.

Dammit. He slapped the side of the truck.

Usually after a couple weeks at home, he was eager to head back to work where he could begin weaning himself from the woman of the week. No problem, he reminded himself. By the time he got back, he'd have two more weeks with Linnet and then she'd leave. Four weeks and he'd be a free man again.

With another scowl on his face, he opened the door and threw the duffle into the back seat of the extended cab pickup. Nearly the same model as Linnet's blue truck parked on the far side of his silver one. The trucks looked good side by side. Just like she looked good tucked up against his side. Patting his pocket, he made sure the flash drive loaded with pictures was secure. There were a couple of her he wanted on his screen saver at work. It had never occurred to him to have pictures of a woman on his desk before.

Manley's tail hit his leg. Creed turned to the dog and bent to scratch his ears. "Be good to her, Manley. Take care of my woman, hear me?"

Manley wiggled under his hands and licked his chin.

"Yeah, you too, buddy. See you in two weeks. Go get Linnet." Creed gave the hand signal indicating where Manley was to go.

With one last wag of his tail, Manley turned and dashed back to the cabin. For a long moment, Creed would have given anything to trade places with the dog.

# Chapter 23

"Would you sit down already?" Hawk complained. "Either that or go chop some wood."

Linnet glared at her brother. The time together had been good, but she was ready for him to leave. The last two weeks had allowed them to become friends in a whole new way. As adults, rather than children. Hawk no longer looked at her warily, but treated her as a competent adult, even going so far as to email the folks with his opinion she was doing just fine. Dad still hadn't quite given up pressuring her to come home, but the efforts now felt more like habit than strong conviction.

Hawk shrugged, not at all cowed by her scathing look. "Or we can do some more target practice, either knife or pistol, but frankly, I'm not sure putting weapons of any kind into your hands right now is a good idea. Just relax."

"If you don't like it, you go chop wood. Or fish. Or find another nail to pound into the sleeping cabin," she groused at him. "Or I could use you as my target."

Hawk snorted at her empty threat even though he knew she was dead accurate with both knife and gun. "I love a riled-up woman."

Linnet turned away to hide her grin. He didn't really deserve her ire, but Creed was coming back either tonight or by noon tomorrow. The last email had been a little vague. It all depended on what he found waiting for him when he got home.

If his family had come through with the errands he'd requested from them, then he'd be here in the next few hours. If something had gone astray, then he'd deal with the rest of the list tonight and come up in the morning. Not wanting to press him, she'd returned an equally vague message letting him know she'd gotten his.

"I'm already busy. Besides, the cabin is done. All it needs is the furniture Willis is supposed to bring, along with the windows he ordered and the door. Hell, you even have the screens done so it can be used right away as long as the weather stays warm."

It was warm now, but temperatures were already dropping at night as the days began to shorten. According to George, the ground could freeze up as early as three weeks from now. The fish runs were winding down fast, the birch leaves were yellow, the fireweed had long since gone to seed, and she'd be stretching it to stay another two weeks. In reality, she should be going back at the end of this week. There wasn't enough going on to keep her here. George made excuses for her, but both of them knew Newbauer wasn't buying. Still, her boss hadn't said anything, which meant there wasn't much for her to do in Anchorage either.

"Linnet, sit down for crying out loud," Hawk groaned from the chair he'd adopted as his. Sitting near the woodstove, he was whittling again. An old habit left over from days as a boy scout, Hawk had once spent hours whittling around campfires. At least tonight, he had newspapers spread out to catch the chips as he chiseled away a partial section from a short split log.

"Do I have to dig out the flask?" He'd tried his hand at carving salmon and eagles into various pieces of wood these past few weeks, but all his efforts so far had ended up in the fire.

"Just what I need, JD breath and a good buzz to greet him with," she grumbled but settled into the chair she'd marked as hers with a book resting on its arm and the knitting bag at the side.

The box of supplies from Mom had been waiting at the Circle post office a couple weeks back. Good thing she'd included a book of instructions and a few skeins of cheap yarn for Linnet to practice on before moving on to the better quality wools. It had taken awhile to remember the intricacies of twisting the yarn around the pointy needles, but so far she'd managed a couple of crude, but serviceable, scarves. Her current project even looked wearable as the lessons from her grandmother surfaced from deep inside.

"What are you all worried about anyway?" Hawk goaded her. "You said this was just a fling. These next two weeks and then you head back to your winter life while he resumes his. No big deal."

Right. Easy for him to say. Linnet ignored him and reached for the needles in the tote bag Mom had also thoughtfully provided.

"You didn't go and fall in love with him did you?"

Linnet glanced up at her brother's horrified tone.

His eyes danced with laughter.

"Stop teasing me."

"Come on, Linnie, we both know you've fallen for him. Handsome dude. Good with the moves if the screams and moans I hear from all over the place are any indication."

Ducking her head in embarrassment Linnet had to admit he had her there. She and Creed had found numerous places to make love the last week he'd been here. Once even with the moose looking on, as they'd discovered one afternoon while enjoying a particularly sweet afterglow.

"Besides, he has a good job, he's a regular guy with a decent sense of honor. I like him, so you can fall in love with him," Hawk declared.

"Why, thank you so much, dear brother. As if it's any of your business or you have the power to grant such a blessing."

Hawk only laughed at her snort of derision. "Well, you need to figure out your feelings before he gets back here."

"Feelings? Who are you and what have you done with my brother? My brother? Talking about feelings?" She gave him a wide eyed look of horror and dramatically placed a hand over her heart.

"Hey, it happens. I can see you have feelings and I'm a sensitive sort of guy. Just can't let the team see it." The smirk he gave her made her laugh. "Come on, sis, you're ready for a real man. One who won't smother you or try to change you. And judging by the last few weeks, Willis won't do that to you."

"Yeah, well George told me Creed doesn't like clingy women. Not my style anyway." Linnet looked down at her needles again and ignored the reference to Henry. That was still an uncomfortable subject and a few emails hadn't dissuaded Henry one bit. He still wanted to come see her.

Instead, Linnet turned her thoughts back to Creed and how she wanted to cling to him in the worst kind of way. Even if it was part of the infatuation. It would wear thin after awhile. Days or weeks, possibly even months, but sooner or later they'd both get annoyed with it, even though, if she were going to be honest with herself, she was ready for his big strong body to hold hers right now.

So, instead of calling him every day and sending him copious numbers of long emails, she'd pretended he was a colleague, keeping her notes spaced out two to three days apart and business-like. Who knew how closely his company monitored personal emails?

Seeking distraction, she'd turned her softer side to sprucing up the inside of the cabin some more. Thinking of ways to block light as well as provide insulation, Linnet had found a pile of cheap blankets at the trading post. A little cutting, a little yarn for decorative trim and the windows all had roll-up curtains. The floor was now varnished, as were the counter tops. Even the old outhouse had been spruced up. Hours had been spent helping Hawk with the sleeping cabin.

After peeling bark from the logs, she'd put the power sander to use on the interior and then coated everything with a wood preservative. As the yarn she was knitting with caught on her roughened skin she had to grimace. The hard work of the last two weeks had toughened her up, but it had taken a toll on her hands and nails. A long soak in the tub late this afternoon and what seemed like half a tube of lotion hadn't entirely repaired all the damage. Maybe Creed would want a hot mineral water soak later tonight. The thought brought a rush of warmth to her face.

"See, you're thinking about him even now," Hawk teased her.

"Yeah, so, tell me again why you're hanging around here bugging me instead of out seeking female companionship yourself?"

Hawk tipped his head backward and laughed. "I'm not ready to settle down. Yeah, I'd like to burn off a little tension, but I'll do that when I get home. I'll have a week to woo the ladies and have a series of short, meaningless, but intensely satisfying affairs."

"In other words, you'll troll the bars and find as many one night stands as you can."

"Only fair to share Uncle Sam's finest with the ladies. Once I decide to retire, then I'll find some sweet young thing to warm my bed and we'll fill the house with adorable babies and I'll learn how to be a Little League coach."

"In other words, it worked for Dad, so it should work for you."

"See? I like that about you, you understand my language." He ducked when she threw ball of yarn at him.

"You're a pig, you know that?"

"Yeah, but I'm the only brother you have so you have to love me."

"There's no law about that."

"Sure there is."

Linnet cast him a long glance, then started laughing with him. "You're still a pig, but I do love you. Just don't break too many hearts, okay?"

"See, I always figured it wasn't fair to leave a wife and kids behind while I went off to war. I saw how Mom tried to put on her brave face while Dad was gone, but it hurt her too."

"Especially when you became a rebellious teenager. So why did you choose the service and SEALs in particular?"

Hawk shrugged and turned his stare toward the fireplace. "I could give you all the standard lines about love of country and duty, but frankly, with the old man, military is what we knew, right? I chose the Navy because it was tradition, but I didn't get high enough ratings to be a pilot, so when my buddies all started eyeing the SEALs, I went along. Four of us made it and we make a good team. I like it and we do good work. Besides, you should see the old man strut around the home town." Hawk grinned sheepishly. "Who knew he could be so proud?"

"He always was; he just couldn't tell us to our faces." Linnet returned the grin. "But I knew. I could see by the way he watched your sports. And when I got hauled up for that Honor Society award in high school I saw the tears in his eyes. He may have been hard ass when he was home, but he was fair too."

"Yeah, he was."

A comfortable silence fell, filled only by the clicking of Linnet's needles and the hiss and crackle of wood burning in the woodstove. A pot simmered on the top of it, a sort of chicken stew. Linnet would add dumplings either when Creed arrived or she and Hawk were too hungry to ignore it any longer.

It was only six now, the earliest Creed would arrive if he was indeed coming tonight. Eight was more likely if she was going to be reasonable about it. Tomorrow would be more practical. Creed hadn't said and she hadn't tried to pin him down. Mom had always said you couldn't hold a traveling man to a precise schedule.

Even when Dad had been stationed at home, one thing or another could always come up and delay him coming home even though he tried to be home by five. Regardless, dinner was on the table at five-thirty every night and if Dad wasn't there, Mom saved him a plate. Both of them had believed in a schedule for the kids.

So why was she holding dinner for Creed? She hadn't told him she would. He hadn't asked her to. And what if he did show with the steak and seafood she'd told him to bring? What then? What if he wanted to eat that and she and Hawk had already eaten? The not knowing was driving her crazy. She wasn't used to thinking of someone else that way. If she held dinner for him would he see her as trying too hard? If she didn't hold dinner for him would he see her as too cold?

"Argh!" she exclaimed, when the churning thoughts threatened to spill out again.

"Easy, sis," Hawk crooned again.

"I just dropped a stitch," she lied, hoping to cover her inner turmoil.

"Sure you did."

Like she could hide anything from him.

# Chapter 24

The last stretch was always the toughest. Creed shifted the truck into four-wheel drive then turned off the highway into the nearly hidden entrance to the rough track leading to the cabin. The first hundred yards was purposely extra rough. It discouraged sightseers from trespassing as did another boggy spot a few more miles in.

All the locals knew the road and preferred to visit by river anyway, respecting the desire to keep the road hidden. There were many such drives taking off from the highway. People valued their privacy out here. Still, until he reached the cabin, he wouldn't breathe easy. Despite the gravel he tossed into the low spots each year, the road wasn't all that improved. The windows for the sleeping cabin were well packed and the small woodstove secure, but a new low spot could slide everything around and waste several hundred dollars of supplies.

Thinking about Linnet waiting at the other end of the drive made it hard to go slow. Unlike every other woman he'd met, this one he'd dreamed of on the Slope and looked forward to seeing again. They'd exchanged emails, probably a half dozen in all, but she'd kept hers short and almost impersonal. Maybe that was just how she was.

He'd seen her get caught up in her work to the exclusion of almost everything around her. Granted, focus was a requirement out on the river. One moment of inattention and disaster could strike. She'd kept most of her emails focused on reporting work on the cabin, which was going well, whatever that meant. Maybe it left her too tired for long newsy love letters, especially since most had been sent later in the evening. Probably as she was winding down for bed as had been her habit when he was there.

Bedtime, now there was a part of the day he was looking forward too. Like most travel days, this one had been long and dull with routine. His alternate had come in, they'd gone over notes for a few hours, then Creed had whiled away some time waiting for the plane to load for the return trip. The flight from Deadhorse to Fairbanks wasn't so bad. It was so routine, now, it was almost akin to catching a cab in New York. Every two weeks, except for the odd four week stint, for the last seven years. Routine. He lived by it, needed it, was comforted by it. Was it about to change?

During his off hours, he'd kept to himself while going about his routine. Laundry, eating, a little more time working out in the gym. Would Linnet notice his slightly more-defined abs? He laughed at himself. As bad as a woman primping for her man. Not that Linnet had the means to do much primping for him, but he imagined she would have spent some time in the tub to be fresh and clean for him. Maybe even fantasizing about one particularly lusty bath they'd shared one evening... he'd certainly called upon the memory as well as the one of her self-pleasuring...

Catching himself before steering into a spruce tree, he laughed again. At this rate his balls would be blue by the time he arrived at the cabin. A glance at the clock on the dash showed he still had a good eighteen minutes to go. The last twenty miles of the trip rarely allowed for a speed faster than twenty miles an hour. Should have asked Linnet and Hawk to meet him in Circle and carry everything up by boat. Nah, just would have meant extra hefting of the supplies. No time would have been saved, though he would have gotten to see her sooner. Just as well.

The CD in the changer ended and shifted to the next one. Yet another old love song from the seventies kicked in. Great. Where had these come from? For the last couple hours, there had been a bunch of new music coming from the speakers—from CDs he didn't even own—most of them soulful love songs and ballads of one sort or another. The rest were about being alone and how much it sucked. George must have been messing around while loading the truck.

Good old George. Needed to take the spare set of keys away from him. He and Dad, with Mom's help, had taken care of the shopping list and had been loading the last items in the truck when the cab dropped him off this afternoon.

Creed had stayed only long enough to check his voicemail, glance through the mail, and grab a snack for the road. All the while dodging questions from his parents. Dad had asked about the new sleeping cabin. Mom had waved Dad off and zeroed in for the kill. She wanted to know about Linnet.

"When is she coming into town?" Mom had asked not quite so casually.

"In a couple weeks. Might come back before me, with me, or after me. I don't know her plans yet. Did you get the steaks?"

"Yes, Costco has great rib steaks. They also had a special on king crab legs and jumbo shrimp. I tossed in a couple rounds of sourdough. So, is she pretty? George says she's tall and very nice."

"Thanks, Mom. Did you find the wine too?" It was tough avoiding the interrogation with his mom standing at his elbow as he double checked the ropes tying down the load.

"Yes, I got a half case. So, she's from California? Blonde? Is she pretty?"

"Brunette. Better ask George if she's pretty. George, didn't you get some photos of her? Mom, the wine glasses? Are they packed too?"

"Yes, and the champagne as well. It's in the cooler surrounded by ice. You've never gone to this much trouble for a woman before. I think I'd like to meet her."

"I don't know if that will happen, Ma." How could he tell her the expiration date of the affair had pretty much been determined already? The very thought twisted his stomach, and he had to stop and take a deep breath. Funny, expiration dates had never bothered him before. They'd bothered the women who were supposed to go away, but never him.

"Yeah, Auntie, she's pretty," George had drawled. "I tried to get some pictures of her, but she seems to have a sixth sense about when a camera is pointed at her. Every time I tried, she turned around."

"Didn't you get a picture of her backside?" Creed had asked. Memories of her fine derriere made him think of the few photos along those lines on his thumb drive.

"I did and I showed them to your dad."

Everyone had turned to look at Dad, who'd just pushed his glasses further up his nose. "She has a very fine backside. I'd like to see the front too."

"The front is even better," Creed had muttered, and vowed to get more and better photos of all her sides while tossing his duffle into the back. It was weird talking with his family about Linnet this way. Didn't seem right that his own father had noticed her fine ass.

He purposely hadn't looked at his mother, afraid he'd see his parents exchange one of *those* looks. Life had never been good for him when one of *those* looks had been shared. He'd usually ended up with extra outside chores, or driving his sister into town for some silly something at the grocery store.

Finally, he'd been able to give Mom a hug, Dad a handshake and George a glare in return for the damned inscrutable look his cousin took on when he was up to something. Could it have been to hide a smirk over the soulful, heart-wrenching love songs that had been pouring from the speakers for a hundred and fifty miles? It had been awhile since he's extracted retribution of some kind on George. Maybe now was a good time...

It hadn't seemed sporting to pick on George the last few years. Ever since his wife had died from cancer, his cousin had been more withdrawn and remote than ever. George had actually emailed Creed on the Slope this last hitch. Mainly to discuss improvements at the cabin. His email report came after going out for a few nights. He'd even gone so far to tell Creed about making arrangements for Linnet to meet him in Circle with the boat.

But there had been news about Linnet as well. George had caught her staring off into space a few times with a dreamy look on her face. Linnet had started knitting in the evenings. Stories told by Hawk about their childhood. The easy relationship between brother and sister. Questions Linnet had asked George about him.

Okay, so maybe he could forgive George for messing with the CD changer. And here was the last rise that eased into the clearing where they parked. Trip completed, safe and sound. He backed the truck into place and shut off the engine. Home always felt good.

* * * *

"What is it Manley?" Linnet asked as the dog's head lifted from the rug near the fire. One minute he'd been snoring, the next he was alert with ear cocked. "Is it the moose or Creed?"

"Probably Creed," Hawk said, as he stood and stretched. He pulled the door open then sighed. "Tourists pulling up on the beach. Want me to deal with them?"

"No." Linnet set her knitting aside. This was the sixth set of travelers since Creed had left. The place felt like a regular truck stop. Why, of all nights, did they have to show up tonight? "I'll go scare them off with my uniform." She stood and shrugged into the shirt with her Fish and Wildlife patch as well as her name tag. Not five steps down the rise toward the riverbank, still buckling on her gunbelt, she heard a whistle coming from behind the cabin. Manley stopped and looked up at her with wide eyes.

"Manley, go get Creed," she said and pointed toward the parking area. "Hawk! That's probably him now, would you go check?" She waited just long enough to catch his lazy salute, then turned to the group in two canoes climbing onto the beach.

A few minutes later she found herself inviting the two couples, both a little older than herself—one Walt and Trudy Garretson and their friends

Pete and Katy of different last names—to camp there for the night. The women looked soggy and weary. Katy in particular had a sour look on her face. She reminded Linnet of a socialite wannabe trying to impress the bachelor of the moment she was prime marriage material.

Rain had chased them most of the day, though the sky was currently clear. But a chill was settling in and an evening in front of the woodstove would do them good. A hot meal as well. It would be a simple matter to double the chicken stew. It would be thin on meat, but dumplings would bulk it up.

With a small smile to hide her disappointment, Linnet left them to unload their boats. Of all the nights to have travelers in need of indoor beds when all the others had used their tents... she huffed out an exasperated sigh. Just par for the course on her and Creed's luck at being alone.

As she approached the cabin, Creed and Hawk came over the rise, their arms loaded with coolers and boxes. She could only imagine how much carrying there was to do. Maybe the visitors would lend a hand.

Lengthening her stride, she smiled at Creed and opened the screen door for him. "Welcome back," she said, her voice a tad huskier than she'd planned. Nerves made her insides feel tight and fluttery.

Her smile widened when Creed paused just long enough to drop a quick kiss on her lips. "Now I feel truly welcomed," he responded with a wide grin, and she felt fluttery for another reason. How were they going to get rid of everyone tonight so they could be alone? Would the tub be their only option for retreat?

"We have company." She nodded toward the beach, then let Hawk pass with his load before following both men into the cabin.

"Couldn't get rid of them?" Creed set his cooler down on the floor.

"Nah. They're wet and cold. It was raining up-river all day. They just got out of the rain about an hour ago."

"Smells good in here; what're you cooking?"

"Just simmering up a pot of chicken stew. Didn't know for sure..." she bit her lip and let the sentence trail off. Didn't want to sound accusatory.

"That's okay. We'll save the good stuff for tomorrow night since I'm guessing you'll offer them a hot meal?" Creed turned toward her and she felt her face warm.

"No time to stand around mooning, you two," Hawk cut in. "Visitors to make comfortable and a truck to unload."

Linnet cleared her throat and looked away. "I'll add to the pot so it'll be ready by the time everyone is organized."

Hawk snorted and pushed out through the screen door. Creed stopped beside her and lightly rubbed her cheek with the back of a knuckle. "I'm hoping we can at least get the bed set up and the door on the sleeping cabin tonight. Would you like that?"

His low voice made Linnet flush with more heat, if at all possible. "I'd like that." She gripped her hands behind her back to keep from grabbing him and dragging him into the woods. Two weeks had never felt so long. The twinkle in his eyes, deep and longing with a hint of mischief sparked a fire of need deep within her. Her heart skipped a beat and she was sure he would haul her into his arms and kiss her. Footsteps on the porch, voices and a knock broke the spell and Creed turned away.

"Good evening folks. Come on in and warm yourselves by the fire." He invited the newcomers loaded down with gear bags.

"Creed? Is that you?"

"Katy?" Creed sounded surprised, possibly even a hint apprehensive.

Linnet could see his shoulders tensing. He knew these people?

"I thought this was your place," one of the men said. "I knew it was around here somewhere, but it's been a long time and I've never approached it from the river. Also didn't expect to actually see you."

Linnet turned back to watch the group enter the cabin one at a time, each one stopping to greet Creed with handshakes after setting down their gear, or in the case of the women, with hugs. Katy tried to cling tighter and longer to him, but Creed pulled back almost immediately.

"Never thought I'd see the day you'd get Katy out on the river for an hour much less a whole week of camping," he joked as he shook hands.

"Hey, she knows I love the outdoors, so she decided to come along this year to see what all the fun was about." The look on Pete's face made Linnet believe the trip hadn't been all that fun, but Katy had her back to him and didn't see it. No, Katy only had eyes for Creed. Interesting.

"Well, I suppose you met Linnet down by the water. She took over for George when he broke his leg," Creed pulled her to his side to make fresh introductions. "I went to school with this group," he explained to her. "Walt and Trudy there have been married since the day after graduation from high school. As for Pete and Katy, always figured you two would get together eventually, but never did I ever imagine Katy in a setting like this."

"Well here I am." The woman tossed a long blonde ponytail over her shoulder.

Linnet noted she wore what looked like old designer jeans. Next to her friend, the comfortable married one, Katy looked like a socialite clinging as hard and fast to her twenties as she could. "Now I get to see what all the fuss is about and what I missed out on when you invited me up here all those times."

Linnet found refuge in her professional voice as Creed's hand squeezed her side. Apparently he wasn't all that thrilled by Katy's presence either. "Pleased to meet you all—again. That was my brother, Hawk, you passed on the way in."

Linnet forced herself to smile. The hairs on the back of her neck bristled and if looks could freeze, Katy's would have sent her into the Ice Age. "Ladies, let's get you thawed out and your gear drying."

Linnet turned away to grab her hot pads and carried the stew pot from the woodstove to the kitchen counter. She couldn't help thinking it was going to be a long night.

# Chapter 25

"So this is where Creed runs off to all the time." Katy eyed the cabin with a critical eye, as Linnet set the pot of chicken stew back on the woodstove.

With dinner once more simmering, Linnet helped the women drape their damp sleeping bags and changes of clothing before the fire. Hadn't these people heard of waterproof gear bags?

They had, Trudy explained with a rueful laugh, but the bags were wet from packing up the camp this morning in the rain. One of the tents had begun dripping and everything had ended up soaked. They'd been thinking to try for Circle tonight, but seeing the cabin, and being cold and weary from paddling all day, had been a God-send. Yeah, Trudy made it clear how thankful they were to have seen it. Had they been traveling closer to the other bank they would have missed the cabin completely.

Sounds from the men carrying supplies from the truck to the sleeping cabin could be heard through one of the windows Linnet kept open. Power tools were heard next as the door was hung and the bed frame, she supposed, assembled. Getting things organized didn't give Linnet a chance to see what was going on.

She had no idea what kind of bed Creed had bought, much less anything else. Probably would have to wait until tomorrow or just before bedtime tonight. Had he remembered to bring sheets and blankets? Pillows? A lantern of some kind?

"What's going on out there?" Katy asked. "What are the men doing?"

"We've been building a sleeping cabin," Linnet reluctantly explained. "Creed brought back some items to finish it up."

"You mean another bunk cabin? Like this one?"

Linnet avoided Katy's laser glare by pulling on her flannel shirt. "No, just a small cabin, just big enough for a couple of people."

"Oh?" The tone implied a raised eyebrow, but Linnet ignored her and slipped out the door.

Unable to stand the suspense any longer, she left Katy and Trudy with cups of tea in hand and prayed they wouldn't follow, to go check on the progress of the sleeping cabin. Creed had just about stepped on the porch.

Surprised, she paused at the threshold. "Hi." Great. Such a witty comment.

"Hi," he returned with a smile. "Want to see?" Creed stepped back, inviting her to join him on the pathway.

"Is it done?"

"Only the windows and the feminine touches are left. Woodstove is even in place."

"That was fast."

Creed's hand settled on the small of her back as he escorted her to the right of the main cabin. Ten yards or so away and a little back from the trail to the creek, the sleeping cabin was tucked between birch and spruce trees, wild rose and highbush cranberry bushes. Further up the slope, blueberry bushes had already been harvested of their treasures. Tonight's dessert was blueberry cobbler made from the last batch around the cabins. There were more, farther afield, but Linnet wasn't sure she'd have time to pick them.

A warm glow came from the open door and a small plume of smoke rose from the new length of black stovepipe above the roof.

"I still can't believe you finished assembling everything in an hour." In awe, she paused at the foot of the trail leading to the porch.

Creed's hand slid up her back to settle over her nape. "Pretty little cabin, isn't it?"

"It is." Hawk had worked hard to keep it rustic looking. Couldn't help the shiny new look of the preservative gleaming in the softening light, but the cabin still looked as if it'd been here years instead of days. Would look even more so when they sodded the roof with the layer of tundra they'd dug up before laying down gravel for the foundation. She'd been amazed Hawk had known what to do, until he'd told her part of his job was building things in order to learn how to blow them apart.

"Sodding the roof will only take a day."

Linnet nodded in agreement.

Hawk opened the door and stared out at her. "You gonna stand there all night?"

"Might help if you stepped out of there. The cabin isn't big enough for a party."

"You heard the lady, gents," Hawk told their helpers.

"Smart lady," the man introduced as Pete said as he exited the cabin. "The girls inside?" He nodded toward the larger structure.

"Drinking tea and warming up as we speak," she assured him as his friend followed him from the cabin.

"Think we ought to give these two a moment," Walt chuckled.

"Thanks." Linnet gave him a smile. "We'll serve dinner in a little bit." She glanced at her watch. "The dumplings will be ready in ten minutes."

"Thank you, ma'am." Both men tipped their ball caps to her and set off to join their ladies.

"I suppose you want me to leave too," Hawk said. He didn't look like he wanted to move, with his arms folded across his chest as he leaned up against the door jamb.

"You can stay... for a minute," Creed told him.

Hawk snorted then stood back from the door to let Linnet in.

Of course she'd been inside, but not with furnishings. The cabin was only sixteen-feet deep and twelve-feet wide, the roof overhang of four feet, more or less, created a covered porch held up by log supports, one of which bulged with a large burl.

Window frames on either side of the door were temporarily covered with screening material, waiting for the paned windows to be secured in place. Excited to see the interior, Linnet ducked under Hawk's arm as he held the screen door open.

Creed followed her. "We still need to put up some finishing touches, such as the molding around the door, but we'll do that tomorrow when we put the windows in. Pete's a carpenter so he got the door set and has offered to help with the windows. That is, if we want them to hang around an extra day."

"That's up to you. Hawk needs to get to town by tomorrow night," Linnet reminded them both. Frankly, she'd rather the two couples left as soon as possible.

For such a tiny space, there was so much to see all at once. The bed, set against the back wall was king sized and looked as rustic as the cabin. The log frame was hand carved with sturdy half posts at the foot and taller posts framing a headboard of more logs. Small bedside tables, each with an oil lamp, matched the style of the bed. For the moment they were empty, but bottles of lamp oil stood nearby.

"It must have taken up most of the room in the back of your truck," she said and smiled back at Creed.

"It did, but it was worth it."

The mattress was bare, but bags of what looked like linens covered the top. One had to be a thick comforter. Cozy.

"We didn't have time to make the bed before dinner," Hawk said dryly.

"Won't take long," Linnet murmured as she turned her attention to the front part. Situated along the right wall, about mid cabin, was the smallest woodstove she'd ever seen, complete with a copper tea kettle on top. It was perfect for the setting. Fireproof backers had been laid on the floor and attached to the wall behind the stove, and a new black stove-pipe run up through the roof. A small window in the door showed dancing flames inside and already she could feel its warmth filling the cabin. A large, red, oval braided rug covered the open floor. A small dresser was set against the front wall to the side of the door and under the window.

"There's room for a couple chairs," Creed said. "They're alongside the cabin and need assembling, but at least they're here."

"It's wonderful," Linnet said as she turned to him. "It's perfect."

"You haven't seen the door yet." Creed smiled as he stepped aside.

"Oh my..." It was the prettiest door she'd ever seen. A wildlife scene was carved into the thick, heavy wood. A small round pane of glass, looking like a full moon, would let in a little light at the top, but not compromise privacy. Or tempt bears, unless they wanted to visit with the carved moose and eagle. "It's magnificent."

Unable to think of better words, she said no more and felt Creed's hands settle on her shoulders, his body warm against her back.

"I have locks for it, but I'll also install a bar holder on the inside. That way if you're out here alone—which I hope you won't ever be again— you can be secure."

Linnet turned to face Creed and also smiled over his shoulder at her brother. "It's perfect. Thank you, both of you."

"Hey," Hawk chuckled, "you worked on it too. Besides, you still have to do the decorative touches, but those will come with time."

Creed was closer so she hugged him.

"Guess I'll just go check on those dumplings." Hawk laughed and closed the door behind him.

The interior of the cabin was dim, lit only by what light came through the window holes and from the woodstove. It was warm and cozy with the firelight dancing around them.

"Feel like shaking out the linens and testing the mattress?" Creed asked playfully.

"We have guests to care for," Linnet chided him softly. "That, and you might like a bath first, though we could make the bed now and test it later."

"Stink, do I?"

"Airplane smell. Antiseptic. Not at all like the smell I grew accustomed to. Aren't you hungry?"

"Only for you, but you're right, I would like to clean up first. Still... there is one thing..."

Creed's lips were soft as he teased her mouth. Mint. She smiled. He'd chewed some of the wild mint growing all around. Staring into his eyes, she forgot everything except how he could make her feel. How his hands and body holding her close to him made her feel. As anticipation built, both of them seemed to be having trouble drawing in enough oxygen. By the time their lips met, Linnet could swear an electrical storm was brewing between them and the contact set it off.

Two weeks of longing and waiting, pent up and strictly leashed, exploded when they came together. Teasing was over as Creed took her mouth, pulling her body so close it almost felt as if they melded. Consumed by the kiss and the feel of his body against hers, she didn't realize he'd backed her up to the bed until they sank down onto it, and pushed the bags ruthlessly to the far side to tumble over the edge.

"Ow, Creed, wait..." she gasped as the bits of her gunbelt dug into her.

"Is that your gun or are you happy to see me," Creed leered over her.

"Stop it," she giggled, and tried to wiggle out from under him.

"Well, would you look at that?" The shrill female voice came from the screened window. "Trudy, you have to come see this. It is just the cutest little love nest!"

Linnet's head dropped back to the bed and Creed buried his face in her neck. "I'm going to kill her," he muttered. "We can hide the body in the muskeg and no one will ever find her, much less miss her."

"Shhh," Linnet soothed him. Frustrated as she was, she still had to maintain a professional demeanor even if his idea held merit and appeal.

"Hey, you all mind if we come in to look around?" Not waiting for an answer, Katy pushed the door open and stepped in, Trudy right behind her.

"Oh dear. Come on, Katy, looks like we interrupted." Trudy at least had the grace to look embarrassed, as she peeked around through the door.

"We came to take a look and let you know dinner looks like it's ready," Katy said standing in the middle of the cabin. It looked as if she had no intention of moving. "Kind of cute, really. Lacking a few essentials such as electricity and plumbing, but not bad in a pioneer sort of way."

"Thank you for that critique, Katy," Creed growled. "Now get the hell out."

"Well you don't have to be so rude about it."

"You drew first rude and opened yourself up to it. Go ahead and start dinner without us. We'll be over when we're hungry or need more supplies." Creed rolled away from Linnet just enough to glare at his friends. "Shut the door on your way out."

Katy arched a thin plucked eyebrow then sauntered out the door. Linnet wanted to send a slug from her pistol after the blonde. Preferably a silver one just to make sure it worked properly.

"I'm sorry," Creed returned to kissing her neck. "I dated her for a while, five or more years ago and she hasn't completely recognized it's over yet. Probably came on this trip because the guys told her the cabin was along the way."

"Creed," Linnet pushed at his shoulders, "this isn't going to work right now. She killed the mood." Not to mention the items hanging off her belt digging into her hip and back.

Creed sighed and nuzzled into her hair. "I know, but I don't want her to know that. The old not-giving-her-the-satisfaction thing. Shall we make up the bed and think great thoughts about later tonight?"

* * * *

It took most of an hour, but at last Linnet was relaxed again. Creed mentally wiped his brow. And he thought he was emotionally insecure. Linnet took the prize and put him to shame. At least she'd tucked her gunbelt into one of the nightstand drawers.

After shaking out the linens, complete with bed skirt for crying out loud, they'd made up the bed with the sheets, piles of pillows, blankets, quilts and denim-covered comforter his mother had picked out. In fact, there were too many layers, and the extras were shoved into the bottom drawer of the dresser. That killed about fifteen minutes, so they'd carried in the parts for the chairs and assembled those. One was a rocking chair, the other an Adirondack style with foot rest. Linnet had spent a few minutes rocking and a small smile had finally crossed her face.

"You think it will work?" Okay, so a part of him wanted the praise.

"Very cozy. I can see spending rainy days right here. Just need a table to hold a lamp for reading or knitting and a cup of tea and I'd be set."

"You look very pretty there." Creed stepped closer and ran the back of finger over her cheek. Not about to say it out loud, he could envision her wrapped in a blanket holding a baby to her breast. Now where the hell had that image come from? Breast-feeding woman? In an effort to reset his mind, Creed cleared his throat. "What do you say we grab our gear, a bowl of grub, and scurry back here? After eating we can go take a bath and then turn in for the night."

Shining green eyes looked up at him and he was most pleased to see the sparkle back. "I'd like that, but let's be quick in the other cabin. I don't want to hang out there tonight."

"I agree. I'd just as soon avoid reliving all our high-school glory days." Which seemed to happen too much when he got together with old friends. The loud growl of Linnet's stomach made him grin. "I'm starved. You?"

When she laughed, her whole face lit up. "Busted. Yes, I'm hungry." She took the hand he offered and stood. It was too irresistible to wrap his arms around her for another kiss. "So, did you really bring steak?" she all but purred.

He dropped a light kiss on her lips then opened the door without releasing her. "I sure did. There's also crab, and shrimp large enough to put on the barbie. And champagne and good wine. I think there's even something chocolate in there.

"Wow. You must like me." She grinned at him over her shoulder.

"To bring red meat into the land of fresh fish? You're damn right I do," he assured her with a pat on her beautiful backside. George may have taken photos of it, but Creed got to touch it. And rub it and do all sorts of wicked things to it. There'd been that evening they'd been panning and he'd bent her over a rock midstream. He could still see her beautiful behind as she'd pushed back against him...

He was still thinking of all those wicked possibilities when they paused before the door of the main cabin. Stalling just a little longer, he cupped Linnet's delicious derriere in his hands, enjoying her arms around his neck. Another kiss and then he'd be ready to face the others. Just to give Linnet that just-loved look to carry with her, of course.

She didn't need convincing, in fact she joined in rather joyfully and the kiss was close to careening out of control. There was the picnic table. He could lay her down on that and feast on her instead of dinner. He backed her up to it and lifted her onto the top, his hands urging her legs to wrap around his waist. If only wilderness girls wore skirts...

Golden light washed over them as the inside door opened, spilling warmth into the rapidly cooling night. At nine, the sun had just gone down and dusk was falling rapidly. Mosquitoes also gathered. The biggest insects, however, being the two-legged sort now not so quietly spying on them.

"Oh look," Katy drawled. "They're doing it again. Do they ever come up for air? Creed, really, you have friends here waiting to visit with you and all you want to do is play with your dolly."

Creed sighed against Linnet's lips. "I tell you, the muskeg will hide the evidence." His hand strayed to her waist, searching for her gunbelt. Damn, she'd taken it off.

"Remember the plan." She kissed him back then let him go.

Licking his lips and giving Linnet his best lascivious smile, he let her go in before him. "And oh, what a dolly," he added for Katy's benefit. Didn't hurt that Linnet blushed and smiled back over her shoulder.

"Hey, Hawk," Creed called out. "Any of that chicken and dumplings left?"

"Yeah, we saved you each a bowl."

"Good. Linnet, need help with your gear?"

"What's this?" Hawk interrupted whatever answer Linnet was about to make. "I'm leaving tomorrow and you're abandoning me tonight?"

"I thought you were leaving day after?" Creed frowned.

"I have the red-eye leaving tomorrow night." Hawk gave him a glare over folded arms.

"Not to mention, we haven't seen you in months," Pete tossed in. "And we want to get to know Linnet." Creed watched as his friend gave Linnet his best charm-the-ladies-grin. "Fabulous blueberry cobbler."

"Blueberry cobbler?" Creed looked at Linnet. "I love blueberry cobbler. From the bushes up the hill?"

"Surprise." Her grin was sheepish.

Going with the surge of happiness filling him, he wrapped his arms around her waist then lifted and swung her in a circle. Just because she had to wrap her arms around his neck to hold on didn't make it a bad thing. A side benefit really. Spinning was said to be good for the inner ear, or so he'd heard.

Breathless and a little dizzy, he didn't let go of her until he'd kissed her thoroughly again. Apparently thoroughly enough to make her breathless and dizzy, too, judging by the starry look in her eyes and her small gasps for air.

"Do you like blueberry pancakes too?"

That husky voice again. He should spin her around more often. For the next several minutes he'd have to keep her plastered to the front of him or the whole world would know just how much he relished the thought of blueberry pancakes for breakfast. "Yeah, I like blueberry pancakes. And muffins, scones, syrup... whatever you can think up to make from wild Alaska blueberries."

"I'll keep that in mind."

He also loved it when she made him promises with her smoky gaze and kissed him to underscore her words. Ungraciously, he wished the cabin's floor would slide open and whisk all their visitors away. Then again, there was a cabin next door with clean sheets on a comfortable king mattress he wanted to rumple up.

"I like blueberry pancakes." Walt spoke up, and Creed shot him a dark glare. Everyone except Katy had evil grins on their faces. Katy wore a scowl.

Only two weeks left to this affair and he didn't want to waste a moment of it. With resignation, Creed dropped his forehead to Linnet's. "I don't see how we can get out of here any time soon."

"I agree." She spoke with reluctance as well. "Maybe we can drop some tranquilizer in their coffee. One moose tranq should be enough for all five of them."

"Evil woman, I think I might fall in love with you if you keep coming up with ideas like that," he murmured against her lips. "You really have tranq darts with you?"

"A couple." The grin she gave him was a little stiff. What was up with that?

"Well hold on to that as a back-up plan. Maybe we can bore everyone to tears with old football and basketball stories."

"Hey, Linnie, what did you do with my extra wool socks?" Hawk tugged on her arm and Creed let her go. "They were on the line."

"I put them on your bunk, dolt." Linnet turned to her brother and slugged him in the arm. Their wrestling ways reminded Creed of his sister, only these days she wouldn't appreciate being held down and tickled. Her husband might have something to say about it if he tried.

# Chapter 26

Instead of being bored, Linnet was feeling down-right murderous.

Creed was talking about falling in love and she had to put up with his friends?

*One more sly remark from that bitch...* Linnet bit her lip. Again.

Katy was making a spectacle of herself and everyone knew it. Pete, in particular, was growing ever more irritated as Katy simultaneously tried to monopolize Creed and find ways to make slight digs at Linnet, all the while reliving what seemed like every moment of the ten-month period they'd dated. Apologetic glances toward her and scowls toward Creed had Pete's head swinging back and forth like a tennis spectator.

Linnet shared an exasperated glance with Creed as he once again shifted away from Katy. This time he did it with an exaggerated yawn and stretch. Katy managed to put her enhanced breast in the way and it looked as if Creed had used the excuse of a yawn to feel her up. He immediately pulled his hand away but it was too late.

"Geeze, Katy, did you leave any silicone for the other patients?" Creed tried to make a joke of it. Everyone but Pete and Katy snorted into their coffee cups. Predictably, Linnet was the only one who earned Katy's glare. That's when Linnet decided she was done and stood.

Trudy had helped with the dishes, so Linnet didn't feel bad about leaving her tea mug beside the dishpan. Everything else could wait. For now, she wanted to sleep. Fortunately she had a place to escape to. Without a word she moved to her bunk and swept the few things on the crate next to it into her duffle. Everything else had been packed earlier, as was her habit when the clothes were clean. She'd worry about the bedding later as she didn't need it tonight.

A looming shadow fell over her as she stood and slung the strap over her shoulder. Just Hawk. "I'm sorry to leave you with the company, but I have to get out here," she whispered.

"I know. I was just coming to get Manley's blankets. Figured you'd want him in the other cabin tonight."

"Yeah, I do." She looked into his eyes hidden by the shadows.

After so many nights of sunshine past midnight, this heavy darkness at ten-thirty felt strange. Already there were four fewer hours of daylight than a month ago. The change of seasons happened more swiftly this far north. And she'd thought Anchorage was fast. The darkness in this part of the cabin made it hard to read Hawk's eyes, but she felt a great sense of restraint about him.

"Creed's done his best to shut her down without actually tossing her ass outside. Once you two are gone I'll try to get everyone to bunk down for the night. I might even sleep outside myself."

"You want the keys to my truck? The bench seat isn't so bad for a night."

Hawk pulled her into a hug while Creed told the others to pick a bunk from the other two sets. "I'll be fine. I can put up with it for one night. The others are okay, but you seem to bring out the worst in one little bitch."

"Funny how that happens. I don't get it," she sighed.

"You're pretty, smart, and fun to be around. You're competition of the worst sort. You make her look bad without even trying."

"Right, that's why I sit alone when I go to bars. I'll remember that." Linnet lightly punched him in the ribs and pushed away. Did she want her bath bucket? There were still all those candles out by the tub, just waiting to be lit. Not to mention the tub had been ready for hours. She grabbed it and the two clean towels folded on her bed. "You can sleep in my bunk tonight if you want. The comfort of an air mattress."

"What? And lose all my tough conditioning? No thank you." Hawk chucked her under the chin and moved away so she could get out of the cabin sooner.

"You're leaving so soon?" Katy's voice was shrill as Linnet reached the cabin door. All she had to do was slip out the door and hopefully sleep late enough the travelers wouldn't wait around in the morning.

"G'night all," she said and waved as best she could with her arms full. "Manley, come."

"Whoa, let me help there." Creed took the duffle strap from her shoulder and another minute was wasted getting untangled. "Give me a sec and I'll grab some drinking water. Do you want the champagne tonight?"

"I just want out of here... like an hour ago," she whispered furiously.

"I know, me too. I'm right behind you."

Without waiting for him, Linnet struck off down the path leaving behind the half-hearted protests that she was going to bed too soon. Thankfully the moon was bright enough she didn't need a flashlight. Hers was in her duffle. With luck, Creed would remember matches to light the oil lamps. Manley, with his superior vision, led the way, then followed her into the smaller cabin.

The screen door had barely slammed shut when she heard the slap of the other one. By the time she had the towels and bath bucket set on the dresser, footsteps sounded on the porch. A heartbeat later, Creed stepped through the door and eased it shut.

"I wish I'd made Pete put the doorknob on completely," he stated. "We'll have to put a chair in front of the door when we go to bed." A plastic gallon jug of fresh water thumped onto the dresser. "Either that or make Manley our doorstop."

"Fine." Irritation made the word short.

"Ah, sweet bird, I'm sorry." Her duffle hit the floor along with Manley's blankets and Creed's arms came around her from behind. Barely enough light came from the woodstove to see two feet and shadows danced in the corners, but it was quiet.

"I know. You didn't know they'd be here." A deep breath and cleansing sigh didn't do much to relieve her tension. "For the most part I liked them." Admitting that made her feel a little better and less bitchy.

"For the most part Katy was a pain in the ass," Creed chuckled. "It would have been a nice evening without her around. I'm so sorry. The other three are decent folks. I could tell Trudy likes you. Walt and Pete do as well, but Katy made it hard for them to get to really know you."

"I don't mind that part. I don't want them to get to know me. All that would do is put undue pressure on you to produce me again for a social situation." Linnet straightened. That admission felt like self pity, but it reminded her, this affair was short lived. Only two weeks, at the very most, were left of it. "We should get some oil in at least one lamp. It's pretty dark in here."

"I'll take the lamps outside and fill them. Can you stick a few more logs in the woodstove?" Creed nodded toward a large basket set in the corner filled with the split wood.

"Yeah, I'll take care of it."

Creed was back a few minutes later and set a lamp on each bedside table. "I forgot matches. We should have a couple boxes in here at least."

"For now we just need to keep the fire going."

"True enough, and a pretty fire it is." Creed wrapped his arms around her again. "We need to let the wicks soak up the oil for a bit. What say we go enjoy some hot water?"

"Yeah." That was what they needed. Hot water to relax and soothe. Wet flesh to rekindle the spark.

Both eager, less than five minutes later they were beside the tub, divesting the rest of their clothes, most of which were already on the floor of the cabin. Linnet lit the candles with the matches she'd left behind earlier that day and soon a warm glow of soft light eased the dark.

Manley found his dry spot to curl up. Familiar with the routine, Linnet bent to scratch his head. He knew they'd be there awhile.

"Let me see the final strip show," Creed said gruffly. His jeans and shoes were already off and he held out a hand to her.

Slowly, one button at a time, she opened the oversized flannel shirt she wore for basic modesty. Each button brought her one step closer to him until the buttons were open and Creed began to ease the shirt from her shoulders.

"I've dreamed of this almost every night," he told her, his lips on her neck.

"Me too," she whispered and dropped her head to the side. Did she dare tell him how much she'd missed him? Would that sound too needy?

Creed followed the falling shirt with his hands and just before it hit the damp ground, he rescued it and put it on the rock. "It's almost cool out here. Ready for some hot water?"

"Yes." In the water where he'd touch her and she'd wash him, teasing him... "You sit in front and I'll scrub your back."

"Wait, let's do this Japanese style and scrub out here, then soak in clean hot water."

"All right." Linnet emptied her bucket. It was perfect to scoop water from the tub to pour over him. "Complete wash, sir?"

"By all means. I'm all yours." Spreading his arms wide, he grinned as she poured the first bucketful over his head. "Ah, I love that water. Always the perfect temperature."

Glad she'd put her hair up to keep it dry since she'd already washed it earlier, Creed made a game out of using his body to rub the soap suds on her. When he, too, was covered head to toe, they took turns rinsing each other with the bucket. Linnet's loofah had been used in many creative ways to make her body tingle and she was eager to make love in the water.

"In with you, wench."

"After you."

Water splashed over the edge as they settled in, Linnet's back to Creed's chest. His arms came around her, feeling so right, as if this was where they both belonged.

"This feels... so good," Creed groaned. "I never want to leave here, unless it's to wrap myself around you in that new bed. I made them get a good mattress."

"You went far beyond my expectations in furnishings. It's beautiful, Creed." The thought she might not ever see it again once she left here was enough to twist her heart. It was the kind of cabin she could see herself in for many years to come. And he'd built it for her... for just a two-week end to their affair. It was enough to make one want to weep, but she'd save her tears for later, when she was alone in her small apartment in Anchorage.

Wanting to hang on to the good times, Linnet turned in Creed's arms and straddled his thighs. Ah, there was the twinkle she loved to see. If nothing else, Creed had taught her to go with her sense of adventure while making love.

*Sex. While having sex.*

"You're so beautiful." The gruff softness of his voice combined with the look of heat in his eyes did wonderful things to her.

Trained well, her body was instantly ready for sex. Creed reached out a hand to play with a damp tendril of hair that had escaped the clip holding most of it up. "With your hair like this, you look so proper, and yet... the little wet pieces hint at the wicked woman inside."

"And you look like a cowboy rogue," she teased back. "All you need is a cigar and a glass of whiskey to complete the image."

"A cowboy in after a long day on the range. Already had the good meal. The cleansing part of the bath is done. Now all I need is the soft woman to fulfill the rest of my needs."

"What if I want to be the cowgirl? What if I'm the one looking for a stallion to ride?"

"I think we can take care of each other, don't you?"

Linnet leaned forward until their chests touched and their lips were separated by less than a half inch. One of Creed's hands circled her nape, the other lazily stroked the side of her breast. Both of them fought to control the urgency of their breaths.

"Oh yes," she murmured. "Yes."

Creed's lips met hers and without waiting, his tongue entered her mouth as eagerly as she sucked it in. Alone, at last, at least part of their fantasy for this evening would become reality. His hands explored as if relearning her body, but also with familiarity. He knew those spots to tease, what pressure to place where.

Wanting him to be as mad with desire as she was, she touched, licked, kissed, and nipped as well. Long, knowing fingers reached between her legs and teased by stroking and tugging, brushing and penetrating. Water sloshed over the side of the tub with greater abandon and Linnet felt herself spiraling upward. So fast, so hot... Creed took her to new and wonderful places and she craved more. Reaching, gasping, she held back, wanting him to fly with her, but he pressed onward with his hands, driving her mad...

"Oh damn, the place is already occupied."

Linnet barely heard the voice or noticed the beam of light in her eyes as she tipped over the edge of no return. Creed held her while she rode the crest, unable to process the fact they had an audience. She heard voices, but Creed's hands never left her until awareness began to return and she collapsed onto his chest.

"Come *on*, Katy," Linnet heard Pete's voice at last and a chill chased away the promised amazing afterglow. "They want to be alone. It's all they've wanted all night long."

"Give us ten minutes, and then you can have the tub," Creed snapped.

Linnet rested her head against Creed's, her nerves tight with tension once more.

"Pete's got her," he whispered, nuzzling her neck.

They both listened as Katy's bitching faded back down the trail.

"Do I have to be nice to her?" Linnet still trembled but whether from fury, embarrassment or lingering orgasmic bliss she had no clue.

"Nah. I'll make the guys help me finish the windows in the morning, take them fishing for an hour, then float their butts downstream. Sound reasonable?"

"Yeah, it does. Don't suppose we could put a life jacket on Katy and toss her in the river. Floating with the current, she could reach Circle about the time they do."

"I love how you think," Creed chuckled.

Damn, that was twice now tonight he mentioned love. Katy had better stay out of the way tomorrow.

* * * *

For the second time in a few hours, Katy had killed Linnet's fragile mood.

Creed was as ready as Linnet to hurt her for it. Instead he helped Linnet clean out the tub then, start it refilling. They blew out the candles before finding their way back to the sleeping cabin.

Inside, with the oil lamps now lit and mingling with the glow from the woodstove, it was cozy inside. All he needed to do was rekindle the mood. He watched as she shook out what looked like dime-store reject blankets. She chose that moment to look up and must have caught the look on his face.

"Curtains," was all she said.

"Ah, privacy." Yeah, he could appreciate that.

"And a touch of insulation, since all we have is screening at the moment."

"Let me help."

She handed him a corner and he copied her by hanging it on a nail over the window. By the time they finished, the cozy feeling had doubled. Or maybe it was the sight of her long legs and the way his shirt rose up to show more of them as she reached over head. Either way, Creed had the strongest urge to go to bed. Immediately.

"Linnet," he growled. The low gruffness of his voice surprised her, judging by the way she turned to him, eyes wide. "Come here. I need you." The hand he held out to her all but commanded her. Only the slightest hesitation slowed her response.

After their bath, all he had left on was his jeans. More than anything he wanted her to remove them, but first he needed to dispel the strange frame of mind she seemed to be in.

Linnet's clean scent filled his lungs as she took his hand and stepped close. Large and luminous in the soft light, her green eyes seemed darker. Some deep thought clouded them and he almost asked what was on her mind. Did he really want to know? This was usually the point in a relationship he started stepping away. Women wanted to talk about things. He just wanted them to be.

A long moment passed as they stared at each other. Shifting emotions in her eyes spoke almost as clearly as if she'd said them out loud. Women needed to base their relationships in something emotional, but they'd agreed the only emotion practical between them was friendship. And friends were concerned with each other's feelings, right? So did that mean he wanted to know what she was feeling? Was it her eyes or his thoughts that made his head feel light?

As he was trying to decide, the clouds vanished from Linnet's eyes and he was staring at the woman he'd laughed with and teased only two weeks ago. The Linnet who had come out of her shell as soon as they'd been left—almost—alone. That should be relief he felt as she leaned towards him, lips raised for a kiss, eyes hooded with desire as she touched his waist.

The physical swamped him. Linnet could do that to him in a heartbeat. Her touch, her taste... his hands sought out and found her nakedness under the shirt. Cupping her ass—her perfect, smooth skinned, firm muscled ass that fit his hands as if molded just for him—he hauled her up against him.

Toothpaste sweet, her mouth was cool and hot all at once as he plunged his tongue into the luscious depths. He felt the softness of her breasts, the points of her nipples through the flannel shirt, her hands trapped between them as she lowered the zipper on his pants. Infinitely careful, she shielded him from the rough zipper and tugged the waistband down over his hips.

Soft flannel, rather than soft skin, touched him. She wiggled, just enough to stimulate him, while easing his jeans down until they dropped to the floor. One kick and he was out of them, wanting her out of the shirt she'd adopted as her own.

Linnet's hand around his cock provided her with a level of control he'd never given to another woman. What was it about her touch that made him lose his mind this way? Willing to go wherever she wanted, he stepped backward as she stepped forward, urging him toward some destination. With their kiss still raging, he didn't notice or care much until the backs of his thighs hit the high mattress of the bed.

"Pull the covers back," she muttered into his mouth.

"But then," he nibbled on her lower lip, "I'll have to let go of you."

"Do it."

"Yes, ma'am." He gave in, and blindly reached behind to pull back the covers they'd turned down not long ago. The cotton sheets were cool under him when she pushed him into half sitting, half leaning on the bed. "What is my lady's pleasure this evening?"

"You will sit," she licked his nose, "and watch."

He would have protested, but at that moment her hand squeezed him, her thumb over the slit where moisture already beaded. Exquisite torturess that she was, she rubbed the fluid around the head of his cock, covering every inch. Before he could vocalize anything, Linnet dropped to her knees on the floor and kissed him on the very tip.

"I thought," Creed gasped as her other hand grasped his testicles, tenderly, but still with business in mind, "you didn't blow."

Don't mess with a woman when she's holding your gonads, his dad had always said. It pretty much meant the same as it was a woman's prerogative to change her mind.

"I changed my mind," she said and looked up at him with a glare of passion. "So enjoy it before I change my mind again."

"I'm enjoying," he rushed to assure her, and followed with a groan as her mouth enclosed his cock. "Oh God," he prayed as green eyes stared up at him. He buried his fingers in her hair and searched out the release of the clip holding it up. There was nothing sexier than a woman's hair draped around him, and around his lap was even better. The slow wink she gave him was followed by a tightening deep in his groin. She was going to take this all the way...

"Linnet, honey," Creed gasped a few minutes later. Leaning back on his arms he was losing the battle for control. He had one last tactic, and that was to beg. "Sweet bird, you've got... to stop... now..." No good.

She wasn't listening, but rather as he tried to get her to back off, she increased her actions. Imprisoned by her mouth, he was enslaved by her hands. She had control and wasn't giving up. In fact, he felt her throat muscles convulse around the head of his cock and squeeze him.

"Too late..." he groaned as his body pushed away his mental restraints. Whether he wanted it or not, the oil had just left the pump station.

# Chapter 27

By the next afternoon, Linnet was regretting her agreement to let Creed's friends stay to help with the cabin. It would have been better for all if the travelers had taken off right after breakfast. Escaping to the riverbank for an hour had helped somewhat, but then Trudy had come looking for her. At least Linnet hadn't had to put up with Katy for an entire week.

When gently encouraged, Trudy had confessed the trip had been a bit of a strain and chances of it ever happening again were slim. Trudy had then asked about berry picking and they'd filled the hours until lunch harvesting everything they could find. Splitting the bounty left them both plenty of blueberries as well as rose hips and highbush cranberries. Trudy promised to write down her cranberry sauce recipe for Linnet.

The true trial had begun after lunch, when Katy decided to join the fishing trip at the last moment. Already crowded, the boat deck didn't allow for much movement. Leaning out over the side, while standing, gave Linnet a few minutes of unease each time she extended the net.

She preferred kneeling for better stability, but there just wasn't room. Hawk's hand gripping the waistband of her jeans helped. Creed was occupied helping Katy pull in a big one while Trudy was getting Pete's help on the far side of the boat.

One minute, Linnet was reaching out with the net, the next she was swallowing thick, breath-stealing cold water as it closed over her head. She reached upward, hoping her life vest would pop her to the surface. Water filled her waders, wanting to drag her down, and with one hand she fought to release the rubber belt straps holding the waders up like stockings on garters. In water this cold, she had only a minute before her brain and muscles began to dangerously shut down.

For a moment, she swore this was the end. Her face cleared the surface just enough to cough out some water and gasp for air. Silt running into her eyes made them hurt, but she was able to see Creed, his hand extended, reaching for hers as the current pulled her down a second time.

Knowing her life could very well depend on it, Linnet fought the cold shutting down her ability to think or move. One vicious kick released a boot and she bobbed upward again, her hands clawing the air, the net already a memory.

Thankfully, large hands clamped around her wrists just before the current pulled her out of reach. Coughing, Linnet could only pray while they pulled her closer to the side. Stiff with cold, all feeling had left her hands and she had to trust they had her.

Looking up, she saw Creed's face, his eyes large, his mouth moving, shouting something she couldn't make out through the rushing sound in her ears, then something large slammed into her from behind and her head hit the side of the boat. Before she could gasp again, the world went black.

* * * *

"Walt!" Creed yelled. "Cut the anchor line and get this boat back to camp!" He and Hawk tugged one more time and Linnet's limp body cleared the gunwales, her legs flopping onto the deck.

"Trudy, there're blankets up under the bow. Everyone else get back on the other side. You'll tip us all over into the drink."

With Hawk's help, Creed laid Linnet flat and started checking for vitals. She was breathing, but just barely. They rolled her onto her side anyway in case she had water to spit out. A fair amount came out with a weak cough.

"Why is she passed out?" he murmured to himself.

"Her head hit the side," Hawk answered gruffly. "The fish hit her in the back."

"My fish!" Katy exclaimed.

"Damn your fish and damn you, Katy!" Creed snarled over his shoulder. At that moment he wanted to toss her over the side and forget about trying to haul her in. Linnet was hurt and Katy was responsible.

Trudy bustled up with an armful of old army blankets. "We need to get her out of those clothes."

"As soon as we get back to shore we can put her in the tub. The water will warm her." Creed shook out a blanket.

"Yes, but we're a good ten to fifteen minutes away," Trudy said calmly.

Hawk reached for Linnet's remaining boot. "She's right. I'll get her jeans, you get her top."

Trudy's calm presence helped them strip Linnet down and wrap her up quickly.

Creed had her cradled in his arms, mercilessly rubbing her with the rough wool, as the boat surged up onto the shingle below the cabin. Hawk leaped over the side and reached for her inert body. Creed gently passed her over, then vaulted off the boat, took her back and raced for the tub.

"Bring her bath bucket and dry towels," he called over his shoulder. "Her clothes are still in her duffle."

"I'll bring them," Trudy called.

By the time he had Linnet in the tub with the stream of hot water pouring over her head, she had begun to stir, easing the fist clenched around his throat.

Trudy arrived just as Linnet's eyes popped open.

"Oh good, she's waking up. Linnet, can you focus?" Trudy leaned over the tub, staring into Linnet's eyes.

"Um, yeah… Trudy?"

"Very good."

Creed heard the smile in his friend's voice and another finger of fear loosened.

"How's your vision? Clear? Or am I fuzzy?"

"Clear. What…?"

"You went for an accidental swim." Creed leaned over the tub and kissed her forehead. "A big fish whacked you upside the head as well."

"That bitch," Linnet growled. "She pushed me in. Her knee knocked me off balance and then she hip-checked me right over the side."

Creed exchanged a glance with Trudy. It was possible. He hadn't been watching because he'd been focused on bringing in the king. Had Hawk seen anything?

"Katy's being dealt with," Trudy said calmly. "We're pulling out immediately so we can dump her off in town faster."

Creed shook his head. "It's too late to head downstream and make Circle before it gets dark. She's not worth endangering the rest of you."

"We'll make it in plenty of time. We'll be out of your hair within the hour. Just as soon as everyone see's Linnet is okay. Especially Hawk."

Hawk was probably out of his mind with worry. Shit. Hawk. Had to run him down to Circle so he could drive out with enough time to catch his plane.

"Yeah, you'd better go tell him she's awake and should be just fine," Creed said and rested a hand on Trudy's shoulder. "I've got her here. As soon as she's warmed up and looking pink again I'll bring her back.

Please make sure the woodstove in the little cabin is stoked, would you? Get one of the guys to do it."

Trudy patted his cheek. "I'll take care of it. They all need something to do to keep from strangling one of our party. Can't say I blame them." With a last wink, she waved and left the two of them alone.

"Linnie?" Creed turned back to look at her deeply submerged in the tub. "Any objection to me crawling in there with you?"

"Not a one. Please do."

That was all he needed to hear. Clothes tossed on the rock, he eased into the water behind her and pulled her close. "I was so scared."

"You were scared?" Linnet's laugh was interrupted by a cough. "Feels like I swallowed a gallon of silt."

"How's the head?"

"A little sore. I'm guessing my forehead hit the boat?"

"Yeah, it was a pretty good clunk if I'm remembering right. All I saw was your face and hands as you tried to clear the surface."

*There* was an image that would strike terror in his heart for years to come. Linnet, white faced, staring up through the water like some horror movie wraith. Just thinking of it sent his heart into panic mode again. He pulled her closer and gently tucked her head under his chin. "You've had a rough shift out here."

"And all due to other people." Still shaking, she leaned against him with a sigh and he wrapped more of his body around her trying to touch and warm every inch of her. "Other than you catching me that first evening, everything else happened because someone thought they were doing something nice for me. Well, except for this last incident."

"And I was there to play hero every time." He had mixed feelings over that. He'd given her the wine that had triggered the flashback. At this point he was amazed she wanted him close, but was greatly gratified when she nuzzled the underside of his jaw.

"Yes, yes you were. You've pulled me out of the river twice now, out of nightmares I don't know how many times, and out of a flashback, and you tended every mosquito bite. Not only that, you taught me to like salmon and how to pan for gold."

"And you made my cabin more comfortable and made living out here more fun than I can ever remember." Needing action before he started sobbing, he reached for the bottle of soap. "Let me wash the river out of your hair. I'm sure that will make you feel better."

"Yes," she sighed. "No one has ever taken care of me like you do. I'm getting spoiled."

Creed's heart thumped in his chest. He wanted to spoil her more. Careful of the bump on her head, he massaged the soap into a low lather, working it through the long strands to make sure every grain of glacier silt washed away. Using the stream from the sluice, he rinsed her hair, taking the opportunity to kiss her neck.

He was still shaking from fear and carefully touched her everywhere he could reach, kissed her temple and cheek, assuring himself she was whole and breathing. Even when he'd been dunked in the river in much the same way, he hadn't been as scared as he'd been when Linnet went under the second time.

The fall had happened too fast. It had been watching her face, white and wide-eyed with fright that had pushed the adrenalin to maximum in his blood. He and Hawk had pulled so hard, Creed was vaguely surprised her arms were still in their sockets.

When Linnet looked over her shoulder, big green eyes staring up at him, it broke his control. He pulled her over so her breasts pressed against his chest and tugged on her thighs until she straddled him.

"Linnet," he whispered against her lips.

"Yes," she answered. "This is... I need..." She lowered herself onto him, bare skin wrapping around him in a feeling so exquisite he nearly fainted.

No protection... the thought flashed through his head then flashed right out again. They'd deal with the consequences later. If there were any. Surely once was safe. His hands wrapped around her hips, pulling her down, pulling her against him, pulling her open more. Thrusting up, he felt the tip of his cock kiss the opening of her womb and a surge of testosterone consumed him. She cried out and rose up, her hands clutching his shoulders.

"Oh... Creed... yes... oh... right... there!"

With each thrust he felt the deepest reaches of her body and she held him there with tightly clenched muscles. The heat, the softness, the friction... it all blended until it felt as if their bodies were molten gold, blending, fusing, melding together. The woods around them faded as a blinding white light seemed to envelope them, transporting them beyond the earthly realm.

It was so sweet, so fine, so completely encompassing... all that existed in that moment was Linnet, and him, in their little slice of heaven. When the climax came, they both shouted and it seemed as if it came from far away. Creed held on to the moment as long as he could, his arms holding her safe as she collapsed on top of him. Silence reigned for long pounding heartbeats and then the world rushed in on a whoosh of bird wings and song.

And that's when it occurred to Creed. Despite all his best efforts to remain unattached, he'd been hooked but good.

# Chapter 28

Creed made sure Linnet was tucked in bed with a cup of tea before he let anyone see her. Hawk was first and he entered with his hands behind his back.

"I have something for you."

She watched as he pulled what looked like a half split birch log about eighteen inches long from behind his back and held it across his chest so she could see it. On the rounded side, an elongated oval had been carved through the bark. Hawk sat on the side of the bed so she could see it better. Carved deep into the oval it said "Linnet's Nest" with blackened letters.

"I used charcoal from the fire, but with a little more time I would have used paint and then sealed it with varnish. It's rough, but in a way, it fits the place."

"'Linnet's Nest'? Where did you get that name?" The oddest sense of wonder filled her as she asked the question, but even before Hawk could answer she looked at Creed. The smile on his face told her exactly where the name had come from.

"I figured you'd started feathering your nest here, making it feel more homelike than it ever has…" Creed's voice trailed off and he shrugged. "He's right, it fits." Creed's smile softened and his eyes warmed. "Just like you fit."

Unable to hold back the tears wanting to spill from her eyes, Linnet hid them by wrapping her arms around Hawk. Nobody let Katy in to say goodbye, but Trudy, Walt and Pete each gave her a hug and a kiss on the cheek. Pete was the most apologetic. Their goodbyes were kept short and Creed followed them out. Hawk sat on the bed one more time for a long, tight hug.

"Take care of yourself," he said gruffly.

"Should be easy now everyone is leaving."

"Ha, ha."

"Honestly, I did just fine before you all started showing up." She cuffed him gently. It was all she could do to keep her eyes open long enough to wish him a safe journey. She barely felt Creed pull the covers up and tuck them around her shoulders. He kissed her forehead and made her promise to stay in bed while he ran Hawk downstream to his rental car. Alone at last, she relaxed into the down pillows and dreamed of blond babies with dark brown eyes.

# Chapter 29

Who knew having fun could take so much energy and concentration? Linnet spent an extra few minutes in the outhouse, where she could at least let her smile relax. She wasn't going to ruin the next few days by letting him see how much this was killing her.

Ever since her swim in the river, Creed had been hovering, waiting on her hand and foot. Pampering her to within an inch of her life. Each cough, sneeze or sniffle had his immediate attention. He was terrified the silt-laden water had gotten into her lungs and would make her sick. Hadn't happened yet, but she loved his attention. Mostly. At times it was a bit oppressive, but mostly it was fun and made her feel better than she ever had in her whole life.

Leaving would be the hardest thing she'd ever done. She'd run from California with few regrets. Resuming her lonely life in Anchorage was going to be downright depressing. But she wasn't going to show Creed. She'd say her goodbyes cheerfully even if it killed her once and for all.

Friday morning. They'd had just over a week to themselves and had enjoyed every waking moment. Or rather, almost every moment—when she wasn't pretending not to be in love with him. Every time she'd been about to tell him how she really felt, what she dreamed of at night, she remembered one particular conversation with George while Creed was on the Slope. George had brought up a load of lumber from town and, while Hawk worked on the cabin, the older man had helped with data gathering.

That clear afternoon, while pulling in fish and cataloging their attributes, she and George had spoken quite plainly. The conversation was crystal clear in her memory. Usually quiet, George had been fussing most of the morning, asking questions about her plans for the future.

"Spit it out George." Linnet didn't have to look at him to know he had something to say.

"None of my business."

"Uh huh." She pulled in the net. The smallish fish didn't give her much trouble. Certainly nothing she needed help with. "Spend much time repeating that to yourself, hoping you'll believe it sooner rather than later?"

"You're a nice girl, Linnet."

"And you don't want to see me get hurt."

"Yeah. Something like that."

"Don't worry," she told him, quite able to work while she talked. "Twenty-five pounds."

"I do worry." He wrote down the number.

"I know the rules. When I leave here, it's over. I know where I stand in the scheme of things. I've given myself permission to have some fun this summer. No strings attached in either direction." She gave George the rest of the vital statistics then waded back into the river.

"You're not the kind of girl who has flings. Creed knows that just as well as I do."

"But he is the kind of guy to have flings. And I'm worse than most of the women he knows. I'm damaged goods." The more she thought about it, the more she was convinced she'd been drugged at least one other time. After Billy. But the details eluded her and she pushed the vague uneasiness away again. "I'm fine for a little fun, but definitely one to run from when it's over. Were we in town, it would be over by now. One night and he'd be gone. It's only because we're out here it's lasted this long and will last a little longer." She pushed the net out into the river again. "Don't worry, I won't hold it against either him or you. I'll still be able to do my job."

To keep George talking, and to remind herself why the rules were in place, she'd asked blunt questions. Respecting her need for truth, George had given in and told her quite plainly how and why each of Creed's affairs had ended. Bottom line—Creed didn't like clinging, whining women, and those were the first signs each one had demonstrated as soon as he started packing to return to work.

Well, she wasn't one of those women. Her father's frequent departures for military duty had taught her to be a brave little soldier. That was one skill she had down pat. Creed, she learned, also hadn't liked the follow-on in the form of phone calls and emails, which was why, George said, he generally didn't contact Creed on the Slope. When Creed was there, he was at work.

So she'd kept contact to a minimum while Creed worked. No phone calls at all, and only a few emails that pertained to the building of the cabin. Not one comment from Creed either encouraging or complaining about the emails, so maybe she'd done well. And since he'd returned, she found herself clasping her hands behind her back more and more to keep from reaching out to touch him. If anyone reached out to do the touching, nine times out of ten it was Creed, reaching for her. The more she danced out of his arms, the more he reached for her. Almost every part of the woods surrounding the cabin had been used for lovemaking.

Sex.

*Don't call it lovemaking.* Keep it impersonal.

She spread her fingers to count. Today—Friday. Tomorrow—Saturday. Sunday. Then, sometime on Monday, they'd both pack up and leave. Creed usually had dinner with his parents the day before heading for the Slope. Linnet decided for sure she'd drop off to visit with George. She'd never dream of taking Manley with her.

While he seemed content to be with her, he belonged with George. Monday she'd take Manley home, then find a hotel for the night. She and George could do the preliminary reports by email and then spend the winter dissecting the data. The drive was too long to head for Anchorage on Monday, so, bright and early Tuesday morning, as Creed was boarding his plane for the Slope, she'd hit the highway south toward her apartment.

Three days left to enjoy her time with Creed. Starting now.

Linnet adjusted her jeans and left the seclusion of the outhouse. The scent of bacon drifted out a window and mixed with the scent of Fall. Nearly overnight, the seasons had changed. Decaying leaves covered the ground and bushes flamed red. The bacon, as much as the beauty, made her smile. At least with all their gymnastics she'd been able to eat without worrying too much about the calories.

Manley met her at the door and she stopped to pet him. "Just a few more days, buddy. Bet you'll be happy to be home with George, eh?" Tears popped into her eyes without warning. No good, she blinked to clear them away. "Come on, Manley. Did that man feed you yet?"

"I did," Creed called out. "And he has fresh water too."

"How are we on supplies?" she asked as the door shut behind her. The mornings were chill enough to require a fire in the woodstove and she wanted to keep the heat in.

"It'll be close, but we're good." Creed turned to smile at her. "If we don't have any unexpected guests we have enough vegetables. If we do, then we make more biscuits and add water to the soup."

Linnet nodded. There were plenty of packets of dried soup mix tucked into sparkling clean glass jars. A casual comment at the store in Circle had resulted in half a dozen waiting for her the next trip down the river. There were jars for potato flakes, pancake mix, rice, beans and powdered milk. Any traveler seeking shelter over the winter would find plenty to keep them fed and warm for a few days. Or Creed would, if he came out on his snow machine. Before the thought could grow on her any more, Linnet stifled the desire to come out in the winter. There were other places she could go. Places far closer to Anchorage, and not nearly as cold as it could get deep in the Interior.

Stomach rumbling with hunger she moved closer to see what Creed was cooking. At least she wasn't expected to cook all their meals. By unspoken agreement they shared the duties, right down to clean up. Though she was the one who invariably washed the dishes, Creed was there to dry and put them away. It felt companionable.

"Here, you'll scare away the moose with all that noise." Creed held a piece of hot bacon out to her. Crispy, just the way she liked it.

"What can I do to help?" she offered, then bit into the salty strip.

"Pour the coffee and get out some utensils. The eggs are almost ready."

The last of the fresh eggs bubbled in the pan. To one side Creed had placed crumbled bacon, the last tomato diced, and some shredded cheddar. Her favorite omelet. The smile she gave him was genuine as she kissed his cheek and reached for the silverware.

"Do I have time to check email?" It had been a few days. Wouldn't hurt to check while George was still in the office. Maybe he had some last minute instructions.

"Nope. Breakfast will be ready before that machine boots up."

"'Kay."

While they ate, her thoughts must have been clear. Lifting his coffee cup with a sigh, Creed shook his head. "Go ahead and start it up. Something's bugging you."

"Hmm?" Linnet looked up from her half-full plate.

"Your eyes keep straying to the computer. Turn it on. I won't have your full attention until you check your email."

"It's been at least three days since I last checked."

"Don't get all defensive. You're right. You haven't been online and I can see it's getting to you." His dark eyes danced with humor. "I want your complete attention for the next three days."

Ah, so he was counting as well. Ruthlessly she stamped down on the small curl of hope. Hope, what good was it? Men couldn't be changed. When his eyes darkened, she had the feeling he could read her like an open book even though his thoughts were hidden. Turning her face away, she concentrated on pushing buttons before turning back to her food.

Omelet finished, Linnet sipped her coffee as email started downloading. Only twenty messages, not bad. Mom, George, and dratted Henry again, she sighed. He wasn't going away, but at least she'd managed to talk him out of flying up for now. Henry would rather wait until she was back in the city again. For that reason alone she was letting him believe she was staying at the river at least another month. Maybe by then she could move and get an unlisted number. Anchorage was big enough that a person could hide in it if they wanted to.

"Anything interesting?"

Linnet glanced at Creed to see him looking mildly interested.

"Looks like the usual. George says he'll be at the office Monday if I want to bring Manley by there when I get to town. Mom is lobbying to get me home for a week or two. Having Hawk home for a few days has made her lonely for old times. Probably wants me to help her bake cookies for Christmas."

"You bake Christmas cookies?" Creed's lifted brow indicated interest. "Then again, considering what you did with the blueberry cobbler, I'd have to say you're probably a very good baker."

"We do all right. Mom starts baking in October and freezes them for giving out at Christmas." Come to think of it, a week in Mom's kitchen would be rather soothing. Might help her get over Creed and help her move on. At least now she felt she could get into the dating scene.

"Anything else interesting?"

"Nothing catastrophic... Wait. Who's this?"

"Hmm?"

"Kerstin Willis?" Linnet pinned her gaze on Creed. "I only know one Willis, is it safe to assume she belongs to you?"

"That would be Mom," Creed sighed. "What does she say?"

"Um," Linnet opened the email. "Uh, well..." The message made her swallow deeply. Just what they didn't need. "Your parents expect to arrive in Circle around two o'clock today and would appreciate it if we took the boat down to pick them up. They have some winter supplies with them and want to spend the weekend out here. If we aren't there by three they'll drive in." Two spots of heat rushed her cheeks. Great. His parents. "Said she got my email from George since she couldn't think of any other way to contact you."

"Well, at least we get fair warning." Creed glanced at his watch. "It's just ten now. We have time. When did she send the message?"

"Last night." Oh God, where were they going to sleep? "I guess we'd better give them the sleeping cabin."

"Why do you say that?"

Without looking she knew his gaze was drilling into her. The burn across her cheeks grew more intense. "Well, it just seems like the right thing to do."

"Linnet."

She knew he wanted her to look at him, but she just couldn't. Maybe it would just be better to pack up her truck now. His parents could help him get the boat downstream and on the trailer for the haul back to Fairbanks. It would save a couple of trips up and down the fragile road.

Creed's finger under her chin made her look up. "That cabin was built for you, and I'm not giving it up to my parents or anyone. Only you and I have a key to it. The cabin is for you to enjoy—hopefully with me."

"But Creed, your parents... what will they think?"

"Honey, they bought the furnishings. They know the cabin was built for you. In case you haven't figured it out, George has a big mouth. He just hides it well from strangers. They know everything George knows about you."

Linnet felt the heat rush from her face to be replaced by icy cold. "But... we only have three days left... before..." *before we go our separate ways.* She couldn't say it out loud. Which made the point about a key moot. Unless she was invited back to work the river next summer, she wouldn't come back. Chances of that happening... her heart sank right down to her toes.

Creed pulled his chair closer without relinquishing his hold on her chin. "Sweet bird, this isn't the end."

"Yes, it is. We agreed before we started..."

"You agreed. You said. I didn't say one way or another."

"No..." A loud buzz from her computer made them both look. An instant messaging window had popped open. Looking away from Creed's intent eyes was a relief, if only for a moment.

"George," Linnet said, her voice too breathy for her liking.

"You can ignore him," Creed said and turned her chin again. "We're not done with our discussion."

"There's nothing to discuss. I'll get the cabin ready for your parents." It took an effort, but she freed herself from his grasp and turned to the computer. "George wants to make sure we got the message." Fingers flying, she responded, keeping a running commentary going for Creed's benefit. "Says he'll call and let them know. He also has a list for me. I have some work to do still..." Could she get it done in the next few hours?

"Also, he wants to know what time we expect to be in town, or rather when I expect to be in town." Babbling, she was absolutely babbling. Anything to redirect his attention. Did she have to make it sound like they were returning to town together? No way. Creed had his routine. Once she drove down that road she was on her own and headed for home.

"Anyhow, I guess I'd better think about that..." she barely got her fingers out of the way before Creed slammed the laptop shut and turned off the sat phone.

"Linnet, stop."

She couldn't. Fingers trembling, she grasped them together trying to hide her nervousness. Creed's friends had been bad enough. How could she face his parents? With that thought she shot to her feet.

"I'll go change the sheets on the bed now." She dodged the arm he held out to stop her end-run around him. "You want me to put the dirty ones in your duffle? You'll need to take them home to wash... well, no, I can wash them." She glanced out the window at the clear sky. "Yes, that will work. I'll go fill the tub now and get them soaking. Everything will be ready by the time they get here. You'll just have to fold and put the clean sheets away once they're dry on the line." She glanced over her shoulder and rushed to the clothesline. Might as well take her clean clothes and pack them now. Last night's fire in the woodstove had dried them quite nicely.

"Linnet." Creed wrapped himself around her from behind and held her arms, his hands making hers stop plucking clothes pins from the line. The one she held dropped to the floor, making a clattering noise as it bounced on the clean varnished planks. "Stop, sweetheart. There's nothing to be upset about."

"I'm not upset. There's so much to do to get ready..."

His lips on her neck worked their usual magic. It wasn't fair he could do this to her. Now, of all times.

"We're not preparing for royalty, pretty bird. It's just my folks and they're used to this cabin. It's already in far better shape than they've seen it in years. What's wrong? You haven't been this jumpy since the first few days we knew each other."

"Nothing's wrong. I just can't sleep in the other cabin, with you, knowing they're in here. I just can't, Creed." He had to understand. It just wasn't done. Just as Creed had slept across the cabin after the first night when her father was there, she couldn't run off to the small cabin while they were here.

"I can see I'm going to have to find a way to keep you busy until it's time to go pick them up."

Traitor that her body was, her breath hitched and heat sluiced through her at the touch of his lips. Gentle teeth bit her nape.

"This isn't fair."

"All's fair in love and war."

"This isn't love," she gasped the words.

"You're partly right, this is mostly war," he growled in her ear. "But love is at stake, and if the war is lost we both lose."

"You've never mentioned love before," she groaned, as he turned her in his arms.

He had, as a joke, but they'd been interrupted by river travelers. His friends.

"Because every time I even think of mentioning it, you find a way to change the subject or distract me." His lips danced over her throat, seeking out each tender spot like a man looking for a drop of water in the desert.

"Creed!" She pushed against his chest. "Stop this, right now." Panic made her voice shrill.

Though he still held her, he allowed her some room, a half step back. Under her hands on his chest, his heart pounded every bit as fiercely as hers. Dark eyes under half-closed lids stared intently at her. He drew in breath and she rushed to fill the silence before he spoke.

"Creed, I'm thankful for what you've done for me, what you've taught me, but if I let you convince me to go to bed now, then it's all lost. I'll be right back there, not trusting anyone, much less any man. Don't ruin it all. It's been wonderful, it's been a dream come true and I'm grateful, but it isn't real and you know it too."

Creed opened his mouth and she covered it with her fingers. "Don't. Don't turn the dream into a nightmare. I've cherished my time here, our time together, but it can't last. Let me go now before things really fall apart. Let me go with grace and dignity. Don't put me on display for your parents, your friends, or anybody else. It's bad enough the river folks all wink and nod when they see us."

Creed's mouth worked soundlessly behind her fingers until he finally set his jaw, lips firmly shut.

"Please, Creed. I'd hoped to put this off until Monday, but my hand has been forced. I can't stay now. I have to leave or lose every bit of my self respect.

Some deep emotion flashed deep in Creed's eyes. Pain lanced Linnet's heart. "It's too late, Creed. We've lost the advantage of a casual, but sincere goodbye. There's nothing else to say." *Nothing but I love you.*

"There's plenty to say." Creed's hands dropped away, and he stepped back. "But I can see you won't believe me." He ran a hand through his hair, a gesture she hadn't seen before but it spoke clearly of his frustration. "What have I done to you? I've never lied to you. Why do you have to throw us away like this?"

Linnet spread her hands helplessly. "You know what I've been through..."

"That's bullshit, Linnet. Something to hide behind." Hurt and angry eyes accused her of being a coward. Well, she was. Always had been.

Unable to face her own pain, much less his, she turned away and blindly jerked pins from her clothes on the line. Too much moisture filled her eyes for her to see properly.

Creed stood behind her, silent and staring. She wanted to scream for him to leave her alone. Somehow he must have got the message because the next thing she heard was him directing Manley to come, followed by the slam of both doors.

Well, she'd handled that well. Not.

Hell, the break up with Henry had been much smoother. Blinking rapidly, she reached the end of the laundry line and stopped at the pair of socks she'd recently finished knitting for Creed. He didn't even know they were for him yet. She'd washed them with her laundry yesterday thinking she'd tuck them into his duffle as a surprise to find when he reached home. She could take them and fondle them, remembering each stitch she'd made while thinking of him and his smile when he found them. He'd teased her about them, watching as she spent evenings talking with him while knitting by the fire. Or she could leave them... Well, they wouldn't fit her, so she left them on the line. It would hurt too much to put them in his luggage now.

# Chapter 30

Creed pushed the throttle to full and, for just a heartbeat, wished it was Linnet's neck with his hands wrapped around it. He'd never done so much for a woman, had never bent so far backward to please one and she'd thrown it all back in his face. Just because he hadn't spent the last two weeks speaking gibberish to her. He was the one who walked away.

No woman had ever used him and then dumped him so coldly before. Maybe it was just as well. As she continuously reminded him, Linnet was damaged goods and he should have remembered victims didn't always really want to be rescued.

The pain from slamming his hand into the steering wheel barely made an impression on him. Dammit! She was *grateful*. He didn't want her to be grateful, he wanted her to be in love with him. He wanted her in his house in Fairbanks. He wanted her in that bed he'd bought for her in that little cabin everyone had worked so hard on. The one with the sign over it declaring it hers. If that wasn't a sign of what he felt for her, he didn't know what else would convince her.

Instead, he was on the boat with Manley, leaving her to do whatever it was she would do. Maybe she'd come to her senses by the time he returned with his parents... he glanced at his watch... in about four hours. Shit. What was he going to do for four hours?

\* \* \* \*

"Hello the cabin!"

The male voice from outside startled Linnet as she smoothed the comforter over the fresh sheets on the bed. Everything was ready for Creed's parents, with an hour to spare. A glance at her watch confirmed it was too soon for him to be back. She straightened and brushed a stray piece of hair off her face. All her gear was in the truck. The washed sheets were hanging by the fire, both cabins swept clean, the dishes done and a stew beginning to simmer on the woodstove in the main cabin.

And now they had visitors from the river. How typical.

She plumped a pillow then stepped away from the bed. She'd hoped to pick some branches with colorful leaves to serve in the place of flowers, but with river traffic there wasn't time. It would have to do. Forcing herself not to look back, she stepped onto the small porch and pulled the carved door shut. She wouldn't let herself look at the sign over the door. Let Creed pull it down. The nest was no longer hers. All she had to do was drop the key off in the main cabin, write a short note and be on her way.

Sniffing back the sentimental blues that had descended as soon as Creed pulled out on the boat, Linnet straightened and headed for the shingle beach where a large yellow raft was being pulled from the water. Two men looked up at the sound of her steps on the gravel as she finished buckling on her gun belt.

"Welcome..." the words died in her throat as she looked up and recognized the two men. Billy and Jack. One she knew had raped her. The other she'd begun to suspect had raped her. The moment she looked into his eyes she knew. The afternoon on the sofa in his office was no nightmare or hallucination. It had happened.

Swallowing back nausea, she tried to regulate her breathing. How the hell had they wound up here? Sure, the trip down the river from Eagle to Circle was popular, but not that popular. There were plenty of other places to fish.

"Hey, Linnet." Jack Weston, her former boss, grinned as if he was truly pleased to see her. Probably was, considering the last time she'd seen him she hadn't recognized him as an attacker.

"Hey, baby," Billy laughed and approached with his arms outstretched. "Aren't you a sight for sore eyes. So this is where you've been hiding your pretty little self. We weren't sure we'd actually find you, and now here we all are."

Frozen in her tracks, Linnet fought to gain control of her body. Ice ran through her veins, cold sweat popped out on her face and soaked her underarms. Still wasn't having much luck with her respiration. Think. Self-defense training. She wasn't a victim. She could control this encounter.

Self talk helped get her unstuck. Remembering she was a state official, she set fists on her hips and forced out the words in her sternest tone. "This is private property and you aren't welcome here."

"Hey, that's not the word on the river. The folks up at the roadhouse said this was a friendly spot to stop." Jack grinned and stepped toward her. "But we already knew that, which is why we picked this river for our fishing vacation."

Remember the danger zone, she heard Hawk's voice in her head. If she wasn't careful, they'd have her trapped between them.

"Yeah, that's right," Billy chimed in. "We were hoping it was you they were talking about."

"I can see we picked a good time to pull off the river for the night. Looks like we're going to have a nice reunion," Jack agreed.

"So, you've managed to convince yourself you aren't rapists?"

Both men stopped and stared at her. "What rape?" Billy asked. "You were begging for it, baby. All night. Each time you came, you begged me for more. Couldn't get enough. You're one demanding woman, baby. Good thing there's two of us here to take care of you tonight. In fact, we're a little ahead of schedule. We have two nights before we meet our ride in Circle."

"Yeah, it will take all of two nights with two men to satisfy her," Jack said, then went on to confirm her darkest fears. "We spent an afternoon and evening together, you rubbing up against me, mewling for more. I had trouble keeping you quiet so nobody would hear us. Used me up for the next two weeks." His grin widened. "By the time I was ready for more you'd left."

"Pity, that." Linnet dredged up more anger which gave her the energy to move. Fortunately, her sheathed knife was attached to her gun belt. Instinct honed by hours spent practicing her quick draw had the gun in one hand, knife in the other. "Stop right where you are."

Jack and Billy both stopped again and raised their hands.

"Whoa there, baby. We're friends, remember? No need to get rough. Unless you want to be tied up this time?" Billy chuckled at his own joke. "Got handcuffs to go with those weapons?"

"You've forgotten that my father and brother taught me a few tricks. Tricks I'm better able to use when I'm not drugged. Is that how you two get your women? Can't do it the old fashioned way?" It was the height of stupidity to taunt them, but she couldn't help it.

"Drugs? What drugs? The hospital couldn't find any when you bullied them into doing a rape kit, remember, baby?" Billy smiled. It didn't look friendly as it had once upon a time.

"On the ground, face down, hands behind your backs," she snapped at them.

"You don't have the nerve to shoot, baby, so put the weapons away," Billy cajoled her.

"Wanna bet?" Linnet squeezed off a round that knocked Billy's hat off his head. "Damn, I haven't sighted this gun in a while. Aimed too high." Another round slid into the chamber.

Billy dropped to his knees, his face white. "Shit!"

"Okay, okay, just calm down," Jack said, both hands in the air. Funny, his unshaven face looked a little pale as well.

"Oh, I'm very calm. On your face while I figure out exactly what to do here. I haven't done target practice in a while, so I'm as likely to blow your balls off as I am to hit you in the heart. Take it from me, boys, you're safer on the ground. Though now that I think about it, I kind of like the idea of making sure you never rape anyone again."

With great satisfaction, Linnet watched both her rapists fall flat on their faces on the cold, wet ground. Hawk was right. It felt damn good to stand up for herself.

Once the men were secured, complete with duct tape across their mouths, reaction set in and she wished Creed were there to hold her.

No. She'd burned that bridge pretty much all the way to the ground. He wasn't likely to forgive her for being an idiot. She already regretted her nervous reaction, but to sit here and wait in embarrassment when they were going their separate ways in just a couple days didn't make sense. Make up to spend the weekend being nervous around his parents and then say goodbye on Monday? No. Much better to leave now and ignore the fact she was running away. Much better to convince herself this would be kinder to both of them in the in end.

Clean break and all that.

Right. If she repeated it enough, maybe she'd believe it by the time she reached home.

\* \* \* \*

Waiting for his parents, Creed was already pacing the public safety office when the call came in. In fact, Dick Winstrom was so amazed, he put it on speaker phone.

"Linnet, repeat what you just said."

"Write this down, Dick." Creed recognized the tone of exasperation over the speaker. "A couple of boaters are tied up at the Willis place. A group from Slaven's followed them downstream and is standing guard over them. The two being held are from California and are perps in a couple of cases of sexual assault. I suppose Creed could also charge them with trespassing or claim jumping or whatever, but they came ashore with the intent to repeat their previous crimes."

"Are you saying these men intended to rape you, but you stopped them?"

"Give the man a gold star! That's exactly what I'm saying. Anyhow, they're tied up and waiting for you. I didn't have room to put them in my truck and I'm already headed for town. I don't know if Creed has left there yet, but you can probably catch a ride up river with him so you can arrest these two. I'll leave details of their California crimes with the Troopers either in Fairbanks or Anchorage. I haven't decided if I'm driving straight through tonight or not."

"Linnet, if you're pressing charges you just can't take off. I need to get your statement," Dick practically shouted when static cut the phone connection. "Dammit! That's a hard-headed woman." He punched the disconnect button hard enough Creed wondered if it would ever work properly again. "Now, do I wait and ambush her when she hits the highway or head up river to take care of the arrest and let her give statements in town? Damn stubborn, pig-headed, pain-in-the-ass, woman!"

"Tell me about it," Creed grumbled. "She got me good. I'm here without my truck, my parents due any moment, and now I have criminals to get off my land." He slammed his palm against a metal filing cabinet. The stinging sensation didn't lessen his frustration one bit. Pretty dumb to go around hitting furniture. Maybe he could get a couple solid punches in on the two yokels tied up at his cabin. That would feel much better. "I'm due back on the Slope on Tuesday and don't have time to go running after her. Well, fine. If that's the way she wants to end it, then that's the way it'll be."

"End it?" Dick looked up from double checking his utility belt. He absently tucked a second set of handcuffs into his pocket and reached for his Kevlar vest and float jacket. "You had a thing going with her? Shit. Lost that bet."

"What?" Creed turned to look at the stocky man.

"I put down twenty bucks that she wouldn't unthaw enough to let any man get close to her. That'll teach me to forget your way with women."

The Trooper's grin made Creed's stomach twist. The river scum were making bets on her love life? Shit.

"Never mind." Creed turned to stare out the window before he decided to take out his frustration on the law man. A familiar truck drove down the street, headed for the boat landing. "Well at least my parents are on time. Need a lift, Trooper?"

"Nah, I've got my own boat. I'll drag a couple of the boys along as deputies. Better call Sally to get the cell cleaned up."

"Nah, not for these two. Put them with the dogs. They deserve worse."

"What'd they do?" Dick opened the door for Creed.

"After-dinner drinks laced with date-rape drugs."

"Well then." Dick pulled the door shut with a slam. "I guess I won't worry about their comfort so much. Trespassing and claim jumping. That ought to add a nice twist to the assault charges. Wonder if they have any of those drugs in their gear."

# Chapter 31

From across the street, Linnet's half of the single story duplex was brightly lit. Eight-fifty on Wednesday night, was she preparing for Thanksgiving tomorrow? Did she have an invitation for dinner somewhere? Or did she have visitors arriving?

Creed watched her through the lace curtains. Sheers, his mother called them. The heavier drapes were open. Didn't she know how much could be seen from the street? Didn't she ever think about inviting personal assault? He could see enough to know she wore her hair in a ponytail. A dark-colored turtleneck hugged her body. Earrings swung from her ears, something sparkly and dangly if the small flashes of light meant anything. Did she have pierced ears and he'd never noticed? Come to think of it, he didn't remember her ever wearing jewelry of any kind.

He really should just climb out of the car he'd borrowed from his sister and go knock on her door. Since when had he become a coward?

Since the day he'd taken off in the boat, leaving her at the cabin without even Manley to guard her. The day he'd spent the better part of three hours staring at the water looking for answers. The only thing that had come to him as he'd downed what little remained of a medicinal bottle of Jack Daniels George had stashed on the boat, was the bare-faced fact that he loved her.

By God, that was it. He'd never truly been in love before, but this was the solid gold, true blue original thing. He'd marry her at the first opportunity. As soon as he got back from his next rotation he'd sweep her off her feet and carry her off to Cancun for a sun-drenched honeymoon. He just had to get back to her before she left. But it hadn't happened. Because of her call to the Trooper's office, he'd known before he'd left the landing in Circle, she was on the road away from him.

Upon reaching the cabin with the Trooper right behind, Manley had jumped off the boat and run to the buildings looking for her. When she hadn't opened either door, Manley had run down every trail looking for her. Hours later, when the excitement of the arrests had died down, Creed had finally found his feet following Manley up over the rise behind the cabin to find her truck gone.

He'd snorted with derision to hide the ache in his heart.

Gone. Just like she'd said. Just as he'd expected. Just as he'd hoped she wouldn't be.

Unable to take it in, he'd returned to the cabin and found himself staring at the sheets and the one pair of socks hanging on the line. He'd fallen to his knees right there and let Manley lick away the tears seeping from his eyes.

Without a word, Dad had tugged him to his feet, then pushed him down into a chair near the woodstove. Linnet's chair. Linnet's empty chair, all signs of her knitting gone. Except for that damned pair of socks hanging on the line. The socks she'd spent two weeks knitting. Why had she left them?

Mom had found the key to the little cabin sitting on the table holding down a scrap of paper with only two words on it.

*Thank you.*

Not a word about how to reach her or even a hint about her feelings for him.

She'd left the key to her cabin. If that didn't say she was through with him, he didn't know what did. She may have left, but in addition to the socks, there were signs of her all over the place.

The cleaned and organized cabin. His parents had exclaimed over the improvements and he couldn't even find it in himself to tell them it was all her. George had probably already told them. Give the man a couple plates of cookies and he became a regular gossip. Mom knew where to get her information.

Then there was the sleeping cabin.

Linnet had done as she'd said she would. Fresh sheets had been on the bed, the cabin swept and a fire made ready to light, and the oil lamps filled with fresh oil. Even the tub had been freshly scrubbed. Creed had found the young moose standing in the woods staring at the tub, an even sadder look on her face. Angry with the mooning moose, Creed had shooed her away.

Linnet hadn't even stayed for the animals. Manley whined for her, his nose seeking out her scent as if he couldn't believe she'd left. He'd stayed by the door, waiting, hoping she'd come through it.

If Creed had left Manley with her that day, would she have left him behind or would she have taken him home to George?

His eyes refocused on the duplex before him as Linnet moved back into his line of sight. She was on the phone and glancing at her wrist. Checking the time but for what reason? Was she expecting someone?

So beautiful.

As soon as his hitch on the Slope had passed, he'd come looking for her. He'd tried email only to have the messages bounce back, and her cell and home numbers had disconnect messages. George had her address from the post office in Circle. Wes had gotten the forwarding information for him.

Address in hand, when Creed had knocked on that door, it wasn't Linnet who'd answered. The college students who'd just moved in sent him to the landlord who swore Linnet hadn't left a forwarding address. She'd given up her deposit and told the man she'd take care of forwarding with the post office. In a town of nearly three hundred thousand people, she'd vanished. Not even her office could tell him where she was.

All they said was she was working from home, her mailing address a post office box. They wouldn't give him her phone number or email. Despair had truly set in and dogged him back to Fairbanks.

How had he stayed away so long? Eight weeks. Last night he'd stopped in Fairbanks just long enough to change planes. His parents had joined him at the airport with an extra bag of fresh clothes then they'd all boarded the plane to continue on to Anchorage. This year he had the holiday off, so it was time to visit.

Terri had taken one look at him, hugged him, then handed him over to her husband. Aaron and Creed's nephew, Kurt, were in charge of cheering up the grumpy uncle. An hour ago, Terri had handed him a printed-out online map with Linnet's new house clearly marked. Not far away, either.

"Go and find her," Terri said, pushing him out the door. "I couldn't get her phone number, but at least George remembered her license plate. Don't know how many times I drove past it before I figured it out. Go and talk to her. Either get her to see reason or find closure, but you need to do this to move on."

Arguing was fruitless. So. Here he was, feeling like a stalker, watching her house. And only five blocks away from Terri's. Linnet had moved five miles across town, only to land in his sister's neighborhood. How funny was that? The decal had given her away after all.

Terri was right. It was time for a new beginning, one way or another.

With a rush of bravado, he pulled the key from the car and stepped into the snowy night. The big flakes from earlier in the day had given way to small dry flakes. Flakes so fine they looked like fog in the streetlight at the foot of her driveway. The fresh three-inch blanket of November snow covered the neighborhood, muting the normal sounds. A hush hovered in the cold air, many degrees warmer than Prudhoe Bay had been yesterday morning, but still nippy to the nose.

Linnet's truck was tucked into a carport at the side of the house. Good, she wouldn't have to try and clear the snow off it and risk slipping on the ice. A garage would have been better. If she'd moved in with him, her truck would have been in a warm garage every night.

For a moment he paused, foot on the first step of her tiny porch. Not much more than the size of a pallet, there was barely room for one person to stand there. A single bulb fixture lit the porch and carport. Not enough light, too many shadows. He could hear her moving around inside. Cheap subflooring.

*Stop thinking, just knock.*

He mounted the second step and pulled his hand from the pocket of his leather coat. Cold metal stunned his knuckles as he rapped twice. Light footsteps approached the door. The distinctive sound of the deadbolt made him nod in approval. Didn't leave the door unlocked when she was home. Good.

The door swung open and there she was, backlit by the entry light over her head, face in shadow, eyes hidden from him. Oh, but she recognized him, that hitch in her breath and the way she froze gave her away.

"Creed?" His name came out of her throat as a squeak, her breath a white fog in the cold air.

"Linnet." At least his voice didn't crack as he said her name.

"How? What?" One hand gripped the doorknob, the other moved to her breast, right over her heart. At least she didn't slam the door in his face. That was something, right?

The scent of her drifted from the open door. Only made sense her house would smell like her. As his body stirred, a brief wave of dizziness assaulted him. "I'm down for Thanksgiving. I wanted to see you."

"Oh. I... I'm on my way... out."

Out where? The fact she was dressed for a date didn't escape him. A casual one, but a date nonetheless. Low-heeled black books encased her feet under the legs of tight black jeans, topped by a dark green turtleneck. Makeup even, if the shadows weren't playing tricks on him. Not much, but enough to enhance already perfect features. Why was she dressed to go out at nine o'clock on Wednesday night? And with whom?

Okay, she didn't have time for him tonight, so no time like the present. "I'd like to extend an invitation to dinner tomorrow. My sister... my family would like it if you don't have other plans."

The hand dropped from her chest. The necklace she wore had a slice of stone artistically wrapped in copper wire hanging from a dark cord. It stoked a memory as he stared at it for a moment.

"I'd love to, but..." she paused to draw in a breath and waved her hand to a suitcase he hadn't seen before. "As soon as my cab arrives I'm heading out. I'm going home for a couple weeks."

As he took in the sparsely-furnished living room he recalled an old conversation about her family. Lake Tahoe was where they lived, she'd said. But where?

"To make cookies?" The words felt dead in his mouth as his eyes swept from the luggage to her face.

She'd shifted just enough he could see her face better. The shadows around her eyes weren't entirely from the lighting. Her pale skin appeared bruised. The tan from her summer had faded leaving her looking tired. Had she suffered too? Her cheeks looked hollowed, as if she'd lost weight.

Linnet cleared her throat. "I suppose we will. Look, I'd invite you in, but my cab will be here any minute now. I need to finish... turning out lights."

"Lame excuse to throw me out before I even say what I came to say." There were very few lights to turn out. Indeed, few items to worry about. No plants, a TV on a bookcase. A rocking chair and a table with a lamp. Damn little else to show the personality of the woman standing in front of him.

"I thought you came to invite me to dinner?" Suspicion clouded her features.

"That was to create an opportunity to talk to you without rushing."

The frown on her face deepened. "So, your sister didn't invite me for dinner?"

"She did, but I was hoping we could talk tonight. Straighten things out between us."

An odd look of panic washed over her features, only to be replaced with a mask of cool indifference. Her cop face, or what she'd tried to cultivate as one.

Irritated that she'd use it on him, he still couldn't help thinking how adorable it was. "There's nothing between us to straighten out. We have some wonderful memories and the chance to someday be friends. That's all."

"Friends," he scoffed. "Hell, Linnet, you don't go back to being friends after being lovers like we were." More than lovers. They'd been friends too, but friendship had made being lovers even better. Which added up to he needed her in his life. He'd never felt as lonely as he had these past weeks.

She stiffened even more and he could almost see the defensive hackles rising on the back of her neck. "I'm sorry. I haven't had a whole lot of experience making friends that way. I was hoping we could spare each other the bitterness. Besides, I thought that's what you wanted. No clinging woman who didn't know when it was time to say goodbye. I'm sorry if I hurt your pride by walking away first. Honestly, I thought it would be easier that way."

Creed leaned against the door jamb and frowned when she moved back a step. Dammit, did she think he'd hurt her? Physically force her? She knew him better than that. Or at least he'd thought she did. Time to stop the assumptions and lay it on the line. Make it so clear she couldn't misunderstand.

"Linnet, I don't know how to say this any other way. I miss you. I want to go back to where we were." Funny how the 'L'-word had stuck in his throat. In his mind he yelled, *I love you*, over and over again, but the words never made it past his lips. Couldn't she read his mind? Couldn't she hear the anguish crying out from his soul? So much for being completely clear.

"I..." She closed her eyes for a moment and drew in a deep breath, her hand covering the stone nestled at the top of her cleavage again. "It isn't possible to go back. There's only forward."

Creed stared at her hand as if seeing the pendant through her flesh and bone. The shape nudged a memory. A lump, in her palm. His palm covering it. Of course. The rock she'd knocked out of the hillside. When polished it was as beautiful as the most precious of gemstones. Her hand dropped, to rest over her stomach this time, and he saw it, polished and secure in a netting of copper wire.

More exquisite than marble, veins colored green, purple, yellow, and quartz white made striking stripes on the roughly two inch square slice of listwanite that showed through the thin wire wrapped around it.

Did she wear it to remember? He glanced at her wrist and more of the stone was set into the band of her watch. Small flakes of gold surrounded the watch itself. The gold they'd found together? His hand curled around the box in his coat pocket.

"Pretty necklace," he said, his eyes on the centerpiece.

The gold earrings dangling from her ears sparkled in the light as she looked down. "It's... thank you."

"It's the stone you found, isn't it?"

"Yes, the one we... yes, the same one. I have a friend with a rock polisher who also sliced it and then I did..." Her hand waved to indicate the wire work. A delicately manicured hand. So different from the often rough-looking hands he'd seen at the river. Somehow the pale pink polish on moderately long nails looked erotic as hell. "I also had the watch made. This is the first time I've worn either," she said quietly, looking over his shoulder.

Creed heard the muffled sound of a car approaching, the tires squeaking on packed snow. Headlights swept over him as the cab turned into her driveway and pulled up behind her truck.

"Look, I really have to go," she said to him as she waved to the cab. "I'm sorry, I can't talk now." Her eyes swept him before she turned and took care of the few lights on in the living room. The rest of the house was dark.

As she returned to the door, he stood back.

Linnet bent to lift her coat from the top of her suitcase and he saw her computer case leaning against it. The coat she pulled on was black leather, similar to his in style, but more like a suit jacket with notched lapels. A sour smile twisted his lips. They were so much alike in their tastes it wasn't funny. If she'd cared to look close enough she'd see he also wore black jeans and a green button-down shirt. Green because it reminded him of her eyes and the woods around the cabin.

She lifted her cases with the intent of setting them on the porch. Creed took them from her, their hands touching for a moment. The energy between them made Linnet look into his eyes before she wrenched away.

Making room for her on the porch so she could lock the door, Creed moved down the steps with her luggage.

"Let me drive you to the airport," he said as she joined him at ground level.

"I don't think... I don't think that's such a good idea."

"I'll pay off the cabbie. Let me drive you there."

Wide eyes stared at him and he watched as she shook off the shock of seeing him. "No. Thank you for stopping by, but I need to leave now. Check-in is going to be hell as it is."

She tried to take her luggage, so he handed her the computer case to hang over her shoulder. Carrying the other bag, he took her elbow and escorted her over the snow piling up on the driveway to the waiting cab. Stopping at the back door, Creed let her go long enough to open the door and set her suitcase inside. Not ready to let her leave just yet, he blocked her way into the car and pulled her into his arms.

"Creed... no," she sighed as his lips touched hers.

Linnet. At last. His whole body tightened and yet relaxed at once. This was right. This was meant to be. "Linnet, please, don't go," he heard himself beg against her lips before taking her mouth again.

She melted against him for a handful of heartbeats, then pulled away. "I have to go," she whispered, her voice breathy with passion, harsh with held back tears swimming in her eyes. No doubt, she wanted him as much as he wanted her. But she pushed against him. She had to go.

Not she wanted to, but she had to.

He had to try again, damn his pride. "I need you. Please, end the torture, for both of us..."

"Hey, you there, are we going yet?" the cabbie interrupted.

"Yes," Linnet said. "I have to go, Creed. I have to." The last was whispered, a searing pain in her eyes as she reached up and touched his face, her thumb rubbing against his lip. "Red isn't your color."

She gave him a weak smile as her warm hand cupped his cold face. "Happy Thanksgiving," she whispered, then ducked into the cab.

Creed shut the door and watched the yellow mini SUV back out of the driveway. Linnet's eyes stared out the window. He watched the tail lights travel down the street then turn and disappear from view.

She was gone.

Again.

How the hell did she keep doing that to him?

# Chapter 32

The trip home was horrible. Long lines, snow delay in Anchorage, topped off by mechanical problems in Seattle leaving her alone with her thoughts for far too many hours. It was noon before she found her father at the baggage claim in Sacramento when she should have arrived by eight-thirty that morning.

Thankfully, the roads were clear all the way to the village of Tahoma on the shores of Lake Tahoe. At least Daddy hadn't asked too many questions. Let him think her silence was due to the exhaustion of red-eye travel. Presumably Mom had already passed on the pertinent details of her broken heart. The latest, of course, they didn't know. Nor did they know the biggest part.

God, how was she going to tell them? She wanted to bury her face in her hands until it all went away, but big girl problems didn't go away when they were ignored. Instead, they tended to grow and become bigger problems.

Creed. On her doorstep. Granted Anchorage was small in comparison to most cities, but for Alaska it was huge. Half the state's population of six hundred thousand lived in the city. It shouldn't have been that easy to find her. Had he put a private detective on her tail? She'd moved, changed all her phone numbers and email addresses. Apparently it hadn't been enough. Should have sold her truck, painted it, removed the decal, or changed the license plate.

But oh, how wonderful he'd looked, his sun-streaked blond hair long and unruly, the snowflakes melting in it making it look like spun fairy gold in the porch light. Must not have cut it since...

Staring out the window of her old bedroom, she shook off the memory of the last time she'd seen him. The horrible hurt and stricken look on his face that haunted her every quiet moment. Without Manley, she'd driven straight to the first hotel she'd seen. A few hours sleep, a full tank of gas and she'd been on her way, reaching home by mid-afternoon Saturday. Three days later she'd completely moved. Traveling light had its benefits. Working from home as well. Newbauer had spent an hour debriefing her in the office then sent her off to analyze the data.

Since then she'd stuck close to home, doing her work, deflecting emails from Henry. How he'd gotten her email again she didn't know, but she'd see him sometime next week. Details just need to be firmed up. For some reason she didn't feel a pressing need to settle those details any time soon. As it was, she had lawyers to meet on Friday and depositions to give.

Just details to close out the cases against Billy and Jack. Hearing about Creed's added charges had made her laugh. Both men had been suspended from their jobs and more women had stepped forward with even worse tales of assault. Linnet's was just the icing on the cake, so to speak, the D.A. had told her.

Had Creed really meant it when he'd said all was fair in war and there was love on the line? Had she lost her one chance at a love to last the ages? Had he changed his mind about not wanting long-term entanglements?

"Linnet!"

Thoughts scattered, she rested her head against the window for a moment. Mom wouldn't be put off for long.

"Linnie?" This time Mom spoke from outside the door and pushed it open. "Sweetie, are you okay?"

She put on the best smile she could. "I'm fine, Mom. The all-night flight is always a little rough, and the delays didn't help." Anything to clear the worry from Mom's face.

New lines creased skin that had always been smooth and blemish free. Liberal streaks of gray highlighted hair that had been solid black only two years ago. Guilt weighed heavily on Linnet's conscience. Worrying about Hawk in the war zone and her in Alaska had surely taken a toll over the last two years. And yet, the news kept on coming. How many more gray hairs would Mom have by the end of the weekend?

"You should have come home a few days earlier. It's just the three of us—we can put off dinner until tomorrow." Mom's hand on her cheek was cool and comforting.

"No, I'm hungry, and the turkey is already in the oven. Besides, I have to go down to Sacramento tomorrow. Let me get a shower and I'll be down to help."

"All right, sweetheart. I'll put on a pot of coffee."

"Thanks, Mom." There wasn't much in this world better than Mom's hug. Scents of sage, onion, vanilla and other kitchen wonders enveloped her. Cinnamon and apple. Pumpkin and nutmeg. All the aromas of a holiday at home. Soothing balm to the tortured soul.

"Half an hour, Linnie. Don't fall asleep in the shower." Mom's smile couldn't quite hide the worry deep in her eyes.

"I won't, Mom. I'll be down soon."

Linnet turned to her suitcase and lifted it to the bed. She touched the handle, where Creed's hand had wrapped around it. It didn't take much imagination to feel the warmth of his touch again. When he'd kissed her, she'd nearly begged him to come with her, or take her into the house... anything but let her leave alone again. But she couldn't do that to him. She'd already turned him away, run away, from him twice. She didn't deserve a third chance.

Tugging on the zipper pull, she opened the suitcase. Though snow frosted the landscape outside, the house was warm. Sweaters wouldn't do any good for cooking in the kitchen anyway. Toiletry case in hand, she stepped into the bathroom. While the water warmed she undressed and dropped her clothes into the hamper.

Stepping into the shower, she savored the comfort of hot water pelting her tired skin. Who knew skin could be tired? The first bottle that fell into her hand was a clean scented gel. It smelled like Creed, fresh out of the tub at the river. Creed in the fresh cold air last night. The tears she'd held back all night would no longer be denied. Hot water mingled with salty drops and she let the memories come. She should have stayed last night, she should have talked to him, explained, begged forgiveness, let him know...

Thirty-two minutes later Linnet couldn't quite make herself skip down the stairs. Instead she glided down as Mom had tried to teach her over and over again. Face bare of makeup, she'd ended up digging deep into her closet where she'd found a comfortable old faded batik wrap skirt and a basic white t-shirt. Soft thick wool socks slouched around her ankles and muffled her steps. Twins to the ones she'd knitted for Creed, they were a deep navy blue, with just enough silk blended with the merino wool to make them soft instead of scratchy.

Their house—hidden back in the woods behind tall lush evergreens—was already fresh with pine boughs laid across the mantel to lend a jumpstart of cheer on the holiday season. The aroma of cooking delights filled her nostrils and a sense of home wrapped around her as she stepped into the kitchen. Roasting turkey, baking rolls and pumpkin pie added their fragrance, making Linnet's mouth water.

"There you are, honey. Taste this filling. It's the blueberries you sent home with Daddy." Mom held out a spoonful of the thick filling.

"Mmmm." Linnet let the rich flavor fill her mouth. It was worth every stain on her lips and teeth.

"I thought we'd try blueberry pie this year instead of apple." Mom poured the mixture into a pie pan lined with her famous flakey crust. Linnet's stomach rumbled even as it flipped over.

Blueberries like she'd cooked for Creed. A memory of feeding each other bites of cobbler filled her throat with a lump. "Sounds great," she choked out and reached for a glass in the cabinet. Water seemed like a good idea.

Staring out the window to the front drive she watched Dad close the garage door while Mom settled the crust cover over the filling. Something made Dad turn toward the road. Linnet tipped her glass and sipped the cool water. Mountain fresh, it soothed her throat as she let her mind blank out while watching a car approach.

"Do you recognize that car, Mom?"

Linnet stepped aside so her mom could look out the window beside her. "Can't say I do." Mom brushed aside a stray hair with the back of her arm. Flour covered her hands. "But Dad seems to know who it is."

Both women watched him cross his arms and stand with legs braced. Not a welcoming pose. The sedan pulled to a stop and the driver's door swung open. Linnet's glass landed with a thump on the counter. That hair...

"Go answer the door, Linnie."

"Okay." It couldn't be. There wasn't time. She would have seen him at the airport or on the plane, but her plane had been booked to capacity. Impossible.

Footsteps sounded on the wide redwood stairs leading from the drive as Linnet approached the front door. Heart in her throat, she flung the door open.

Creed stopped on the top step and stared at her, the look on his face as raw as the red rimming his eyes. It looked as if he hadn't slept since closing the cab door last night. He couldn't have slept to make it here this close behind her.

"Creed?" Her voice couldn't manage more than that, and even his name had come out sounding strangled.

"Manley sent me." Creed shoved his hands into his coat pockets, his eyes dark and unreadable. Golden three-day beard made his jaw look scruffy, dangerous and sexy. How had she forgotten how gorgeous he was? "George can't do a thing with him. He stares out the window, whines at the door to be let out, then turns right around and whines to come in. He snarls at everybody and won't let anyone comfort him. He's off his feed and looking pretty scruffy. This is so not like Manley. He's always been a clean dog, you know."

Linnet folded her arms against the cool air and to hide the trembling of her hands. "Poor Manley. I miss him terribly."

"I had to catch the red-eye to San Francisco and then spent the last five hours driving up here with only the GPS for company. But I'm willing do that for my favorite dog. He wants you back in the worst way. I've never seen that dog moon over a woman before. His loneliness is making not only him, but everyone around him, miserable. He's just a shadow of his former self."

A tear welled up and trickled down her cheek. Was he really talking about Manley, or himself?

The tear seemed to undo Creed. He took a step closer to her, his worried gaze searching her face. "Linnet, don't shut me out. Manley isn't the only one who needs you. I need you." He took another step closer. "I should have told you weeks ago, and I would have if I'd been able to find you."

Linnet took a step out the door. "Why didn't you fly to Sacramento?"

"The only seat available out last night was to San Francisco. I didn't have much choice."

"Linnet?" Mom's voice came from behind her. "Is everything okay, honey?"

"Creed?" Linnet took a step closer, matching the step he took. A mere three feet separated them now. "I... I don't understand." She wanted to believe, she really did, but she wasn't going to assume, not something this important. *Let him say the words! Please!* And then she'd have to tell him...

"Linnet, I'm here because I can't stand it anymore. I love you, I need you. Don't send me away, please. Don't run."

Linnet's heart pounded against her chest and she pressed a hand over it. He loved her? "For true? You don't just want a fling?" She had to be sure.

"No, sweet bird." Creed's dark eyes stared into hers as he took another step closer. Two feet. "I want much more than that. I want a fling every day. I want kisses and hugs every hour. I want you in my arms every night. Life doesn't mean anything without you. Please, tell me you feel the same, pretty bird. If you turn me away this time I won't make it. I'll turn into a nasty old hermit and let my teeth fall out while raving at stray tourists on the river. Just me and the moose. It won't be pretty."

Half-laughing, half-sobbing, she covered her mouth with a shaking hand then dropped it to cover her bare arm again. "I can't let that happen." She took step toward him and he matched her. Twelve inches. "I suppose you need me to save you from a hideous fate."

"I do."

"Oh Creed, I've been so stupid, please..." She gulped. He'd gone above and beyond. It was her fault, but he'd come for her three times now.

Another step and the toes of Creed's boots touched the tips of her socks. Following her gaze, he looked down at their feet. "Nice socks. I have a pair just like them. Best socks I've ever had."

Nodding let her avoid speaking. Behind her she heard Mom and Dad muttering in the door way. In front of her, Creed's body heat reached across the inches separating them and warmed her in the chill mountain air. She shook her head. She had to say it.

"I've been so stupid..."

Creed's finger on her lips stopped the words. "No self recriminations. That time is past, Linnet. Don't string me out any longer here. I love you. I need you in my life. I know we can work out my schedule. I'm willing to do anything to make you happy. Just tell me there's hope." He pulled his finger away and shoved his hand back into his coat pocket.

Linnet watched his hands twitch inside the pockets. He was as nervous as she was and for once she felt a twitch of humor, misplaced as it was, take a hold of her. "I don't know, I kind of like playing you on the line." Fighting the grin trying to take over her face she looked up at him. Anguish and uncertainty made him look haggard. Probably the long travel hours contributed a fair amount too.

"Marry me, pretty bird. Spend your life with me," he whispered, his voice rough. "I'm dying here, have mercy on me." In the hand he'd pulled from a pocket was a small velvet box. A ring box. He opened it and held it between them. "I had these made from some of those rocks we dug out of the ground."

Linnet looked down to see a full wedding set. Two thin bands of gold, coated with nuggets, one with a large diamond set on top of it. The third band was thicker and larger. A man's ring.

"Gold we found together," he said. "I tried to make earrings for you, but the gold wanted to be made into rings."

"I don't remember finding so many nuggets or any that large." They were so beautiful. She reached out a finger to lightly touch the obviously male ring. Strong, without being ostentatious. Just like Creed.

"So, I palmed a few of them." A crooked smile made her heart beat faster.

Lifting a trembling hand, she touched the lines on his face, soothing them as the clouds of their breaths mingled in the cold air. "Creed, I think I've loved you from the moment you and Hawk ran to rescue me from the moose. I'm sorry for being so dense. It's just that I never dreamed..."

Creed's lips cut her off, his arms squeezed her an instant later. She was in his arms again, her own around his waist, the warmth of his coat and body covering her. The only place she wanted to be. But she had to know. Had to ask the question that had been tormenting her for a week now.

"You have to answer a question for me first," she mumbled against his lips.

"Anything. I'll give you anything you want."

"You've already given me a gift... and I want so very much to share it with you." She felt him stiffen. "I need to know if you want it... want to share it with me."

Creed leaned back so he could look into her eyes. "I gave you a gift? When?"

"I'm not exactly sure when, but I can pretty much pin it down to a certain two week time period... most likely one afternoon in particular..." She watched him frown, but it only lasted a second. In an instant his eyes cleared and a grin started to lift the corner of his mouth again.

"I hope I'm not wrong... but there was one time..."

"When we forgot..." She gulped, fully aware her parents stood in the doorway behind her. Did she really want to mention the missing condom in front of them?

"Yeah, we did, didn't we?" Creed's grin widened. "I think we gave each other the same gift. One that will stick around for a very long time."

"Unless we kick it out of the house when it turns eighteen."

"Right. Like your parents did. Like my parents did." The smile he gave her was wry.

"Yeah. Just like that." She couldn't help smiling at him. The fisherman who'd caught her heart. The man who'd taught her to love and trust again. He dipped his head and she pushed up on her toes to meet him half way. She so loved kissing him.

"Well, Dovie," Dad's voice drawled behind her. "That would be, Creed."

"The man from this summer?"

"Yeah. Has great potential as a son-in-law. What do you think of the name Linnet Willis?"

"So he's the one who pulled her and the big fish from the river?"

"Yup."

"And wooed her with wine in the wilderness?"

"Has a fair taste for California vintages. Even got her to eat king salmon."

"Impressive. I think it looks likes she's been hooked, Falcon."

"Nah, I think she's sunk. I mean, really, he's not even military. And if my guess is right, they already have an anchor tying them down. Good thing there's a get-married-quick-chapel, or two dozen, on the other side of the lake."

Creed pulled back just enough to mutter, "Mmm, blueberry. Tasty." He licked her lips before commenting on her parents. "They always provide analysis like that?"

"Yeah. Dad always wanted to be sports announcer, like John Madden."

"I think he needs to stick with the day job." Creed kissed the side of her mouth.

Linnet tightened her arms around his waist. "Doesn't matter. If we're living in Fairbanks we won't see them much."

"Sorry, but your family will have to see us at least twice a year. Maybe more if we can entice them up to the river for the summer."

"Creed?"

"Yes, honey?"

"Shut up and kiss me."

"Just as long as you promise to feed me. I smell turkey with all the trimmings and I passed up dinner at my sister's to chase you down for Manley."

"We'll feed you, now shut…"

Linnet couldn't have said another word if she wanted to. Creed's mouth closed over hers and his arms pulled her close. He kissed her like a starving man, his tongue delving deep as a moan rumbled from his throat. As the kiss eased, Linnet could swear he was humming a certain tune... and when he put his lips to ear, she was sure...

*"There's a berry tasting girl, who sets my heart awhirl, and soon she'll live up on the Yukon far away…"*

# Meet the Author

Morgan prefers to live under her pen name. An everyday woman, she's a wife and mother like many out there. She doesn't feel there is much that makes her stand out from the crowd, with the possible exception of her imagination.

Inside her mind live characters who look normal, if almost a little boring, on the outside. Inside they have passions and hungers that would shock their preachers and next door neighbors.

Kinky? Maybe. Twisted? Warped? Definitely—but in a fun way. Bloodsport is not her style. Leather and lace? Oh yeah. A sexy stare-down, a thorough tongue lashing, bubbles and petting. Champagne and hot tubs. Morgan lives for decadent luxury and love. Ripped abs, smooth warm skin, and tight butts on her heroes a must. Strong arms on strong men with lusty appetites.

Morgan doesn't consider her day successful unless she's had a good belly laugh and warped her teenager in some way. Luckily, both are relatively easy to accomplish. Or is the teen warping her? She's noticed an increasing trend of rap music on her iTunes lately. When does the parent become the child?

Let your inhibitions go and step into Morgan's world. Erotic adventure often mixed with danger-laced action keeps the pages turning.